A Country Villag

Suzanne Snow writes contemporary, romantic and up-lifting fiction with a strong sense of setting and community connecting the lives of her characters. Previously, she worked in financial services and was a stay-at-home mum before retraining as a horticulturist and planting re-designed gardens.

Living in Lancashire and appreciating the landscape around her always provides inspiration and when she's not writing or spending time with her family, she can usually be found in a garden or reading.

Also by Suzanne Snow

Welcome to Thorndale

The Cottage of New Beginnings
The Garden of Little Rose
A Summer of Second Chances
A Country Village Christmas

SUZANNE SNOW

A Country Village Christmas

CANELO
US

San Diego, California

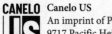 Canelo US
An imprint of Printers Row Publishing Group
9717 Pacific Heights Blvd, San Diego, CA 92121
www.canelobooksus.com

Printers Row Publishing Group is a division of Readerlink Distribution Services, LLC.
Canelo US is a registered trademark of Readerlink Distribution Services, LLC.

This edition originally published in the United Kingdom in 2021 by Canelo.

Published in partnership with Canelo.

Correspondence regarding the content of this book should be sent to Canelo US,
Editorial Department, at the above address. Author inquiries should be sent to Canelo,
Unit 9, 5th Floor, Cargo Works, 1–2 Hatfields, London SE1 9PG, United Kingdom,
www.canelo.co.

Publisher: Peter Norton • Associate Publisher: Ana Parker
Art Director: Charles McStravick
Senior Developmental Editor: April Graham
Production Team: Beno Chan, Julie Greene, Rusty von Dyl

Library of Congress Control Number: 2022932413

ISBN: 978-1-6672-0223-5

Printed in India

26 25 24 23 22   1 2 3 4 5

To Stewart, who loves Christmas

And my dad Barry, for all the meals and memories

Chapter One

Olivia Bradshaw closed the door, heading out into the November afternoon with a rush of something she knew was a mixture of guilt and relief. She hadn't planned this latest visit to her dad properly, and the wool peacoat she usually wore for the office was no match for the dreadful weather. The wind seemed to be trying to lift her clean off her feet and carry the bag from her hands as icy rain slashed at her face. Christmas lights had been wound around a fir tree close to the entrance of the retirement flats, but she barely glanced at it as she ran past.

She reached the car and flung her bag onto the passenger seat, already feeling for the phone that was in her coat pocket and never far from her hand. She unlocked it as she tugged her reading glasses down from her hair and checked the number of unread emails she had, already nineteen more than an hour ago. Another one landed in her inbox as she stared at the screen; sometimes it seemed like they arrived as often as she blinked.

She sighed, resisting the impulse to open them this minute and deal with everything she knew they would contain. Weather notifications were more of a concern right now and she clicked on one, not really needing its warning to inform her that the rest of this awful day was now at the mercy of a winter storm threatening chaos.

Olivia didn't often bother with a forecast and it wouldn't have changed her mind about this visit to her dad if she did. An online client meeting had been postponed and she'd jumped in her car to get here. Opportunities between her work hours were few and far between, and she'd taken this latest one in spite of the weather.

Starting the engine so as to activate the heated seat, she put the phone down and pushed her glasses back into her hair. She was only fifty miles or so from home and she ought to get going. At this time of day, in this weather, with rush hour traffic to come, the journey would take at least a couple of hours and probably much more. Her phone was already ringing but she ignored it.

The call was from her business partner Julian, and he would have to wait. She expected a voicemail to follow, hoping she would still make their planned dinner this evening. She guessed he was ringing to update her about the meeting he'd had earlier with a new and high-profile client.

Pulling out of the car park and onto the road, Olivia settled in for the drive. She loved her quick, sleek Jaguar, although her dad had expressed concern earlier about her driving back through the Dales countryside in such weather and in a vehicle not built like a Jeep. She'd dismissed his unease with raised eyebrows and a gentle reminder that as the mother of a grown-up daughter, she was long past his needing to worry about her. They both knew it didn't stop him, though.

She had been thirteen when her mum had died and until she had given birth to her beloved daughter Ellie in her late twenties, it had always been just her and her dad looking out for one another. Boyfriends had come and gone, and university had brought a first-class degree in law followed by professional qualifications in human resources. She'd balanced her career with unexpected single-motherhood, finding the strength firstly to cope and then to thrive by herself.

Once Ellie had settled at university, Olivia had felt a gradual return to those days of just her and her dad. It was one of the reasons why she hadn't yet got used to visiting him in his new flat instead of tucked up in his old house in Thorndale with his beloved books and his friends around him. Ellie came up when she could, but Olivia knew her daughter's life was flourishing as her finals drew near and Ellie had already organised a year outside the UK to gain her master's degree. They shared a number of characteristics and a desire to achieve was just one of them.

Olivia felt a spike of anxiety as she headed out of town, trying to avoid water gathering into deepening puddles on the roads. The wind was still battering the car, and it was four o'clock and dark already. She made a quick decision to avoid the motorway she would normally use, instead taking a route she knew well and one she was certain would bring less traffic.

The wipers were flipping furiously in an attempt to keep the windscreen clear while she drove steadily on. As the town disappeared behind her she passed through darkened countryside, saw the odd person still about, the few houses brightly lit and bringing a brief sense of not being entirely alone out here. It was six miles or so to the next village and she breathed out a sigh of relief when she saw the welcome glow of lights and a sign hanging outside a pub blowing in the gale.

Once through here, it was less than ten miles to the main road before she could join the motorway after that.

It was a horrible journey alone in the dark, and a glance at the screen on her dashboard told her she had virtually no phone signal barring the emergency number. The buildings were petering out and she shrieked, jumping on the brake as she saw a huge tractor rearing up in her headlights.

Her heart was still thudding as she realised the tractor wasn't actually moving but parked across the lane instead, barring all exit and further entry from the opposite direction to this new village. Someone was sitting inside the tractor and Olivia watched, despair mounting, as a man jumped down from the cab and ran around to hammer on her window. She opened it enough to reveal a worried face beneath the hood of his yellow waterproofs, greying hair plastered to his forehead.

'You can't get through,' he yelled, waving his arm to the trees framing the road and threatening to buckle beneath the wind. 'River's burst its banks half a mile on and flooded t'lane. I've parked tractor here to keep folk from tryin'.'

'But I need to get home and it's the quickest way now.' Olivia had to shout as well. 'I don't know if I can still get through if I go back and it'll mean a huge detour.'

'Aye, well, I wouldn't even be tryin' if I were you.' His voice lowered slightly, and she saw him point to the pub nearby. 'Best sit it out, lass. Get yourself inside and stay put, home'll 'ave to wait. Don't suppose you'll want to see your car floatin' down t'river or sat in three feet o'watter.'

She wanted to scream, despite knowing he spoke perfect sense. She'd seen enough clips on the news of cars washed away in swollen rivers and sandbags piled up outside houses, trying to keep the worst of the water from their doors. She couldn't risk it. She clearly couldn't leave

4

the village by the route she'd intended unless he shifted the tractor and there looked to be little chance of that. And neither did she really want to have to retrace her steps and risk a longer drive across lonely moorland or spend hours crawling back through town.

Olivia thanked him worriedly, backing her car up and turning around. The pub was only a hundred yards or so away and she parked behind it and grabbed her bag.

The torrential rain hadn't relented for even a moment and her coat was sodden by the time she'd run to the door and shoved it open, bursting inside with a gasp of relief at the sudden heat and light. She shook the water from her hair, feeling its chill slipping down her neck. A few heads had turned to see her arrival but she ignored them as she approached the bar.

She knew nothing about the pub. She couldn't have named it and right now it didn't matter whether the food was up to standard or the service average: there were lights, a roaring fire and something that smelled like shepherd's pie being carried past by a waitress. Olivia's stomach rattled with sudden hunger; she'd forgotten to eat lunch before she left the office earlier.

A quick glance around revealed subtle Christmas decorations arranged throughout the room and she could hear the inevitable seasonal music playing. She guessed the building had been recently renovated, judging by the modern decor still retaining a traditional element to its Georgian history. A stone-flagged floor and white-painted beams interspersed with oak sat nicely with leather chairs at the tables and high-backed stools dotted along the length of the bar.

Most tables looked to be occupied by people tucking into hearty platefuls of food and Olivia had already noted that the pub offered rooms. She made an enquiry, not really expecting one to be free, and somebody went to check. Looking around, she couldn't see an empty table, wondering how long she might be stuck here.

A cheerful young woman came to tell her that she was in luck, they had two rooms available and Olivia accepted one immediately, following the woman to check in. Her business bag contained a few basics that would see her through until tomorrow. She could do nothing more with her clothes other than smooth them out when she went to bed. Once in her room she hung up her wet coat, thankful that her understated, knee-length green work dress was still more or less dry.

She picked up her phone, glancing at the email app and ignoring the number sitting there as she listened to Julian's voicemail. It was indeed about their new client, his enthusiastic voice quickly outlining the client's require-ments. But she didn't want to speak to him now and be drawn into a long conversation about business. She wanted something nice to eat instead and sent a text to let him know what had happened, apologising for not being able to make dinner tonight.

She put the phone down and took in the room with an experienced eye. Attractive oak furniture complemented a king-size bed, and she noted subtle modern touches in cream and grey, with floor-length curtains concealing the darkness and the storm outside. She freshened up, dislodging her glasses to run her fingers through a layered, caramel-blonde bob, and reapplied the plum-coloured lipstick she used for work, making her feel more present-able. She left the room and returned downstairs.

In just the short while Olivia had been gone the pub had filled further still as people lined the bar. She spotted a corner booth near the fireplace, the leather seating wrapped around a small table, and nabbed it before someone else did. There were already menus on the table and she scanned the drinks list, ordering a gin and tonic when a waitress came over. Seasonal music was still playing and a Christmas tree flickered in a corner, brightening the atmosphere into something jolly, mocking the madness outside.

So now Olivia had a free evening, one she hadn't expected, and she took her phone and a notepad from her bag and unlocked the screen, pulling her glasses down over her eyes. There was a message from Ellie about her plans for Christmas and Olivia replied to it first, scanning her daughter's latest images on the family chat group of a weekend away with her boyfriend in Cornwall.

'Excuse me?'

Olivia's glance shot up – and up – to find a man standing beside her table, his smile apologetic, a glass of something that look liked whisky in one hand. She took in dark brown hair flecked with grey and smart jeans worn with a navy cashmere jumper that seemed to highlight intensely blue eyes. He was probably a little older than her.

'Would you mind?' He had the most beautiful voice, as inviting and luxuriant as the fire blazing nearby and somehow she felt it was another layer of comfort on such a horrible evening. He pointed to the empty space opposite her. 'I really wouldn't bother you, but there are literally no other seats and I'm desperate for a square meal.'

'Me too.' Olivia couldn't help her own smile, liking the intelligence she'd already identified in his expression and the courteous manner of his approach. She normally avoided such encounters like the plague, but this afternoon had been far from normal, and it would be mean in the extreme to deny him the empty seat at her table. It wasn't like they had to make conversation; she was perfectly capable of closing down such attempts when she didn't want to talk. 'Please, sit down.'

'Thank you.'

Then he was opposite her, placing a phone and a paperback on the table followed by his glass. It was a booth made for three, four at a stretch and Olivia felt perturbed by his proximity, unable to completely remove him from her vision. Her gaze was back on her phone as she sipped her drink, aware of him picking up the menu she had discarded earlier.

'Caught by the storm?' She smoothed her still-damp hair with a hand, wondering why she'd asked the question. The unsteady note in her voice was a surprise and she cleared her throat, telling herself firmly it was just the result of leaving her dad in his new place earlier and the drive through appalling weather.

The man looked up and Olivia saw his surprise as he considered a reply, the menu still in his hand. 'Yes. I'd been visiting a friend and then my train only made it to this stop before it was cancelled.' He paused. 'You as well?'

'Yes. I hope you're not inconvenienced for long.' She preferred the usual brisk efficiency in her tone this time. She wasn't about to try and draw him into a conversation neither of them wanted.

'Thanks. You too.' His eyes held hers for a second before resuming his exploration of the menu.

Olivia returned to her phone, aware of her companion replacing the menu with his book, settling back against the leather with an ease she could no longer match. She travelled regularly for work and often found herself alone at dinner, much preferring her own company to the alternative. She used such occasions to go over her day and prepare for the next one, and despite the presence of this handsome man now opposite her, she saw no reason for this evening to be different.

Nevertheless, she found her eyes covertly darting to glimpse him again. There *was* something slightly familiar about him… She dismissed the thought; she didn't have time to wonder about such things.

The waitress was soon back, iPad at the ready, and Olivia's smile was casual when he too ordered shepherd's pie. He glanced at her, an acknowledgement of their shared choice but nothing more. They both ordered red wine too, and the waitress suggested a bottle. It seemed to make sense and he waited for Olivia to decide, accepting her choice of a red that promised to be full-bodied and delicately spicy.

When the bottle arrived a few minutes later, Olivia tasted it and nodded her acceptance so the waitress could pour, her companion still absorbed in his book. The waitress gathered up the menus and disappeared, leaving them alone in their corner.

Olivia frowned as she scanned through an email. There was a problem with one of her clients and her assistant hadn't been able to reach her. She began to compose a reply, her thoughts running over the negotiation she'd conducted just yesterday. It was too late to make any calls tonight, even though her client was in the States and would expect a response this evening.

She brought up her calendar and rearranged her morning appointments to deal with this new problem before her time was swallowed up by everything else. Her sigh was irritated, and she knew her dad wouldn't be impressed if he could see her now. He'd told her in no uncertain terms earlier that if she stared at her phone just once whilst she was with him, then he was going back to his reading and she could leave, the visit over. But he only had her best interests at heart, and he was worried about her, no matter how often she told him—

'Are you alright?'

'I'm sorry?' Olivia's head jerked up and she dropped the pen in her hand. She'd almost forgotten that her companion was there until he spoke, her mind flitting from her client to her dad and back to work again.

The man indicated her phone before bringing his eyes back to hers. 'You looked distracted and a little upset. I hope it's not bad news.'

There wasn't exactly a question in his words and she dismissed his concern. 'I'm fine. It's just work, you know how it is. Everything's twenty-four seven these days.'

'Isn't it just.' There was a suggestion of cynicism in his tone, his fingers cradling a glass of wine, the whisky gone.

'Oh?' She could've kicked herself. Damn, that was a nuisance. He might be rather gorgeous with a quiet charisma she wasn't going to admit she found attractive, but now she'd definitely made her reply sound like a question and she should've known better. He'd think she wanted conversation, wanted to while away their enforced hour together and make small talk.

Olivia returned her focus to her phone so he'd realise she wasn't interested and picked up the pen. He seemed to be of the same mind and nothing followed, leaving her free to concentrate on her new problem. She pressed send on the email she'd written.

'Oh, thank goodness you're here, we'd almost given you up.'

Olivia's attention switched from her phone again to find a woman hovering at the table now. Her concerned expression was darting between Olivia and the man sitting opposite her, and it soon became a beaming smile. She wore a plain blouse and black trousers and Olivia saw her name, Sally, written on a badge pinned to her top.

'The weather!' Sally was rushing on, pointing to the storm beyond the window. 'So awful, and we were thinking you must have got stuck somewhere and we'd not heard. Anyway, here you are and many congratulations to you both.'

'I'm sorry, I think you might...'

'Oh, don't worry about being late.' Sally waved away Olivia's attempt at explaining and dropped a key card on the table. 'I know you've already checked in online and the honeymoon suite is all ready for you.' Sally's glance became impish. 'We did think you might rather have dinner in your room, though. Just the say the word.'

Her cheerful gaze went from Olivia to her companion across the table. 'Gosh, you look just like that chap, what's his name, from that show? I bet you get that all the time.' She giggled again, adding a wink for good measure. 'The champagne's on ice.'

With that Sally hurried away, the card on the table between them. Olivia stared after her, momentarily lost for words as the older woman was swallowed up by the crowds at the bar.

'Well, that's a first.'

'I'm sorry?' Olivia swung her eyes back to her companion. He seemed amused, his expression easing into something more friendly.

He pointed to the card. 'I've never been offered a honeymoon suite in a pub before. Sally has clearly mistaken us for a couple about to spend their wedding night here.'

'So it would seem.' Olivia felt her lips twitching, the card sitting between them. She liked the new pleasure on his face, the warmth in his few words.

'I don't know what's more worrying, though. That she didn't bother to check who she was giving the key away to, or that we look so unlike a honeymooning couple should. I was reading and you were engrossed on your phone. Not exactly a picture of newlyweds, surely.'

Olivia laughed and it was only a second until his grin followed, softening the lines around his eyes and mouth. 'I'll take the card back and explain.' She stood up and made her way to the reception area, finding someone to help. Cue a swift apology and she waved it away, it was a mistake and they'd both found it funny.

She returned to her table, weaving through the crowd enjoying Christmas music, surprised to find her companion's gaze on her and liking the quick anticipation she was feeling at the thought of re-joining him. She slid into the booth, replacing her bag on the leather seat.

'All sorted? The real newlyweds still got their room?'

'I think so.' She reached for her wine. 'If they ever make it here through the storm. I wouldn't have minded the champagne, though.'

'Me neither.'

The waitress arrived with their meals and Olivia swallowed down a moan of greed as steaming plates of shepherd's pie and seasonal vegetables were set before them. The young woman topped up their wine glasses before leaving them alone. They began to eat, the silence a little easier than before and it wasn't much longer before Olivia amazed herself again.

'Where are you returning to when your train is rescheduled?'

'London.' He was eating more quickly than her and paused to answer her question, amused again. 'Are we doing this, then? Abandoning our city habits to make conversation?'

'How do you know I live in a city?' She felt a new relaxation in her shoulders, liking his lighter tone and matching it.

'I've lived in London most of my life and I know the signs.'

'Not bad. Five minutes and you're already giving me your life history.' London wasn't a surprise, he carried an air of sophistication that suited his elegant voice, indifferent one moment and curious the next, and Olivia reached for her glass. 'But I'm not *from* a city, I live in one. I'm actually from a small Yorkshire town.'

'Which one?'

'Castlebridge.'

'The book festival town. I know it well.'

But *that* was a surprise and Olivia knew it had registered on her face as he continued. 'I worked in Sheffield for a time and I visited the literary festival whenever I could.' He took a sip of his wine before continuing. 'So, which city do you live in now?'

'Manchester. It's not quite Yorkshire but it's near enough for family and I've got used to having everything on my doorstep.'

'Is that where you were heading before this awful weather intervened?'

'Yes.' She had eaten enough and put her cutlery down as she saw him doing the same, his own plate empty. 'Let's hope the storm blows itself out and we can both be on our way tomorrow.'

She was struck by a new impulse; one she would never normally have acted on in such circumstances. But tonight she was surrounded by a blazing fire, the backdrop of lively chatter and seasonal cheer, a handsome and intriguing man opposite her, and her arm reached across the table. 'Seeing as we're apparently married you should probably know I'm Olivia.'

His hand was already holding hers and his eyes narrowed in a way she really liked as they shook firmly, the little table between them. 'Tom.'

Chapter Two

'How did we meet, then? Before we apparently got married.' Tom leaned back in the booth as their hands separated.

'Online, of course. You swiped right first.'

'Oh, I did? Not you?'

'Well, I probably would've done.'

'Thanks for that.'

They both laughed again, an ease Olivia hadn't expected already beginning to find them through their conversation.

'What did we do for our first date? Did I plan it or did you?'

'Oh, I did,' Olivia said airily, pushing her glasses into her hair. 'You said that it was up to me and you'd take me anywhere I liked. It was wonderfully romantic.'

'Was it?' Tom was sipping his wine, his smile wider. 'Actually, I remember now, it's all coming back to me. I suggested Paris for the day, and you said that you'd much prefer a trip to that funny old museum, the one about operating theatres.'

'But didn't we have a lovely time.' She was loving making up all this nonsense, couldn't remember when she'd last laughed like this, and that was a shock. 'The museum was closed and we had coffee in that strange little cafe near the market instead. You bought cheese from a stall and it stank the whole time.'

'You told me to buy it, as I recall. Said it would work perfectly with pizza,' Tom replied dryly. 'It's a wonder we made it all the way to marriage after a date like that.'

Olivia was laughing so much she hiccupped, and stopped abruptly, embarrassment filling her face as he grinned.

'Sorry,' she said from behind the hand covering her mouth. She used her free hand to point to his paperback instead. 'Tell me about the book you're reading.'

'You like to read?'

'Absolutely.' There was a wistful note in her voice, thoughts of her dad and his bookshop coming back to her. 'I've always meant to read Payne but never got around to it,' she said, referencing the novel on the table. 'Are his books as emotional as people say?'

Tom reached for the wine bottle to empty the last of it into their glasses. 'As a generalisation I'd say yes. Personally, I think he writes with a lot of honesty about the ability of people to care and how we often make the wrong choices before learning to identify the right ones. He's brilliant at placing recognisable characters at the heart of his writing and showing how, in the end, all of life really comes down to love. How it's all we really share when there's nothing else left. What binds us.'

Olivia saw the quick flash of sadness on Tom's face, the slight reveal telling her that he understood, believed, the truth of his reply. She'd worked with just about every kind of person throughout her career and couldn't miss the emotion he was now trying to disguise with a smile.

'Tell me about the last book you read.'

'Ah, well, it's been a while. Quite a while, actually.'

'And why's that, Olivia?'

She didn't want to like how her name sounded when he spoke it in that deep, unhurried voice quite as much as she did. 'Too busy with work, I suppose, I've let myself get out of the habit. I really need to start again.'

She heard the words, knew them for the excuse they were. Her mind was always full of work, and it was easier when she dropped into bed to scroll through her phone or her iPad rather than pick up a book. 'You've made me curious, though, I'm going to try Payne's books when I get the chance.'

'I'm happy to hear it.'

Her phone was flashing with another incoming call, and she ignored it. It was her assistant and anything urgent that Olivia needed to know after not picking up would result in a text. She waited a few moments and when no such message arrived from him, she put the phone in her bag. Her dad would've cheered, and she felt a quick stab of guilt for not having done it when she was with him earlier.

'Are you sure I'm not keeping you from something you need to do?' Tom glanced at the notepad still on the table, her pen beside it. 'You were busy when I came over before.'

'No, it's fine, it's just work.' She dismissed his concern as she pulled her glasses from her hair to rest them on the notepad. She was enjoying his company too much to return to her emails and the problems they contained. 'Some of my clients are in different time zones and I frequently work late, I can't switch off at five o'clock.'

'What is it that you do?'

'Property.'

'As in development, or selling?'

Whenever Olivia tried to explain most people assumed it was estate agency and she was quite happy to let them think so. In reality her job was so much more, and it increasingly demanded even further reserves of her time and energy. 'As in finding. I'm a director of a company which locates property for clients with little time and specific criteria.'

'That sounds challenging, as well as interesting.' Tom's curious gaze was fixed on hers, as though she was a question he hadn't quite worked out the answer to yet. 'Have you been doing it for some time?'

'About six years. I met my business partner when I was head of human resources for a legal firm and he approached me with an offer. I was ready for a change and I love every minute. Except maybe the midnight ones,' Olivia said dryly. 'He and I have developed the business to offer a full service, finding anything from an interior designer to a security guard, a chef or a nanny. I'm sure you get the picture. So what is it you do, Tom?'

There was only the merest hesitation before he replied. 'I fundraise for a charity.'

'What kind of charity?'

'A shelter for young people who've ended up homeless, for all the usual, awful, desperate reasons.'

'How sad.' It couldn't have been more opposite to her own work, quietly searching out the most expensive and magnificent properties the country had to offer for the wealthiest of clients, some of whom had more money than sense. 'Not your job, I mean. Just that it needs doing.'

Their wine was finished, and they both refused dessert when the waitress came back to offer it, and she suggested coffee instead. Olivia knew this was the moment when she could make her excuses and leave, head to her room and catch up with work before falling asleep. But she had enjoyed her time with Tom far more than she had expected, sure her attraction to him was reciprocated, revealed by their laughter and conversation, the glances they had exchanged.

He seemed to be waiting for her to decide when the waitress asked again, clearly ready to be on her way. Olivia accepted, a quick rush of happiness following as he agreed to join her. The pub was beginning to quieten as people left, the festive music still a pleasant background to the night, reminding her that she had yet to start on her Christmas shopping. She ignored the thought – it had no place in this unusual evening. Instead she drew Tom back to the fun they had been having, wanting to see that flirtatious gaze on hers once again now that the waitress had left their coffees on the table.

'So seeing as we're apparently spending our wedding night here, where do you think we'd go on honeymoon?'

He was already smiling, leaning back to consider her question and pretending to search for a serious answer. 'Well, we disagreed on that one.'

'We did? I'm not entirely surprised.'

'You wanted sun and I wanted snow.'

'Ah. Who won?'

'You, obviously, a beautiful villa in Cape Verde. As your husband I'd aim to please.'

Olivia blushed furiously, something she hadn't done in a really long time. She'd rather have hiccupped again than let him see how much that simple comment had affected her. She gulped a mouthful of coffee and followed it up with a cough. Infuriating.

'Don't tell me you're a romantic, Tom.' She kept her tone light when she had recovered, toying with her cup, her pulse still hurrying. 'Happy endings, and all that.'

'I will admit to having romantic tendencies, although I'm rapidly learning that my new wife probably doesn't. Tell me the worst romantic gesture you can think of. Just so I can be clear. For the future of our marriage.'

'Okay, for the future of our marriage. I have a few.' Olivia thanked the waitress as she returned with a bill that she left in the centre of the table. 'But the worst must be a cheesy night out on Valentine's Day in some overpriced restaurant trying to dredge up meaningful conversation whilst musicians are hovering at your table.'

'Agreed. And the rest?'

'Have you really got time?' she teased, pulling the bill towards her and reading the amount, neatly halving it in her mind. She felt certain he was enjoying their bantering conversation as much as she was.

'Try me.'

'Okay. If you're sure you're happy to hear them, given that you've admitted to having romantic tendencies.'

'I am.' Tom's phone flickered and he ignored it.

'Fine. Going down on one knee. Dancing. Watching any kind of movie that professes to be romantic. Cute little meaningless gifts. Boring date…'

'Stop, please.' He held up his hands in defeat. 'You're right, we don't have time for a list that long.'

Olivia put the bill down with her cash and he reached into his jeans pocket, pulled out a wallet, added his money to hers.

'What's your best romantic gesture, then?' His voice was softer now, his eyes fixed on hers. She dragged her gaze away to take in his hands; elegant, a ring on the first finger of his right hand, one on the middle finger of his left. 'I think we have time for that as the list must be shorter.'

'For the sake of our pretend marriage?'

'Of course.'

'The only thing I can come up with is the perfect gift I haven't had to choose myself. What about you?'

He didn't reply at once, eventually offering a glimpse into his thoughts that Olivia wasn't expecting. 'Someone who understands my life.' At once his tone lightened as he covered his comment with something less personal. 'I'd settle for an espresso Old Fashioned made with my favourite bourbon.'

'Have you been married before, Tom?' Serious, direct, personal her question this time, and she wondered if he would answer, if she'd gone too far.

'Before you, you mean?' They both smiled at that. 'Yes. Divorced now.'

'Me too. One ill-advised marriage and I have a lovely daughter in her final year at university before her masters. Do you have children?' Olivia was still thinking of Ellie, living life at a hundred miles an hour, just like her mum, before she realised that perhaps she shouldn't have asked Tom about family.

'No.' A quiet melancholy in his voice this time and his smile was quick, gone. 'We wanted to but it didn't ever work out.'

'I'm sorry.'

There was nothing more Olivia could add. She'd heard the emotion layered into his words and sensed he didn't want to linger now on loss. Her fingers touched his for a second and she saw his brief nod, his acceptance of her understanding. She wondered what time he was leaving for London tomorrow, whether she would catch him at breakfast before they went their separate ways.

She stood up and Tom was on his feet the moment she was, leaving the booth as she slipped her bag over her arm. How to part, she asked herself, how to say goodbye when she wasn't really sure she wanted to quite yet. Holding out her hand for the second time this evening, he took it. She liked the feel of his fingers around hers, his thumb brushing her skin and bringing an awareness of someone else's touch she'd almost forgotten how to appreciate.

'I suppose it's time to say good night.' There was a trace of regret in her remark and she forced herself not to fidget as their hands finally separated. 'Thank you for sharing dinner with me. Safe journey tomorrow.'

A passing couple were staring curiously at them and Tom turned slightly, almost shielding her from view, his back to the room.

'You too. Thank you for your company, Olivia. It's been a really enjoyable evening, not at all the one I expected.'

'Me neither.'

His eyes were still holding hers, sending her stomach into a dive as she recognised that he too didn't want to part, to end their evening. The words slipped from her mouth, light, casual, a suggestion she hadn't been certain she would voice until it was hovering out loud between them. 'Walk with me upstairs?'

'Of course.'

They left the bar and Olivia threw a glance at the receptionist, who was mercifully uninterested in them as they crossed to a staircase. Tom felt tall and unfamiliar at her side, holding open a door as they reached a landing on the first floor. She thanked him as she darted through, resisting the urge to run. Either to him or from him, she still wasn't sure. The light in the corridor was faint and the silence felt piercing as they walked together. He smelled of wood smoke from the fire and something headier, filling her senses with ginger and cinnamon spices.

'This is me.' Olivia paused, made a point of reaching into her bag for the key card. Her pulse was racing as Tom waited for her to unlock the door. A nightlight was on beside the bed, and she dropped her bag, leaning against the door to keep it open. 'What time are you leaving tomorrow if the trains are back to normal?' Her voice sounded different again: breathy, low.

'Around seven.' There was an evenness in his tone, at odds with the intensity in his eyes. 'I'd like to be back in London after lunch if the weather has improved. How about you?'

Olivia didn't really want to think about her morning now, about the problems piling up and the clients demanding her attention. Attention she was normally happy to give them, her life built around her career since her daughter had left home.

'I ought to be going early too. I have to speak with a vendor first thing, renegotiate an offer, view a property in Cheshire and then meetings until late.' Perhaps thoughts of work were just what she needed in this moment, a means of disrupting the direction the evening might have been taking and she aimed for brisk instead. 'I think you'll be fine. I've heard the storm will pass overnight and the restaurant opens at six thirty, so you won't have to travel on an empty stomach.'

'Appreciate the public service information.' Tom grinned and she wondered if she was imagining the regret

23

she thought she saw in his face through the shadows. 'So. I think this is goodbye. Again.'

'On our wedding night? I suppose we are running true to form after Sally found us, me working and you reading.'

Olivia felt her breath quicken as he leant forwards. Never had she laughed, flirted with a stranger quite like Tom before. Enigmatic, charming when he chose, cautious, intelligent, handsome. All words she would attribute to him and she was sure there were more besides. She relied on being in control to keep her balanced, but felt it deserting her now in the desire to let go, to both lose and find herself in someone else. Her pulse was roaring and she felt desire falling in her stomach, the urge to reach out and touch him ready to overwhelm her.

'I suppose we are. In other circumstances that would be a shame and something I'd hope we'd both want to rectify.'

'Other circumstances?'

Her words were no more than a whisper as he left the lightest of kisses on either side of her face. His reply to her question was to gently cup her cheek with a hand, his mouth still distractingly close as he touched his forehead to hers. His jaw was already shadowed and Olivia let her fingers reach for it, brushing her thumb over the roughness she found there, the touch of his skin against hers the one she had been longing for all evening.

She was barely aware that she'd turned her head until she placed a soft kiss on his palm and heard the groan he tried to subdue. His other hand was light on her shoulder and hers found their way into his dark hair, trying to bring him closer still. She sensed she and Tom were both thinking of offering a gentle exploration with their lips but they were beyond it already.

Only one person before had she kissed and been kissed by in return, with such endless passion, promise and skill, and Olivia knew she was matching Tom in everything they offered the other. His hands were discovering her with an urgency she recognised and she was doing the same, finding the unfamiliarity in his frame and letting her fingers commit him to memory, the open door against her back, her heart slamming against his chest.

Someone was passing along the corridor and Tom sprang away from her, one hand against his face as he swiftly put a new distance between them. 'Olivia, I'm sorry. I can't do this.'

She heard his ragged breath, the words he was forcing out, furiously at odds with where they seemed to have been heading. His voice was a distracted mutter, and she couldn't fathom the reason for his abrupt pause as she stared at him in appalled silence. Until this moment she had been certain that he wanted her too and she saw the new apology in his expression as he rubbed his face distractedly.

Shocked now by a halt she had not anticipated, she went to move away, the reality of being alone in her room with someone who was a stranger suddenly crashing into her. One of Tom's hands gently caught hers, trying to keep her close, the tenderness still evident.

'I'm not… I can't…'

Her mind registered his mumbled comments and her lips tried to form an answer, but she couldn't find the right reply. She wasn't able to explain how she had never done this before, had never kissed a stranger on the threshold of her room and wanted him to stay. She snatched her hand from his as she fumbled for the control she had always been able to summon when she needed it. Horrified by the tears gathering at the humiliation and hurt, her voice was a frantic plea. 'But why?'

It was a moment before he answered, despair and regret chasing across his face. 'I'm not what I've let you think I am, Olivia. And I already know you deserve much better than me.'

He gave her a sad, sorrowful smile and spun away, gone, the door banging behind him and shattering the new silence.

Chapter Three

Olivia left her car in the garage and dragged her case to the front door of the house, rifling through her bag for keys. It was freezing and her fingers were cold, hindering her search. She'd meant to arrive in Thorndale earlier but had been delayed at the office as usual, no allowance made for it being a Friday night. All she wanted now was to curl up in bed with a book and sleep for eight hours straight, if such a thing were possible.

Frost was glittering on the wrought iron railings bordering the shallow front garden, edged by a row of neat box hedging. December was a few days old and she hadn't known until she'd got here that tonight was the big Christmas switch-on, when everyone in the village and plenty from beyond it gathered to light up the huge tree lashed into position on the green. It wouldn't have mattered if she had, she couldn't have arrived any earlier and it was years since she'd joined the switch-on with her dad.

The noise and merriment across from the house were definitely at odds with her mood. She'd eaten a quick sushi takeaway at her desk a few hours ago and she could smell the food from the stalls drifting across to her now, the promise of a hot mulled wine, something tasty and filling to eat. Her mouth watered at the thought – maybe the book and bed could wait for a bit longer.

Olivia unlocked the front door and stepped inside the darkened house. It was pleasant enough, the ancient oil-fired central heating managing to just about keep the winter chill at bay. She still couldn't get used to seeing the house without her dad here. Until six weeks ago he would have been comfortable in his library when she arrived, surrounded by his books and warmed by the fire he lit almost every day.

Or he'd be in the kitchen, making her a welcome supper as he knew she wouldn't have already stopped to eat. They'd taken care of each other down the years, and he still loved to spoil her whenever she came to visit: making sure she had a hot water bottle to keep her warm in the night, a hot toddy before bed, a book he thought she'd love already left beside it.

Now there were no lights, no fire, no Dad. Not here, anyway. No milk heating on the range for the coffee and whisky she drank, no hearty goulash in the oven, eaten with the chunks of bread he'd make fresh every day, smothered in creamy butter from a local dairy. Now he was getting used to his new life in the retirement flat in the town where he'd worked all his life.

Olivia had found the flat for him, had taken care of the details, arranged the move and saw him comfortably settled in. He loved Thorndale but she also knew he adored being able to wander around the town where he was still well known. He had his favourite coffee shop, two doors along from his old bookshop, and most mornings he was to be found there, nattering with regulars over a bacon sandwich they made just the way he liked it.

And now, there was this house to sort out. It was far too big of a job for her dad to manage alone, and even with Olivia's help they were going to require professional clearance at some point. She dreaded the thought of emptying his home of its history, packing up the details of his life into boxes small enough for their two flats. Where to start, she mused, with a life lived nearly eighty years.

She carted her case straight up to her room and left it there; unpacking could wait until tomorrow. She borrowed one of her dad's best chunky scarves – hand-knitted for him by his neighbour, Mrs Timms, who liked to keep an eye on the comings and goings of the village and her dad in particular. It always made Olivia smile and him exasperated, but she knew he appreciated the attention and friendship really.

She switched off her bedroom light and, heading out, locked the house behind her. The loud chatter and the Christmas carols being played by a brass band with head torches and lights pinned to their music stands was different to the usual quiet in the heart of the village as Olivia wandered through the crowd. Children were dashing around excitedly, clutching bags of sweets and gifts that she guessed had come from the Santa Claus she could see parked in his sleigh near the post office, a couple of reindeer safely penned nearby.

She spotted Mrs Timms too, manning a stall selling cakes, and Olivia quickly darted into the nearest queue for food, unwilling to be drawn into how her dad was and whether she was planning to stay beyond the weekend. She reached the front of the queue a few minutes later, stamping her feet to keep warm, and couldn't resist ordering a festive sandwich that sounded amazing. Toasted white bread – she smiled wryly at that, she hadn't eaten white bread for years – filled with turkey, stuffing, pigs in blankets and cranberry sauce.

She'd have to come back for the mulled wine: this sandwich was going to take two hands to manage. She'd missed the Christmas tree being switched on and its lights were now shimmering white through the darkness as she found a quieter spot to eat what she soon decided was the best sandwich she'd ever had. Maybe it was the cold, or the season, or the lack of a welcome from her dad, but it was incredible, and she finished the lot.

The local fell rescue association headquarters had their doors open and Olivia hurried along the green, realising that she didn't need to rush for once, and the thought was a surprise. She knew a few of the volunteers and spotted one she recognised; Jon Beresford stood by a rescue vehicle, his wife Annie in front, leaning against him. He had his arms around her, his hands resting on hers as she held her large baby bump, and Olivia smiled at the picture they made.

'Are you sure that's a New Year baby you've got there and not a Christmas one?' she called, seeing Annie's head turn towards her. 'That's quite the bump.'

'Olivia, how lovely. I didn't know you were coming to the switch-on.' Annie moved away from Jon to give Olivia an awkward hug, her bump making it more difficult. 'Officially New Year but who knows. I've been getting a few Braxton Hicks and Jon's nervous, threatening to keep half the fell rescue on permanent standby in case I go into labour in the middle of a snowstorm or something.'

Olivia had met Annie just after the younger woman had married Jon and moved into Thorndale Hall. Annie had arrived in Thorndale, the village where she had spent much of her childhood, after her godmother Molly had died and left her cottage to Annie. Molly and Olivia's dad, Hugh, had met for supper every week for years until Molly had had to leave the village.

Annie had been kind enough to carry on the supper tradition at the Hall, and she and Jon had become good friends of Hugh's. Annie and Olivia kept in touch, mostly unbeknownst to Hugh, and Olivia really appreciated the eye that Annie had on her dad. Olivia had visited them at the Hall several times since and was thrilled about their baby.

Jon joined them, smiling at Annie and also giving Olivia a quick hug, bending down to fold her into his arms before straightening. 'Just an advantage of volunteering and turning out at all hours, and we've got a new snowplough now.'

'What he means is, he's desperate to try it out.' Annie was beaming at her husband, and he slipped an arm around her shoulders.

'Yes, but preferably not when you're in labour. A nice little practice run with the plough would be fun but I don't want any hold-ups getting you to hospital.' The note of anxiety in Jon's voice was a surprise, and Olivia saw the reassuring glance Annie gave him.

Jon was wearing a Christmas jumper beneath his red fell rescue waterproof jacket and holding a fund-raising bucket, and he thanked a passer-by who dropped some change into it, the man glancing back at him. The American accent Jon retained from his childhood in the United States still took people by surprise in the depths of the Yorkshire Dales.

'Me and bump will be fine,' Annie told him, reaching for his free hand. 'We've got weeks yet.' She turned back to Olivia. 'How's your dad, have you seen him today? I really miss seeing him in the village, but it's lovely having

31

the bookshop open again. I'm planning to pop down and visit him next week.'

'Not if it snows, you're not,' Jon told her firmly, and she rolled her eyes at Olivia.

Olivia was distracted, removing money from her purse to drop into Jon's bucket. 'He's good thanks, settling in and making new friends. I haven't been to the flat for a couple of weeks but we Zoom every few days and he looks well.'

'Have you decided about Christmas? He did say he'd like to spend it here if possible. One last time and all that.' Annie was sad for a moment. 'He doesn't want to come to you?'

Olivia thought about her penthouse apartment in Manchester, realising with quick surprise that she'd never spent Christmas Day there yet. One more Christmas in Thorndale was just something she and her dad needed to get through, and then they could move on. Put the memories behind them. 'He would like to be here, so I think that's what we'll do.'

'That sounds good, Sam always says it won't seem quite like Christmas if he's not reading at the carol service.' Annie smiled. 'So are you here for the weekend? He did tell me you were coming at some point to sort out the house.'

'Actually I'm planning to stay until Boxing Day.' Olivia thought of the work ahead with a sinking heart. 'He's adamant he wants me to start sorting the contents before Christmas and it's going to be a mammoth task.'

She heard the frustration in her voice and dismissed it. December wasn't the worst month to have a little time off and she planned to work much as usual in Thorndale. Decent Wi-Fi was at least something her dad's house did afford, and she needed to take some of the annual leave she had piled up.

Jon excused himself to return into the barn housing the fell rescue headquarters and Annie took his bucket. 'How's the sale progressing with the arts consortium?' She thanked someone who made another donation. Fundraising this evening was certainly made easier by the festive cheer and relaxed mood enveloping the village. 'I know he's excited about them taking on the house.'

Olivia was thinking about the home where her dad had spent so many years. She was aware of the local group that had formed and was searching for somewhere to base their developing arts programme and writers' retreat. Her dad adored the idea, enthused by the prospect of selling his house to the group and making it the permanent home for everything on offer.

'It's well on its way. He's accepted the offer in principle – he didn't want it to go to sealed bids and risk them losing it. There are some technicalities to sort out before contracts are signed but I expect it will be finalised in the New Year.' Olivia knew she sounded a bit flat. 'I still haven't got my head around him leaving the house if I'm honest. I wasn't convinced he was ready but obviously I was wrong about that.'

'I think he was, Olivia.' Annie touched a gloved hand to Olivia's, her voice understanding. 'It was the same when Molly left the cottage. She seemed to be coping perfectly well and then one day she called me and said the decision was made. She moved out the following week. Once she'd accepted that she couldn't manage on her own she wanted to get on with it, not linger on what she couldn't do. She hated seeing the garden becoming wild.'

Annie's flash of sorrow was gone as her voice became lively. 'Your dad's had quite a few visitors from Thorndale already from what I hear, including Mrs Timms. Apparently she's insisted that he can't do without her cakes so she gets on the bus and goes to see him every Wednesday afternoon.'

'She has been good to him.' Olivia felt a dart of humour as she thought of her dad's friend, who helped to run the cafe in the village. Cynthia Timms hadn't been in Thorndale that long, but she had positioned herself at the heart of much that went on. She loved to bake, knit and natter, and time was the one thing she seemed to have in abundance, especially for Hugh.

'And there's a good reason why she goes on a Wednesday too.' Annie was shaking her head. 'She's got a soft spot for Ben, who drives the bus every other week. He's lovely; his partner Daisy is our accountant. Mrs Timms swears it's nothing to do with him but I'm not convinced, I don't know if she bakes any of the other drivers their favourite flapjacks. He used to be a banker but you'd never guess it from the long hair and cowboy boots.'

Olivia laughed as Jon came back to join them and she excused herself, leaving them to their fundraising and still pondering Annie's comments about her dad. She bought some mulled wine, using it to warm her hands as she strolled amongst the few stalls set up for the evening. The brass band had finished now, and she saw them packing up, folding music stands and instruments into cases. She caught the conductor's eye, and the woman gave her a cheerful smile, which Olivia returned.

Plenty of people were still milling around and seemed in no hurry to leave just yet. She chatted to a few people she knew, most of them asking after her dad and how Ellie was getting on. Olivia hadn't lived in Thorndale for years, but some faces were familiar and many of them had a long and friendly association with Hugh.

The Courtyard, formerly a working farm, was now a thriving craft centre, a jumble of studios converted from the old farm buildings and filled with local craftspeople each occupying their own space. It had stayed open later this evening, attracting an influx of visitors ready to shop, and Olivia made her way over, checking her phone on the way for anything urgent.

She had done nothing for Christmas yet. No planning, shopping or decorating, and since Ellie had left for university that wasn't unusual. Ellie had met her boyfriend Logan, who was from Western Australia, in her first year and they'd been together ever since, spending that first Christmas with his family in Kimberley. Olivia had missed Ellie terribly, being so far away while she'd been here in Thorndale with her dad, quietly eating a ready-prepared dinner and watching repeats on television.

Ellie's father, Olivia's feckless ex-husband, usually travelled and worked right up to the holidays and his time with Ellie even when she was a child had been sporadic. But they were still in contact, and this year Ellie was heading to the Caribbean to spend the holidays with him and his extended family in Tobago, Logan going with her. Olivia had a weekend with her daughter and Logan to look forward to before they left at the end of term, and she needed to get a move on with her Christmas shopping.

Five stocking fillers and half an hour later, Olivia strode up the lane back to her dad's house and let herself in. She took off his scarf, hung up her coat and went straight up to bed. The mulled wine had made her surprisingly drowsy and she always slept better when she was in Thorndale, although this would be the first night she had spent in the house without her dad in an awfully long time.

The house was silent, as though it had breathed in and wasn't quite sure how to exhale again without him there. She unpacked her cosy pyjamas and sighed. It was never that warm here, and yesterday she'd ordered the first pair she'd found online that could be delivered to her office this morning. The pyjamas were navy, long and snug, and she did her best to ignore the dozens of dachshunds in Christmas hats and jumpers printed on the fabric.

The bed felt cool when she slid between the sheets and she jumped out again, hurrying barefoot to the bookcase on the landing to find a book from the dozens of choices facing her. Her hand reached for a childhood favourite and she was back between the sheets in no time. It wasn't even ten p.m. when she finished checking her emails and fell asleep, the paperback still in her hand.

It was the thud that woke her. Some part of her mind thought she was dreaming, and she lay still in the bed, her senses suddenly alert. Olivia didn't know the house that well at night now and she took a deep breath, reassuring herself that it was just a tree outside, or someone shutting a car door. She turned over, willing the sleep she'd already had to find her again.

When the second thud came, she knew it was in the house and that she wasn't alone. She hurriedly gathered her phone and keys, slid them into her bag and got out of bed. The carpet felt thin and cold beneath her feet as she moved to the door and slowly twisted the doorknob, praying it wouldn't squeak.

The tiny peep that followed as she turned it wasn't any louder than her own heartbeat roaring in her ears and she listened. Footsteps now, crossing the hall. She slid the strap of her bag over her shoulder and tiptoed onto the landing in the darkness, reaching for the bookcase. Her fingers found a heavy hardback, something that felt as big as an atlas.

Olivia heard the footsteps climbing steadily, passing the stairlift, nearing her. They'd reached the little landing beside the picture window now, where the stairs turned, and she saw a shadow moving in the faint light, framed for a second by the glass. Her heart was pounding so fast she was ready to scream, and she bit her lip to stop the fright escaping.

She would use the book, aim low and take them by surprise, then leg it out of the house to her car. She'd back it straight through the flimsy wooden garage doors like James Bond if she had to. He – she was certain it was a man – was only two feet away from her now, crouched as she was beside the spindles in the darkness. The hardback in her grasp, she lifted it with two hands, ready to strike.

The light came on, flooding the landing with brightness and making Olivia squint. Shocked, she dropped the book before she managed to land a blow and it hit the floor with a resounding clunk. There was a terrified yell and she saw the intruder leap about a foot in the air and spring away from her.

'What the bloody hell?' he roared as the glass in his hand fell to the floor, spilling water and shattering into dozens of pieces. She saw the recognition dawn in Tom's face at the same time as hers and gasped in horror. His wild eyes narrowed suspiciously as they shifted to the atlas near her feet. 'What were you planning to do with that?'

'You would've found out if you hadn't switched the light on.' There was a shaky note in her retort and she swallowed, trying to rid herself of the tremble in her hands.

'If you want to kill me, Olivia, there are probably kinder ways to do it. Don't move,' he ordered, pointing to the mess between them. 'Your feet are bare and there's glass everywhere.'

So he'd remembered her name. She was too shocked to move, other than to slump against the spindles, her bag sliding to the floor beside her. She'd forgotten about her feet; a run across frozen gravel without shoes to her car wouldn't have been very nice.

A dozen thoughts were chasing through her mind and she tried to arrange them into some sort of order. What was Tom doing here, in her dad's house? Did they know one another? Had he followed her somehow, found out who she was and where she was going to be? No, that one was ridiculous, she told herself. They'd exchanged no personal details and there was more than one high-end property-finding company in Manchester.

She hadn't seen him since he'd rushed from her room that night in the pub three weeks ago and she hadn't expected to see him again ever. The morning after she had made sure to be up and away by dawn so there was no chance of bumping into him again, the humiliation of his exit and what they'd almost done still so raw. She'd worked even harder since then, pulling more hours, scheduling more meetings, trying to forget she'd ever met him.

But it hadn't been easy, forgetting. Every so often reminders of their conversation had come back to her, made her smile. Then she'd remember his eyes and the fun, the flirting as they'd discussed a first date and talked about that honeymoon. The look on his face the second before they'd kissed, and she'd been pressed against the door. Then the disappointment, the regret when he'd halted all they'd shared and she was certain they had both wanted.

Tom stepped past her, running down the stairs. He was back in a few minutes, a cloth, dustpan and brush in his hand. She watched him clear up the mess, trying to make sure he had gathered up all of the shattered glass.

'What are you doing here?' She found her voice and stood up, crossing her arms and giving him the best outraged glare she could manage in Christmas dachshund pyjamas. He straightened, the dustpan in his hand and Olivia saw the tension again in his face.

'I was about to ask you the same thing.'

'Me?' she replied incredulously. 'This is my house. I have every right to be here, whereas you...' She tailed off, feeling a bloom of satisfaction as she registered his astonishment.

'Your house? Doesn't it belong to Hugh Bradshaw?'

'It does,' she told Tom coolly. 'Hugh is my father.'

'Your father?' Tom let out a breath that turned into a sigh. 'Right. I knew he had a daughter but I wasn't expecting her to be you.'

'So it appears, and I certainly wasn't expecting you either. But what I still don't know is why you're actually here and creeping around his home in the dead of night.'

'He hasn't told you?' A note of anxiety in Tom's voice, one that was still doing things to her senses that it absolutely shouldn't.

'Obviously not.'

'I see.' A beat of silence followed as he rubbed his jaw. 'So you probably don't know then that Hugh and I are good friends and he's, er, he's very kindly offered me the use of his house for a few weeks.'

'He's what?' Olivia wished she'd toned down her shriek, longing to reach for the atlas again and chase this man straight outside into the night and far away from her. She should be asleep, not confronting the person responsible for disturbing it every time she laid eyes on him. 'He can't have! He knew I was planning to stay so why on earth would he let you be here as well?'

There was a defensiveness crossing Tom's face now and she had the impression he didn't want to answer. He wasn't getting away with that. He was technically still a stranger to her and she waited. 'Well? And how come you're such good friends and I know nothing about it?'

'Does your father know all of your friends and when you see them?' Tom countered.

Olivia couldn't refute that, feeling her adrenaline finally beginning to settle and finding it difficult to make eye contact with him. Her dad had made so many friends through his shop down the years and she knew he was still in touch with some of them.

'You can either tell me and leave in the morning or you can leave now without explaining. It's up to you but your stay is over. If you're here to look after the house for him then there's no need, I'm taking over. I'll be seeing him soon and I'll let him know you've gone, it's too late to call him now.'

'That would be difficult for me.' Tom was apologetic as he faced her, waiting for the challenge she was sure he was expecting. The wretchedness in his voice took her by surprise and she felt herself softening for a second, lowering her defences for reasons she couldn't begin to fathom.

'Which? Leaving or explaining?'

'Both.' He carefully placed the dustpan on the floor beside the cloth and straightened up. His eyes found hers and she steeled herself against the glimpse of panic and pain she saw in them, the effort she suddenly knew he was having to make to speak.

'Because I'm homeless, Olivia. I have nowhere else to go.'

Chapter Four

'You must have.' Olivia hadn't meant to sound so sharp,
blinking rapidly. 'I mean, surely, you must...'

Tom shrugged, hunching his shoulders against the
hurt. She felt herself wanting to go to him, to reach out
and apologise, to say – what? She had no idea and she held
back, unwilling to offer more in this moment. Who was
this man really, and how was he friends with her father?
How had Tom crashed into her life, twice now, and rattled
her in ways she wasn't used to?

'You look, I mean, you don't...' She couldn't find the
words, couldn't explain how a man who seemed as he
did – handsome, successful, charming, capable – could
possibly be homeless. She stepped back to lean against the
spindles. She was used to being the one in control, able to
command her emotions and settle them as she chose, but
the ability had deserted her in this moment following his
revelation.

'Don't look the part?' There was bitterness in Tom's
voice and he was twisting the ring on his right hand. 'No,
I don't suppose I do.'

'And Dad's letting you stay here? Because you're homeless?'

Olivia didn't like the word, didn't like to pin it on Tom,
didn't like the way it made him look and her feel – sad
and sorrowful, a new thread stitched into her thoughts

of sympathy, possibly even pity. What had brought him to this? His words that night came back to her. That he wasn't what he'd let her think, believed he was less than she deserved.

'He knew I needed somewhere to go and was kind enough to offer me his home.' Tom was staring at her, and she sensed he was forcing out just enough words to provide a plausible explanation. 'I'm writing a book and he thought it might give me space to think without worrying for a while.'

'You're a writer?'

'I was,' Tom corrected her. 'Used to be. Trying to be again.'

Olivia dismissed that. 'My dad always says if you write, you're a writer.' She hesitated, remembering again that night in the pub, the things they had talked of. 'What about your job? The charity?'

Tom was leaning against the wall and she felt sure he didn't like being questioned. Didn't like being obliged to confess the poverty of his position but felt compelled to, given the circumstances in which they had both now found themselves, and she really couldn't blame him. But she need to know more, to get everything straight in her mind, her order to him to leave made moments ago already wavering in the light of his admission.

'I didn't actually say it was a job,' he replied quietly. 'I said I fundraise for a charity.'

'I assumed, and you let me.' Olivia knew he had not been untruthful, simply economical with it, and she wondered if she might have done the same, in those same circumstances. 'You meant that you're a volunteer?'

He nodded. 'I'm sorry for that. We all tend to make our own assumptions about one another and I was happy

43

to let you believe that my status was different to the reality.' He paused. 'But you're right, we can't both stay here. I'll leave in the morning if you don't mind. It's a bit late for a train now.'

'Tom.' Olivia hadn't even realised she'd moved until her hand was on his arm, much smaller than him now in her bare feet. At once she felt the flutter of the attraction she'd recognised the moment he had settled opposite her in the booth that night. 'We can talk about it tomorrow. I wouldn't make you leave now even if there was a train.'

'Because you feel sorry for me?'

She couldn't entirely deny it. Who wouldn't, confronted with a man who appeared the epitome of success only to find out it was a shell he wore, perhaps keeping the world at bay and letting it make its own decisions about him, just as she had done.

'You really don't need to, Olivia. It's my problem and I'm working it out.'

'But where will you go?' She didn't want to be worried about him, couldn't seem to help it now. 'Surely you must have friends, or family...'

Tom looked weary and it was late to be having this conversation. She was surprised to see her hand was still sitting on his arm and she withdrew it. 'We should probably both try and get some sleep. We can work out what we're going to do in the morning.'

He nodded and the panic on his face from before had been replaced by relief in the reprieve she'd offered, however temporary. 'Be careful,' he said softly, glancing at the carpet. 'There might still be glass around.'

'I'm fine.' She was still standing in front of him and saw him taking in the cheery Christmas pyjamas. That night in the pub suddenly flared between them again and she saw the flash of awareness in his eyes before stepping back quickly. Whatever had taken place then was over and she wasn't about to go there again.

'I'll bring you some more water, it was my fault you lost the first.' She turned away, his reply following.

'I'm glad it was just the glass that got broken and not my kneecaps. You were crouching there like some sort of ninja about to deliver a fatal blow. I'll fetch the water, you've still got bare feet. That kitchen floor is freezing.'

He passed her, heading down the stairs. Olivia returned to her room, shivering, her feet like blocks of ice as she huddled between the sheets, an old patchwork quilt covering them. She heard Tom coming back upstairs, knew then he was sleeping in the room next to hers as the door opened and then clicked shut.

Used to living in a busy apartment block, the silence in the house seemed to be shouting, making her restless. She picked up her book, resisting her phone and the work she would find there. At some point Tom crossed to the bathroom; her every sense was alert to his movement, aware of another night in the same building with him. A second night of disturbance, a second night of thinking about him.

–

When Olivia woke in the morning she reached for her phone and glasses first, as ever. She quickly checked her emails and messages, glad to see that there wasn't anything so urgent that she ought to deal with it in the next hour or so. Last night and finding Tom in the house was at the front of her mind, and she got out of bed, checking the landing for signs of him before she darted across to the bathroom.

That would be another problem if he were to stay. There was only one bathroom on the first floor and a basic cloakroom downstairs. She was so used to her own functional and organised space and didn't relish the thought of sharing, like being a student in digs all over again. After a hurried shower she went downstairs, sitting at the kitchen table with coffee and her phone.

She missed her dad in the house, how it felt empty now and yet full still of almost everything he possessed. The thousands of books he couldn't bear to part with, many of them stashed in the little annexe at the bottom of the garden that he'd turned into another shop.

When she'd tried to persuade him not to, he had declared he missed the day-to-day trade of customers, even though hardly anyone knew the shop was there. Until the move into town he had propped himself in the annexe a couple of afternoons each week and lit the fire, happy to chat to whoever found him. Apparently a few visitors even bought books, something that always made him happy.

Tom's presence in the house now was something else. Olivia felt hyperaware of him, as though she could sense him through the silence. She didn't want to think of the fun and flirting they'd shared when they'd been mistaken for newlyweds, their amusement over a fictitious first date and the choice of pretend honeymoon.

She didn't want to be reminded of how their attraction was as mutual as it was compelling, or remember their hands exploring one another so urgently. How she'd loved discovering the shape of him and the way they had kissed. And she especially didn't want to still be thinking about kissing him as he walked into the kitchen.

'Morning.' His gaze found hers for no more than a moment before he removed it. He was about to help himself to coffee from the cafetière she had made, and Olivia saw him pause, his hand hovering above it. 'Would you mind?'

'Of course not.'

There was a familiarity to his quiet movements around the kitchen as he found a cup and opened the fridge to add milk to the coffee she already knew he didn't drink black. To Olivia's experienced and professional eye the room looked dulled, a blue range clashing with the dark green walls, the colours unsuited to a west-facing aspect. No morning sun troubled this space, with its mismatched range of cupboards spelling out their history.

Despite the room's lack of cosmetic appeal she could still appreciate its generous proportions: the large window overlooking the small, paved garden leading to the annexe at the bottom. She'd tried a few times to get her dad to update the kitchen, to bring it into this century from the last one but he'd always stubbornly insisted he could manage perfectly well without a few modern appliances and better heating.

Tom pulled out a chair opposite her, and a glance was enough to recognise the tension in his face, the tautness across his shoulders. How to start, how to find the beginning of this story, she wondered, when they seemed to already be in the middle of it?

'So.' Olivia's voice was her usual crisp, professional one, even though she was irritated that she was finding it hard to meet his eyes. She'd met hundreds of people during the course of her career and didn't want to be concerned about the worry she expected to find in Tom. 'Maybe you

47

could start by telling me a bit about yourself and how you know my dad.'

'Olivia, it's fine,' Tom said firmly, an edge to his tone. 'I really don't want to be interviewed like I'm applying for a job; I've had enough of those. I've thought about it overnight and I can't stay here. Your dad was very kind to invite me but I think he must have forgotten that you were going to be here too.'

Olivia doubted it very much. Her dad was certainly frailer than he used to be but that was in body only. His mind was sharper than hers half the time and she was quite sure he knew what he was doing. Which was more than she did right now, her plans for work on a short pause.

She watched as Tom took a sip of his coffee. 'So where will you go?'

There was an evasiveness now too in his face and she knew he didn't like being questioned. She couldn't really blame him, most people would object to having to reveal their most private and possibly wretched circumstances to anyone, least of all someone they'd met once in a pub. 'Tom? I can't just let you leave if I don't know what you'll do.'

'You can't actually stop me. And it's not your business either, is it?' There was a resentment in his words he didn't attempt to disguise.

'It sort of is,' she replied reasonably, slipping her glasses off. 'You're already an invited guest and it's not my house. I don't get to pick and choose who stays or goes, that's my dad's prerogative. Even if I am being forced to share.'

'You sound almost as though you don't want me to leave now. Have you had a change of heart?'

Olivia's heart was already softening towards Tom in a most unusual way, that was the problem. She'd liked him, had been attracted to him that first evening, and seeing him again had made her realise that both of those things had not changed. But she was far too busy for anything else, and he was, well, what was he? She still didn't know. But she could do this. She could work, meet clients, order in a basic Christmas meal for her and dad. Here, with Tom staying. She'd have to. She couldn't clear the house from Manchester and they were running out of time.

'You surprised me last night, Tom, that's all. You can imagine how shocked I was to find someone else here, and then to discover that it was you, after that night...' Her gaze was elsewhere again and she decisively brought it back to face him. 'But what happened between us was just a moment of madness and if we're both staying here then we have to make sure there isn't another one.'

'Absolutely.' Tom sounded perfectly clear about that.

'Good.' Reassured, though slightly disappointed by the ease with which he'd agreed, Olivia carried on. 'I'm really busy with my work, I don't have time for any distractions and I have to make a start sorting this place out soon. I'll be back in Manchester at some point. You'll be...'

His laugh was short, without humour when it followed her pause. 'Neither of us really knows the answer to that one, do we?'

'Stay.' She felt ridiculous, almost pleading with him now when last night she had been ready to sling his bag straight after him through the front door. He was her dad's friend and that meant he must trust Tom. It seemed she would have to do her best to put up with it.

She'd faced far worse in her time than sharing a house with a handsome man. Olivia knew her dad would feel she had let him down too if she were the reason for Tom leaving, especially when she had her own home to return to and Tom apparently didn't. And why he looked slightly familiar, she still couldn't work out. She was certain she had never seen him here before.

'Please, Tom. We're both busy and the house is big enough for us to keep out of one another's way.' She pointed at the window and waved an arm to the weather, hating the thought of him with nowhere to go. 'It's freezing out there.'

She wasn't prepared for the rush of relief in his face that he quickly disguised or the way her breath caught at the sight. She tried to lighten the moment with something more friendly and relaxed. 'We'll have to draw up a rota for the bathroom, though. I don't want to be crashing in when you're showering or vice versa, and there's no lock. Dad never got around to replacing it when it broke.'

Olivia didn't really think she'd mind crashing in when Tom was in the shower and gave herself a silent telling-off, reaching for a loaf of bread on the table so that he wouldn't notice the sudden flush plastered on her face.

'Would you like some toast?' Two pieces were as easy to make as one but it was something else they'd need to think about. She didn't really cook and she wasn't going to be planning meals for two, even if they did go straight in the microwave. 'My dad makes the best marmalade and there's still some left. And er, sorry, this must be your bread. I haven't been shopping yet.'

'It's fine. Thanks.' Tom waved that one away, refilling his coffee and she nodded when he pointed to her cup. 'He gave me a jar the last time I was here, it's really good.'

'You've stayed before?' Olivia slid another piece of bread into the toaster and found a second plate. Her dad had clung on to the dinner sets he'd had since her mum had died and there were only about four side plates left, half of them chipped. She knew it was one of his ways of remembering his wife, the life they'd lived before she'd been lost to illness far too soon.

'Yes, usually when the literary festival was on in town.'

'Of course, you mentioned that. Visiting the festival.' That night, but she didn't add those two words. She put the plate and Tom's toast down in front of him and he smiled at her in way she could really do without, especially given they'd just agreed to avoid each other as much as possible.

She retook her seat, the beginnings of relaxation following, a strange relief that Tom wasn't leaving the house and she the reason for it. Her phone was flashing with a call and she let it go to voicemail. 'So you know about Dad running a bit of a retreat here then, during the festival? You were part of it?'

'Yes, I was lucky enough to be included in his famous hospitality.'

'What, the dodgy sausage rolls he made himself and the weird salads?' Her dad was better than her in the kitchen these days but only just.

'You've missed out the prawns served with sultanas and lentils.'

'I'd forgotten that one! I was convinced he only invented that dish to try and put people off coming back.'

'Even that couldn't keep them away. He's a great host, Olivia.'

She and Tom were both smiling now, a quick recognition of the humour they'd shared in the pub as their eyes met then moved away.

'I only came a couple of times during the festival.' Olivia had finished her toast and sipped the last of her lukewarm coffee. 'Was it as lively here as he used to say?'

'Absolutely. Writers, artists, journalists, everyone was welcome and I loved it.' Tom was wistful, one hand resting on the table. 'There were some great debates and a few fireworks over the years. If these walls could talk, and all that. I think a few highly successful deals were done here.'

'And you've stayed friends with my dad? You mentioned you're a writer.'

'We have, he's been really good to me. Supported my book when it came out, invited me up for signings, asked me to speak at the festival. Promoted me wherever he could.'

'That sounds just like him. His absolute favourite thing is discovering a brilliant new writer and he loves to champion them. And you're writing a second book? A third?' Olivia heard the pensive note now that her dad was no longer in his beloved shop, at the heart of the bookselling trade he adored. 'Are you a really famous author and I don't even know it? You still haven't told me your full name.'

She saw Tom lean back in his chair, becoming evasive again as he crossed his arms.

'Come on, Tom.' She made her voice deliberately warm, adding a confiding tone as she tried to draw him out. They were sharing a house after all, and she deserved some details. His name at least. So much for years of human resources and managing interviews, she wasn't doing very well with him. But then, she reasoned, she hadn't ever kissed the candidates who had sat before her to talk through their applications.

'You won't have heard of me,' he said lightly. 'My book's not that well known.'

'Try me.'

'Okay. My name is Tom Bellingham.' He was watching her through eyes that seemed to be waiting for some sort of recognition, and Olivia grinned.

'You're right, I've never heard of an author called Tom Bellingham. Sorry.' She thought for a moment, the few words he had offered prompting a memory. 'Wait, isn't that the name of an actor, that guy from some period drama who drove everyone crazy when he took his shirt off? I never saw it but I do remember people in the office going on about it. Someone even tried to put up a poster!'

She saw Tom's faint smile, the hand he lifted to push through his hair, heard the quick sigh. Her eyes widened and she stared at him. Tall, dark hair, probably the right age now, a few years on, if she remembered correctly what she'd overheard at work. And definitely still gorgeous. It fitted.

'No! It's not! I mean, you're not... Are you?' Olivia was aghast, babbling, and he nodded slowly. Her gaze shot away from his face to roam over his shoulders, the briefly famous chest, safely covered in a chunky sweater, before landing back up somewhere near his right ear.

She was furious to find herself blushing, remembering how they had kissed, the feel of his frame beneath her hands. *Well*, she thought wildly, *the surprises just keep on coming*. No wonder he was such a great kisser, he'd probably had plenty of practice. It really was a good thing she hadn't kneecapped him last night with the atlas.

'And that's why it's always better not to tell people who I am if they haven't already worked it out.' Tom stood up and collected their plates, took them to the sink. 'Years of training and professional roles and it all comes down to my shirt. Or the lack of it,' he finished dryly.

Chapter Five

> Tom Bellingham!!! You didn't think to tell
> me?

Olivia fired off the text to her dad, shaking her head.
She'd left the house and found a table in the restaurant at
The Courtyard, which was busy with shoppers wandering
through the studios or sharing brunch. She settled
down with her laptop and phone at hand, ignoring the
Christmas music softly playing and the beautiful decorations scattered around the light and modern building.

She ordered coffee, noticing that most people seemed
to be appreciating the festive atmosphere, unlike her. Her
client in the States was anxious and she scheduled a call
with them for this afternoon. She had planned to go and
see her dad but it would keep until tomorrow. Heavy snow
was apparently forecast but she ignored the notification
from her weather app. She hadn't got time for that either.

She had a property to view in Cumbria on Monday
and the elderly vendor was concerned, checking the time
of the appointment again and whether she would actually
come if it snowed. Olivia already had a client in mind
for the house so she smoothed things over, assuring the
vendor that she would be there except in the absolute
worst of the weather.

Sipping coffee, she picked up a flyer advertising the seasonal activities taking place in Thorndale, surprised by how much was going on since she had last bothered to take note. There was the carol service that Annie Beresford had mentioned, and at which Olivia's dad usually did a reading.

She hadn't known about the Christmas tree sale the fell rescue volunteers were holding each weekend outside their barn, offering refreshments in return for buying a tree to support the association. She wouldn't have minded having a go at the cocktail workshop here in the restaurant, but she definitely wouldn't be turning up for the wreath making one or the cookie baking classes. She slid the flyer back between a small poinsettia plant and a menu.

Christmas Day was only three weeks away and she had plenty of work to get through before she could think of taking some of her annual leave, never mind the shopping she still needed to do. A reply arrived from her dad and she clicked on it.

> You wouldn't have come if I had, Liv, we both know that. Tom is a wonderful writer whose life has not always been easy. He deserves another chance and I'm glad I can help. Looking forward to seeing you but don't come in that ruddy car if it snows. Love Dad.

He always made her smile, the way he finished his messages with 'Love Dad', as though she had no idea who had sent them. Olivia forced away her irritation of how he had manoeuvred her into a corner over Tom by not telling her he had invited him to stay. It wasn't *all* her dad's fault; he didn't know about the night in the pub with Tom and how awkward things were between them.

Her lovely dad knew her so well and he had such a good heart. Better than hers, it seemed. She sent him a grimacing emoji that she knew would make him laugh. She didn't want to go back to the house yet, so she ordered brunch, almost drooling when the plate of eggs Benedict with juice and a decaf coffee arrived not long after. She had no idea how Tom was spending his time here, other than writing, and wasn't quite ready to bump into him again just yet.

Two women appeared at the table beside hers a few minutes later and she lifted her head long enough to give them a brief smile of acknowledgement. They replied in kind, settling down and chatting noisily above the Christmas songs. Olivia tried to ignore them but it was difficult; they were enjoying an early glass of Prosecco and she couldn't help catching some of their conversation as she ate.

'Nope, no social media, not a single one.'

'There's that group on Facebook, the fan one.'

'That's nothing to do with him, though. He probably doesn't even know it exists.'

Olivia heard the dismissiveness in the first woman's reply. She saw them scrolling through their phones, presumably on social media, carrying on their conversation without looking at one another. Her juice was gone and she was happy to linger over coffee, her most important emails done.

'Are you absolutely certain it was Tom Bellingham you saw?'

Olivia sat up a little straighter, only pretending for once to be interested in her phone. The two women were quite loud and it was impossible not to hear what they were saying from where she was sitting.

'Of course I am. I was about to turn onto the high street, and I had to pull over so he could cross the bridge. He was in running kit, all muddy and messy. I didn't realise it was him until he caught my eye and then he did that thing, when he sort of smiles but doesn't, all sexy and mysterious. He's such a stone-cold fox for an older guy.'

Olivia's lips twitched. She wondered what the two women would've made of Tom smiling at her over the breakfast table a couple of hours ago and felt her own pulse patter a little faster at the thought. She shook herself crossly.

'I know, right? But what's he doing in Thorndale?'

'No idea. He hasn't acted for ages, he's supposed to have given it up so it can't be filming unless he's planning a comeback. Family maybe? Or he's moved here? I might check out that Facebook group, see if anyone else has noticed him.'

'What's the betting his series will be repeated over Christmas. They always show it.'

'Your mum will be happy.'

'She's not the only one.'

Their conversation moved onto something else and Olivia tried her best to tune it out this time. She opened the family group chat of just her, her dad and Ellie to see some images from her daughter. Ellie was good at keeping in touch, knowing that her grandad missed her and therefore dropping anything in the group she thought would interest him – books and bookshops mostly. Her dad had already replied to Ellie by the time Olivia had looked at the messages, her thoughts still flitting through the comments she'd overhead about Tom.

There was another message too, from her best friend Gina, who lived near Ripon. She and Gina had met in the first year at high school and had been friends ever since, despite the years, marriages, divorce, house moves, children and differing careers in between. They didn't catch up in person as often as they'd like, their messages an ongoing conversation no matter how many days in between.

Whenever Olivia wanted a brief time-out, she would head to Gina's messy home, filled with her partner and four teenage boys, and Gina herself busy with her dog training business. She and Gina would walk the dogs for miles, catch up, de-stress, then sit up late and drink wine together as they put the world to rights. Being gathered into the heart of this large family was so different to Olivia's more solitary life in the city and she always felt rejuvenated by the fresh air and hearty home cooking.

She would reciprocate when Gina wanted a bit of city sophistication, fewer demands on her time and considerably less mud. Her friend would head south on the train to Olivia's apartment in Manchester for lazy mornings drinking coffee and wandering around the city before cocktails and a night out in the Northern Quarter, often in the bar managed by Olivia's assistant's boyfriend.

Now Gina wanted to know if Olivia had arrived in Thorndale yet and how her dad was, checking in with typical haste and usual care. Olivia replied but made no mention of Tom. There was little to say, other than *Hey, did you know Dad's got me sharing the house with a writer and famous actor who I might accidentally have kissed in a pub?* That would bring a reply straight back and the thought made Olivia smile to herself.

She'd have to tell Gina at some point; she would be bound to find out and Olivia knew it should come from her. She wouldn't mention the kiss or the pub, though. Not unless it was unavoidable.

Her coffee finished, it was time to go. She had another explore through the studios, taking a picture of the Pilates one with its dates and times, hoping she might make classes whilst she was here. She would miss her gym sessions but running was something she enjoyed, and she would try to keep that up, shuddering at the thought of being outdoors in a Dales winter instead of on the usual treadmill.

She collected a couple of meals for one from the cook-shop, feeling a quick stab of guilt, shopping for just herself, as she remembered Tom. What had her dad meant, she wondered, when he'd said that Tom's life had not always been easy?

The house was quiet when she returned and she glanced in at the dining room on the way to the kitchen. It had always been a bleak sort of a room, chilly, lit by a window that allowed in a cool westerly draft. A dresser filled with china stood against one wall, and there was an old-fashioned dining table to seat six, which could be extended to fit ten. Photographs hung on the pale blue walls alongside some good art, and of course there was another overfull bookcase.

A hoodie was slung on the back of one chair facing the window, a notepad, empty glass and a laptop on the table, a small stack of books and no Tom. It was going to take a couple of days' work to pack and clear just this room and the thought was enough to make Olivia's head ache.

She dropped a reminder into her calendar to call someone next week about the furniture. They'd already filled her dad's new home with bits and pieces from here, most of it oversized and unsuitable for a modern flat.

She carried on to the kitchen and left her meals in the fridge, glancing at the other provisions she saw there. The usual stuff and lots of vegetables, plus a couple of foil-covered dishes that looked as though they could be leftovers.

Still no sign of Tom and she thought he must be out unless he was in his bedroom. Next to hers, and that was a reality she still hadn't got her head around yet. She'd heard him in there this morning as she'd dressed, feeling almost as though she could sense his movements around the room. Did he sense hers too, she wondered? Did he think about her, as she thought about him?

Work was beckoning and she was at the sink beneath the window, filling the kettle to make a peppermint tea, when she saw two unfamiliar men leaving the annexe. One of them was holding a bag and they were chatting, in no hurry as they strolled across her dad's garden to the drive and disappeared from sight. Olivia realised she had overfilled the kettle and quickly turned the tap off.

She looked at the annexe. The lights were on and that was another surprise. She put the kettle down, opened the back door and darted through the freezing air without a coat, rushing into the building and halting the moment her feet were over the threshold.

'What's going on?'

Tom was standing behind the desk that passed for a counter, holding a book, and his lips twisted wryly. 'I'm guessing your dad hasn't told you about the shop either?'

'What do you think?' she countered. She took in the cheerful fire burning, a man sitting in an armchair beside it with a book in his hand, someone else browsing along a shelf of hardbacks. 'I assumed it was shut.'

She hadn't been in here for months, not since they'd emptied her dad's old shop in town, and he hadn't been able to bear the thought of letting someone else clear away his books as a job lot. They'd brought them here instead, despite her protestations, and she realised now with fresh horror the size of the task ahead. There were mountains of stuff to move and it was going to take months, probably, not a few short weeks before Christmas to sort this place out.

Tom put the book down. 'Your dad suggested I might want to open the shop now and again, and I liked the idea.' He gestured to the teetering piles of stock. 'I thought it might help to sell more books. Reduce the load.'

'Like that's going to make a difference. You'll need a decade of "now and again" to shift this lot,' Olivia retorted. She remembered the comment Annie had made last night about the bookshop being open again. It had been niggling her and now she understood what Annie had meant. Olivia pointed helplessly at the shelves. 'Look at it all! I must've been mad, letting him fetch everything here.'

The man on his chair had finished his comfortable read and got up, leaving the shop without a word or the book, irritating Olivia even further. What were they running here, Tom and her dad? Some kind of free reading room? They'd be offering coffee and cake next, and a regular book club if she didn't watch out.

'Shouldn't you be writing?' There was still a sharp note in her voice that Tom couldn't miss, and his eyes narrowed.

'Not that it's anything to do with you when I work, but I write all morning and then open up here on Thursday, Friday and Saturday afternoons. The rest of the time I write all day and sometimes into the evenings as well. Is that hours enough, do you think?' He was glaring now. 'Are you hoping the quicker I finish the book, the sooner I can be on my way?'

He crossed the room, no mean feat among the clutter, and replaced the book the previous chap had left on the armchair back on its shelf.

'Sorry. I just didn't realise you would have time for this.'

She stared around the annexe again. It had seen all sorts of uses in its time and after her mum had died it had somehow filled up with everything her dad didn't want in the house but couldn't quite bring himself to part with. There was a tiny kitchen next door and another large room off that, and she assumed Tom must have been doing some tidying of his own.

Olivia saw now that he had made it resemble more of a sitting room than a bookshop and she had to admit, at least privately, that it did look a lot better. He had brought in two armchairs and placed them either side of the fireplace, and lit the wall lamps, chasing away the reality of the dull winter afternoon outdoors. The mantelpiece had books all along it, held in place by a sturdy brass candlestick at either end.

The shelves on one side of the fireplace were history, military, railways and politics; the other fiction, from Penguin Classics to a few children's books at the bottom. A coffee table held books on gardening and some on cookery, two more had been pressed into temporary service as homes for travel writing and sports respectively. Local interest was stacked on the desk where Tom was once more engrossed in the book back in his hand. There was even a little Christmas tree glittering merrily on the floor opposite the door.

'Sorry if I was a bit snappy,' he said, looking up to give her a smile Olivia found distracting. She wondered if he was doing that sexy little thing the two women from the restaurant had mentioned earlier. She wasn't sure, but it made her blink, twice.

'That's okay. Me too.' She was doing her best to ignore how handsome he looked in that chunky navy sweater and tried to think about the shop instead. 'So let me get this straight. Three afternoons a week, is that it?'

'Usually. I am thinking of opening maybe another afternoon as it's getting close to Christmas and some of these books are just waiting for the right home.'

'You sound like my dad.' Olivia's phone flashed with a notification and she realised how quickly the day had moved on. 'I've got to go, I need to make a call and I can't be late. We can talk about this later.'

She hurried back to the house and grabbed her laptop, shutting herself away in her dad's library. It was another two and a half hours, not the one she had scheduled, before she re-emerged, feeling suddenly exhausted. Her client was moving from the States to Yorkshire to take over as the CEO of a manufacturing company and they were starting to become a real nuisance, calling her at all hours of the night as it was still day for them and leaving urgent messages if she didn't pick up. Checking in again about the private school she had found and was it really up to scratch for twin boys aged eight who loved sport and drama respectively. Was she absolutely certain that they'd get planning permission to knock down a barn and build a gym?

No had been the answer to that one and she was beginning to think that she would prefer them to pull out. The farmhouse they were supposed to be buying was exquisite and she knew she would find another buyer in a heartbeat, long before it ever reached the open market.

Olivia wandered into the kitchen, ready for a glass of wine. Tom was already there and he gave her a nod, returning his attention to the meal he was preparing. She found a bottle of Malbec from her dad's collection, remembering that Tom had liked red wine when they had shared a bottle before. 'Would you like a glass?'

'You don't mind? I don't want to presume or drink your dad's supply dry.'

She was smiling as she uncorked the bottle and found glasses. 'Are you trying to tell me that my dad hasn't already invited you to help yourself to anything you want?'

Tom's silence told her that she was right and she passed a glass to him. He thanked her, chopping herbs as she watched from the table, strangely soothed by the process, her phone nearby. 'What are you making?'

'Just a vegetarian rice dish.'

'Right.' It looked amazing as he sliced peppers, chilli, onions and garlic with a practised hand. 'So you like cooking?'

'I do, I find it relaxing.' He paused to try the wine. 'Would you like to join me? I can make it stretch.'

Olivia was already refusing his offer in the tilt of her glass. He couldn't have missed her two little microwave meals for one in the fridge when he'd fetched his own ingredients. 'Thanks, but I wouldn't expect you to share.'

'Why not?' Tom was heating a pan on the range, adding oil and letting it get up to temperature as it sizzled noisily. 'You're sharing the wine.' He gave her a quick grin. 'But I can see you've got supper sorted. You don't need my made-from-scratch, spicy Mexican rice dish served with fresh coriander and lime.'

'Oh stop it,' she wailed. 'How do you expect my ready-made spaghetti carbonara to compete with that?'

'I don't.'

'Have you ever done adverts,' she muttered to his back as he slid the vegetables into the pan, her stomach rumbling unhelpfully as the smell drifted across. 'I bet you could sell anything.' She'd nearly said 'with that voice' but stopped herself just in time.

'Is that a yes?'

'Yes. Please.'

She set the table for them; it was useful to have something to do as he cooked, adding chopped tomatoes and stock to the pan once the rice had joined the vegetables. It smelled wonderful and Olivia found she didn't mind the lack of conversation until they were facing one another across the table.

'This is incredible, thank you.'

'You're welcome.'

She was finding it impossible to forget the last time they had shared an evening meal and how that night had ended. Maintaining eye contact and generating simple chat seemed beyond her as she refilled their glasses, and she settled on practicalities instead.

'We should probably decide about shopping seeing as we're both here now.' She thought again of those two sad little ready meals in the fridge, trying not to love Tom's cooking too much. 'It's very kind of you to have made enough for me tonight but I certainly don't expect it.' She hoped that comment would make it clear she wouldn't be doing the same for him. 'I'll wash up. I was always telling my dad he should have got a dishwasher with all those people he had to stay for the festival.'

'But that was half the fun.' Tom reached for his wine, holding the glass with a hand Olivia remembered had touched her face just as gently that night in the pub, making her skin feel warm.

'If your dad wasn't cooking then someone else would be and we'd all pile in here, take turns at whatever needed doing. The only strict rule he imposed was that the clearing up had to be done the night before and the table laid for breakfast. He hated coming down to a tip, he wanted to find guests already tucking into something and ready to chat.'

Ready to chat. She had used to chat with him too, something she seemed to have done less and less of as the years had moved on. Her phone was blinking at her and she ignored the notifications. After her mum had died, Olivia remembered how she used to go the bookshop in town after school and do her homework there. Her dad would have a hot chocolate waiting and something nice from the bakery across the street.

They'd found a simple peace in creating that new routine, finding a way into the future. She'd wait for him to finish work for the day, and they'd go home together to the house silenced by sadness. She'd moved on, college, university, a brief marriage, a daughter, a career, whereas her dad's life had remained on the path he had chosen over forty years previously. Had seemed to shrink as hers had expanded, or so she'd thought.

Now she realised that it hadn't shrunk at all, he'd simply surrounded himself with people he loved to talk to, shared their world, been at the centre of it with them for a time, supported their careers and championed their work. How had she got so busy, so focused on work that this man opposite her now knew more about her dad's routine than she did?

'How lovely.' Olivia was sorry now she'd missed it, even though she'd never really been a part of the literary community he'd created here. She tried to push the guilt away, bring her mind back to practical matters again. 'So, the shopping? I'm planning a weekly delivery and it seems silly to have two lots of everything open at the same time.'

A thought occurred to her, and she tried to find a way to frame it, hoping to make Tom realise that she wasn't trying to make him cough up half of what she decided to spend. She had no idea what the state of his finances were and didn't want to add any extra pressure.

'I'm happy to cover the delivery and obviously I'll replace any of my dad's wine we drink. We've got at least three weeks here and we're going to need something to get us through.'

At once she was aware she'd got it wrong as Tom's lips tightened and he glared across the table as she rushed on. 'I've already booked the first delivery so I thought it would make sense if you agree. Unless you think it's better that we just divide everything in half or work out exactly what we've each used and pay accordingly?'

She'd always hated doing that, adding up item by item in restaurants rather than just splitting the cost and sharing more than a meal. She'd offended Tom now, that much was clear as he shoved his empty plate away.

'I might be homeless right now, Olivia, but I'm not destitute yet. I'll pay my own way. Half of everything we share.'

He stood up and left the kitchen, banging the door behind him, and she dropped her head into her hands, mortified. That hadn't gone as well as she'd hoped.

Chapter Six

Olivia saw the moment she opened her curtains she had been wrong to ignore the weather notification yesterday, and she let out a frustrated groan. Snow was piled up in wavy drifts, disguising the usual view of the small garden from her bedroom. She did have to admit it was beautiful, draping everything in a thick, white blanket and adding another layer of seasonality to the day and the village.

But it was still falling steadily and would play serious havoc with her plans. She checked the landing for signs of Tom before rushing into the bathroom and singing loudly to make sure he would know she was in there. She didn't much care if he liked her rendition of 'Proud Mary' or not, she'd always had a nice singing voice and that was something else that had gone by the wayside these past years.

Breakfast was excruciating as she waited for him to make an appearance. Every time she tried to find a way to apologise about the shopping the words got muddled in her head. She truly hadn't meant to offend, only help. She'd cleared up alone last night and set the table, a tiny homage to her dad, which she hoped Tom would realise if he came down first. She could hear him moving around upstairs and she was washing her single plate and coffee cup by the time he came into the kitchen.

'Morning.' Olivia made herself sound friendly, busy with emptying the water from the washing-up bowl. She could feel his presence in the room, all through the house, as though it were an invisible cloak draped over her. 'There's coffee if you'd like some.'

'Thanks.'

She found a tea towel and began to dry the plate. She would be finished in a minute and could leave him to his own breakfast in peace. She needed to work, to rearrange her week, given the weather conditions.

'Olivia?' Tom was beside her now and she set the plate down, picked up the cup. 'I'm sorry. I know you were trying to be kind. Generous.'

'That's okay.' She still wouldn't offer him her eyes, afraid of what she might give away. Her feelings for him seemed to be altering hour by hour. Attraction, desire, laughter one moment; embarrassment, sympathy, disappointment, anger the next. 'I'm sorry if I offended you.'

'You didn't, truly. It was my fault.' He cleared his throat, touched a hand to her shoulder then let it fall away. 'I don't find it easy to accept help, I never have. And especially not now, here, like this. With you.'

Olivia's fingers had stilled on the cup, hoping he might share, help her understand how and why he was here. His attention was fixed on the garden, the shop at the end, everything covered in snow as the seconds drifted by, and her reply was quiet. 'What do you mean?'

'Do you ever think about the night we met?'

Tom turned, pushing his hands into his pockets. His words were sharper, quick, and she knew she had given him her reply in the surprise racing across her face as he stared at her. She didn't need her training and years in human resources to recognise the misery clouding his eyes, the dark circles around them, most unusually finding herself wanting to reach out to him again.

'I can see that you do.' He paused. 'So do I.'

'What about it?'

Her pulse was starting to rush again and the dryness in her mouth made her words feel thickened. They were standing close together, almost as close as they had been that evening on the threshold of her room. Olivia put the cup down carefully, dredging up thoughts of loving someone and being left behind, the determination never to allow herself to place her happiness, her peace of mind in someone else's power ever again. She had no reason to trust Tom with anything beyond a few weeks of sharing a house and needed to ensure it became nothing more. He had told her as much himself, that night. That he wasn't what he'd allowed her to believe.

'That I regret leaving you. Wish I'd stayed, that things were different. For me.'

'We can't go back, Tom.' Her words were barely more than a whisper. 'It would be a mistake.' She wanted to believe it, ignoring the way her body was trying to change her mind for her. She could feel the tremble in her fingers, the way she wanted to touch him, place her hand on his face, smooth away the sadness.

'I know that. Nothing's altered since then, with my situation.' There was an edge of frustration in Tom's voice, and she recognised the tension in his shoulders. 'I'm a poor prospect for anyone, let alone you, Olivia.'

'Me?' It was a moment before she understood his meaning. 'What, you think I wouldn't want you because of your being…'

71

'Homeless? Out of work? Finished maybe?' There was weariness there now too. 'You can say it, I know how it sounds.'

'You actually think that makes a difference to how I see you?'

'Are you telling me it doesn't?'

'Of course I am.' Was she, really? Would any of that matter if they acted on the attraction she knew they both still felt? She had a highly successful career, a luxurious apartment, a daughter, her dad, a busy life, barely any time. And he had, what, precisely? No home, no proper job, perhaps no family to fall back on. Would she seriously consider dating a man like that had his profile popped into her dating app? She knew the answer and felt the shame swiftly following.

'So we're, what? What does sharing this place make us now? Housemates? Friends?' Tom's gaze left hers to dart across the garden to the shop at the end again. 'More? Less? How do we categorise our relationship, especially now you know why I'm here?'

'I'd like us to be friends. I think we could do that.' Olivia was still battling the shame, wanting to offer something that was kind.

'I suppose that's better than housemates.' He breathed out a sigh, staring at the snow still falling.

'You trust my dad, don't you? You're letting him help you.'

'Yes.' Tom's smile was brief. 'He's been a true friend to me and I value his support more than I can say.'

'If I can help too…' Olivia wanted to show Tom that he mattered, not the circumstances he found himself in. A chance to make herself believe it too, to be better than someone who measured the man against his position. If her dad liked and trusted him, then she could trust him too and be his friend. 'I mean, I can't cook, not like you, but if there's something else. Please Tom, I'd like to help.' She saw a glimmer of hope amidst the sorrow lingering in his gaze.

'There's nothing you can do, Olivia. At least not in the way you think. But thank you for saying it. I'll find my own way, I always have.'

Suddenly her arms were around him before she barely even realised she'd moved. She wasn't sure Tom would want her holding him in quite the way she was but then his arms were around her too, and they were hugging tightly, an acknowledgement of how they felt, what they'd shared. What they'd missed. She thought that this wasn't perhaps what her dad had had in mind when he'd invited her and Tom to stay at the same time and then decided maybe it really was.

Her next words escaped with a quick laugh before she could prevent it. 'I've just realised I've never hugged someone famous before. I usually manage to restrict myself to a handshake with my clients.'

She didn't seem to be managing to restrict herself around Tom very much at all and loved how he felt against her: strong, firm and smelling wonderful. His chin was resting lightly on her head and she felt the serious moment pass into an easy light-heartedness following her teasing. 'Can I have a selfie?'

'That might depend on what you're planning to do with it.' He drew back to look at her, and she liked the flare of amusement in his expression.

'Turn it into a screensaver maybe? Instagram? Twitter? Which would you prefer?'

'Oh Instagram, definitely. I'm not sure how I'd feel about you staring at me on a screen all day.'

'I'd never get anything done,' Olivia replied at once without meaning to, a sudden blush threatening to render her even more embarrassed. 'I mean, it's just, you're him, aren't you? Of course I know you're not, I was just...' She was perfectly aware that she was making her hasty confession worse.

They still seemed to have their arms around one another and they both let go at the same time, as though surprised that they were still embracing. Tom set about making toast and Olivia decided to have another coffee. She poured one for him as well and he thanked her as she settled at the table with her phone, putting her glasses on. There was still a slight awkwardness in their presence together and she wondered if he had revealed a layer of himself he had never intended to.

She needed to get on and make new plans. She definitely wasn't going to be seeing her dad today in this weather – she doubted she'd even be able to get the car out of the garage, never mind the village. And there was the house in Cumbria to see tomorrow; that would have to be rearranged after all.

She emailed her dad to say she was really sorry and included a Zoom link, suggesting they chat at four. He would have had his afternoon snooze by then and it would give them around an hour before he liked to eat. His happy reply almost brought her to tears and she wished she'd put her client off yesterday and gone to see him instead.

She also emailed her vendor in Cumbria, smoothing them over and promising to be there just as soon as she could. Olivia assured them she had a buyer in mind and that they should still be able to sell quickly. Nothing from her client in the States so far today and that was a relief. But their day had yet to start and they might still track her down, even on a Sunday. The snow was definitely a nuisance she could do without, and she'd almost forgotten about Tom opposite her until he spoke.

'Problems?'

'Sorry?' She looked up, startled from thoughts of work. Julian had messaged too, asking if she could view a property as soon as possible for a high-profile footballer who was switching clubs. This wasn't unusual; her team covered the north and Julian's the south, which suited them both. She'd have to fit it in this week as for clients such as this they always viewed the properties personally.

'You look concerned.'

'Oh, it's just work.' She ignored Tom's eyes sharp on hers.

'It's Sunday. Don't you ever take a whole day off?'

'Of course I do.' Did she? Olivia tried to think back to the last day when she hadn't sent a single email or replied to an urgent message. She couldn't find one. 'This bloody weather isn't helping. I was supposed to be in Cumbria tomorrow and now I've got to go to Northumberland before the end of the week, which isn't looking very promising with snow and all the meetings I have sched-uled.'

'You need a bit of time for yourself, Olivia. You shouldn't work every single day.' Tom stood up, carried his things over to the sink. 'It's just snow and we all have to adapt. It'll pass.'

'Try telling my clients that,' she replied, cross with the change in her plans as well as his rational response to the conditions outdoors. 'Half of them think they can command the weather as well as me.'

Irritated, she got up and went to the overfull coat stand in the hall, finding her dad's battered waxed coat and the scarf again, wrapped them around her. 'I'm heading out for a bit.' She might as well take some photos for Ellie and Logan; snow was pretty much the one thing they were guaranteed not to have in their Caribbean Christmas. Olivia stepped into her dad's wellies too, his feet not much bigger than hers, and took her phone outside.

Children were haring around the green, shrieking excitedly and throwing themselves into drifts, lobbing snowballs into the frigid air. Two boys were building a snowman and a couple of small girls were sprawled on their backs, adults nearby to capture it all on their phones. A snowplough was scraping its way along the high street, shunting piles of snow onto the side of the road. Olivia checked to see if it was Jon Beresford driving and realised it wasn't.

Everyone was wrapped up in scarves and hats, and she soon recognised Charlie Stewart, the young, ex-rugby-playing vicar, and his wife Sam playing on the green with their little daughter Esther. Charlie and Sam had also been good friends to her dad and Olivia went over to say hello. They were happy to see her, wanting to know how her dad was and if he would be coming to the carol service to do his usual reading, which she told them was likely. Hugh might have moved out of Thorndale but he hadn't left the village entirely behind.

As a board member of the arts consortium planning to purchase Hugh's house, Sam was up to speed with the bid and excited about implementing the workshops planned for next year, including drama, which she taught in college. Olivia also learned a bit more about the consortium's search for a part-time director to manage the programme of events for the writers' retreat.

Sam also casually dropped in that she and Charlie had had Tom around for supper recently and asked how Olivia was finding sharing a house with him, a merry glint in her eye. Olivia replied that it was fine, which was – for the most part – the truth. It was almost time for church and the young couple gathered Esther up and said goodbye, stomping off through the snow with their daughter squealing in excitement.

Olivia pulled out her phone and, busy capturing images for Ellie, shrieked furiously when something heavy whacked her right on her bottom and exploded in a flurry of snow. She whipped around to see that Tom had followed her out of the house. He had a coat on too, his hair tucked inside a beanie, and was already bending to gather more snow in his hands.

'Don't you dare!' She was half amused, half horrified, and didn't think for a second he was going to take any notice of her warning – he looked far too determined for that. 'What do you think you're doing?'

'Isn't it obvious? I thought I'd pelt you with snowballs as retaliation for nearly clouting me with a massive atlas. Seems a shame to waste the opportunity.'

'But I didn't even do it!'

'That's not the point. You were going to.'

'Right.' Olivia bent down, moulding the freezing flakes between her fingers and trying not to gasp at the cold. 'You're going to regret this.' She only just managed to jerk out of the way of his next shot, hindered by the snow clumping around her feet.

'I'm not sure I will.'

She didn't think she'd ever had much of an accurate aim, and he was laughing until her first shot landed on his left shoulder. She thought it might have slipped beneath the collar of his coat, judging by his roar. It was her turn to laugh now as he tried to dislodge the last of the snow before it melted on his skin.

It was pointless trying to run – she couldn't get away quick enough. He was advancing, catching her on her right arm with his next lob and knocking the snowball clean out of her hand before she had time to launch it. She yelled a protest and bent to gather more, managing to duck out of the way of his follow-up shot. Tom was much faster than her at making missiles, so she was delighted when her next hit him square in the chest.

She fought back as hard as she could until they were both plastered in snow and almost doubled up with laughter, their shots missing more often now than hitting their targets. Her hair was drenched where he'd landed a particularly good throw on the side of her head and his jeans were completely soaked.

Still they fought and when Tom was worryingly near he made a grab for her, tripping her easily and depositing Olivia on her back in the snow. She waved her arms and legs merrily, his expression unfathomable. She couldn't remember when she'd last had so much fun that hadn't gone in her calendar beforehand.

'Haven't you ever seen a snow angel before, Tom?'

'I was never much of a one for games.' His reply was murmured, that flash of sadness back in his face.

'Is that right?' She reached for his leg, tugging as hard as she could with both hands until she managed to unbalance him, and he landed in the snow nearby. When he saw that she was about to gather more snow to pelt him with, he trapped her hands, pulling her so that she was lying half on top of him.

She could hear the shouts of others playing across the green and yet it seemed they were alone in the snow suddenly, staring at one another. She wouldn't have to move far to drop her mouth onto his and she made herself wriggle away, standing up and holding out a hand to him. He took it and she helped pull him to his feet, watching as he shook the snow from his coat. They were still holding hands, their fingers reddened by the snow.

'I should get some more pictures to send to Ellie. She and her boyfriend are coming up in a couple of weeks and it'll be gone by then.' Olivia casually freed her hand from Tom's. 'I'll send some to my dad too. At least I've got a valid reason for not being able to visit him today.'

Tom was starting to shiver, his coat much lighter than hers, and she pushed his chest gently. 'Go and get changed.' Her reply was soft, concerned. 'I don't want you to get double pneumonia, even if you did start it.'

'You were such an easy target, standing there, phone in hand. I couldn't resist.' He set off to the house, threw another comment back over his shoulder. 'But it was definitely the most fun I've ever had in the snow.'

Olivia followed him soon after and went up to her room to change out of her wet clothes. She supposed she ought to be clearing some of her dad's things ready to recycle but she couldn't face it. She didn't know whether it was Tom's presence in the house, or her dad's absence, that was making her so unwilling to get on with what needed to be done. She sent the images she'd taken to Ellie, who was very much hoping for more snow when she and Logan came to visit. He'd only ever seen snow a few times before and was desperate to go sledging.

The dining room door was firmly closed when Olivia returned downstairs and she heard Tom tapping away at his laptop as she passed. So he was presumably working on a Sunday too. She made a cafetière of coffee, poured herself a cup and splashed some whisky from the drinks cupboard into it. She took a second cup, did the same, and knocked on the dining room door, hoping she wasn't disturbing him too much. She stuck her head around when he called come in.

'Hi, sorry to bother you. Made you a coffee with whisky in it case you're feeling chilled.'

She walked over to the table, saw him nod distractedly. Putting the cup down, she backed away – she didn't much appreciate being interrupted when she was working either. He thanked her quickly as she closed the door and left him to it. She returned to her own laptop on the kitchen table and started rearranging her calendar for the week.

Once she had checked the forecast, she provisionally scheduled her Cumbrian visit for Tuesday, hoping that the promised thaw would come. Somehow she fell into more work, replying to emails and when she checked the time again it was almost four. She logged into Zoom, smiling the minute her dad's face popped up via his iPad.

They had a lovely chat and of course he wanted to know how things were with Tom. Olivia told him casually they were fine, and the man himself appeared a few minutes later, wandering into shot behind her and rubbing bleary eyes. Hugh was delighted to see him and insisted that Tom join them and talk about how his writing was going.

Tom seemed surprisingly happy to talk and it wasn't long before Olivia began to feel like a third wheel in the exchange. The two men discussed the bookshop, who was buying what, the level of interest in what they were doing by opening up again. She was dying to say there was virtually zero interest and what was her dad planning to do with it all when he sold the house?

But she also recognised her dad's pleasure, the easy way he drew Tom into conversation, and she couldn't miss the sincerity of the friendship they obviously shared. After nearly ten more minutes, her dad seemed to remember that she was still there, and Tom stood up to make way for her.

'No, don't go, Tom.' Her dad's voice always took people by surprise, the largeness and certainty of it at odds with the skin thinned by age, the speckled hands and narrow shoulders. His bright eyes reflected the intelligence and humour always apparent in his face. 'I want to speak to you both whilst I've got the chance. This concerns you too, Liv. It wasn't exactly how I planned to tell you but seeing as the opportunity has presented itself...'

Oh no, what now? Olivia tried to stop her heart sinking any further as she wondered what new plan he'd dreamt up. She wouldn't put it past him to be trying to buy more stock and start up the shop again full-time and put Tom in charge.

'I've asked Tom to work through the books in the shop, as well as everything else that's there. Some correspondence and suchlike from home has found its way to the annexe over the years and I've specifically given Tom permission to read and catalogue anything he finds however he chooses. Obviously, his writing has to come first and the shop mustn't be allowed to interfere with that.'

Okay, that didn't sound too bad, and a glance at Tom's expressionless face told her that they both knew there was more to come.

'Liv, I know you mean well but you simply haven't the time to go through the annexe as well as the house, and we both know that's a big project on its own.' Olivia thought yet again of all her dad had accumulated over the course of his life: the wardrobes full of secrets, drawers heavy with history. 'There are thousands of books left, including those in my library in the house, and some of them are extremely valuable.'

Hugh was staring straight into the camera on his iPad. 'Tom understands what my work has meant to me over the years, and he's my friend. So that's why I'm signing over the entire collection to him just as soon as my solicitor has finished drawing up the necessary paperwork.'

Olivia felt Tom shift, sensed his look going to her before racing straight back to her dad.

'Hugh, I can't, really. I wouldn't...'

Her dad held up a hand, halting Tom. 'I want you to have it, Tom, and that's that. No arguments. I think the three of us know that Olivia wouldn't want it.'

Wouldn't want it? She could've cheered. Not only would she have less to sort out, but her dad's cherished books would be going to a wonderful guardian, and she was thrilled for Tom. Her dad was right; much as she'd loved the shop over the years and having so many books to choose from, there were only so many she could take to her apartment. Hugh seemed to be reading her mind when he spoke again.

'There are a few, maybe more, that I think Liv will want to keep from her childhood, Tom. Please let her choose.'

'Of course.' Tom still seemed stunned. 'But Hugh, please, I'd feel much happier if you…'

Olivia saw her dad grin. 'That's just it, isn't it? You understand. I know you don't want to see them dumped in a skip or carted off for pulp. Whatever happens with the arts consortium, the house sale will take some time and you can stay as long as you like to sort through it.

'It also goes without saying that the collection is yours to do with as you please, Tom. I suggest you sell it and use the proceeds for whatever you wish. I will be perfectly satisfied, knowing that you have done it with care. And that's the end of it.' Hugh yawned and Olivia was sure he was doing it on purpose. 'I'm tired now, I'd like a snooze before it's time to eat. Liv, come over when you can but not in that ruddy car if it's still snowing. And if Tom's not too busy, bring him with you. I'm glad you're getting along. I thought you might.'

Hugh took himself off out of the meeting before either she or Tom could say another word.

'That,' she said, closing down the meeting and logging out of her laptop, 'was a masterclass in manipulation.'

'Ah, so that's where you learned it from.' Tom slowly got up from the table; he didn't seem to know quite what to do next.

'Don't be so cheeky. I'm good at getting what I want, usually people don't even notice it happening. Congratulations, by the way. I'm really happy he wants you to have his collection because it means the world to him.'

She gave Tom a reassuring glance to back up her words and prove that she meant them, but he still didn't look convinced, his eyes sliding guiltily away from hers.

Chapter Seven

Monday wasn't as awkward as Olivia had thought it might be with Tom, trapped in the house by the snow. She'd sensed the beginnings of a tentative friendship between them over the weekend, especially after the snowball fight, and they mostly managed to avoid each other during the day. He was already working in the dining room by the time she came down for breakfast. She had lunch before he did and didn't like to exclude him, so left sandwiches in the fridge and a note on the table.

Her online grocery shop had been delayed until tomorrow because of the weather, so she nipped down to the post office to stock up on a few things to tide them over until then. It had stopped snowing last night but everything was still covered in its thick white blanket. Quite a few snowmen had popped up on the green, making her smile as she remembered the fight with Tom yesterday. She saw Mrs Timms in the cafe and made as hasty an exit as she could before her dad's friend waylaid her for too long.

Back at the house Olivia worked at the kitchen table, setting up appointments for the new year and trying to bring some online meetings forward as travel was out of the question for a couple of days. But not everyone she wanted to pin down was available so instead she made herself go into the room where Ellie usually slept and started clearing some belongings.

There were books in every room, and she was about to sort through those in here when she remembered her dad's gift to Tom, realising they would no longer be Hugh's or hers to decide upon. She removed a few and put them in her room, saving some for Ellie too. She was making a peppermint tea when Tom came into the kitchen, dressed in running gear. She hadn't gone out herself yet, deciding to wait until the snow had cleared.

'I'm guessing you don't want one of these?' She gestured to her mug and the kettle.

'No thanks.' He zipped up his jacket and pulled finger-less gloves and a head torch from a pocket. 'I need to get out for a bit.'

'Right.' She poured hot water into her mug and swirled the teabag around. 'How was your day?' Olivia was astonished she'd spoken the words out loud; she couldn't remember asking someone that particular question very often before.

'My day?' Tom raised his eyebrows. 'It was fine.'

'Is your writing going well?'

'Is that what all this questioning is about? Are you still trying to find out where I'm up to, how soon I can be out of here?'

'I thought we were past that, I was just making conversation.'

'You don't seem like the kind of person who has time for idle chat, Olivia.'

'Nor you for a polite one apparently,' she threw back, stung by his rebuff of her attempt at friendliness, especially after their conversation yesterday morning. 'I'm not concerned how long you're planning to stay, I was just interested in your work.'

'No need, there's nothing to tell.' He drew a beanie on, fastened the head torch in place, checked his watch.

'Tom, it's dark outside.'

'So?' He was pulling the gloves on now.

'So is it a good idea to be running in the snow at night?'

'I'm fine, I can look after myself. And before you say it, no, I don't know how long I'll be or where exactly I'm going.'

'Don't you think you should tell me?'

'Why? Are you worried I'll get lost?' Tom was at the back door and he gave her an exasperated look. 'I'm not used to checking in with anyone, Olivia, and I see no reason to start now. But as its dark and you seem concerned for me, forty minutes or so, towards Ellerby Moor.'

Sixty minutes later Olivia was only the teeniest bit concerned, expecting him back at any moment. Though she had no idea why her skin was beginning to prickle with alarm and anxiety seemed to be lodged in her stomach. Her dad had informed her that Tom had been in Thorndale for two weeks now and he must have run here before now; the conversation she'd overhead in the restaurant confirmed it. There was no need to be nervous.

Twenty minutes after that she was at the kitchen window and googling how long to wait before reporting a person missing in snow. There didn't seem to be a conclusive answer unless the person was vulnerable, and Tom wasn't. At least not in ways she could easily explain or identify.

By six p.m. it had been two hours and Olivia was seriously worried. She didn't believe he would have stayed out in this weather just to prove a point and she hoped he had taken his phone with him so he could call for help if he needed it. The phone wasn't in his hand anywhere near as often as her own was and she checked the dining room. No sign of it and she ran up to his room, hesitating before walking in. His phone was sitting on the bedside table, on top of a book, and she felt her anxiety increase.

She was absolutely certain Tom wouldn't thank her for dialling 999 and calling out the entire fell rescue association on his behalf. However, there was no harm in a casual, quiet word with Jon to alleviate her worries, surely? She had Annie's number but not Jon's, so she gave her a call and Annie passed her phone straight to Jon when Olivia quickly explained what had happened.

Jon didn't hesitate. He told Olivia to stay in the house in case Tom returned and was already using his own phone to call it in to the fell rescue as an emergency. She thanked Jon, feeling relief at the thought of a search underway, and an increase of apprehension that Jon believed it necessary. If Tom walked back through the door this minute, then she could well imagine his dismay at what she had set in motion.

She couldn't settle anywhere, finally lingering in the library with its view of the village, the shutters open to the night. The fell rescue headquarters opened up across the green in sudden activity, lights blazing through the darkness and a Land Rover raced out into the night, searching for Tom. She felt a spike of real fear then, wondering if she had left it too late. What if he'd fallen, knocked himself unconscious? Slipped into the river and drowned in icy water? She couldn't bear to think of it, and she watched, waiting, her heart racing and stomach sick with dread.

Olivia snatched at her phone when it rang forty minutes later and Annie's name flashed up, almost missing in her haste to answer it. Annie quickly informed her that Jon had called to pass on that Tom had been found. He had tripped on his way back from his run, lost the head torch he had been wearing and taken the wrong route. He was mildly hypothermic, and the volunteers were in the process of warming him up and trying to persuade him to go to hospital.

Olivia couldn't have explained why she was ready to cry as she thanked Annie gratefully. Within fifteen minutes a fell rescue vehicle was pulling up outside the front door. Olivia grabbed a coat and stuffed her feet into wellies, rushing outside to see Tom. Wrapped in blankets, a volunteer was on either side, one supporting him into the house through the snow, and she saw the relief and the apology in his face. Jon had been driving and he jumped down to speak with her.

'We're satisfied he's only mildly hypothermic as he was actually moving, trying to find his way back, and he's adamant he doesn't want to go to hospital. He didn't lose consciousness, he's not drowsy or confused and his temperature is improving.' Jon lowered his voice. 'If you have any concerns or there's any change for the worse, call an ambulance, okay? No matter what Tom says. If there are any delays call me, and I'll come. Annie will text you my number.'

'Thank you so much. I'm really sorry to have had to call you out.'

'You did the right thing and don't let Tom tell you otherwise.' Jon sounded weary and he ran a hand over his face. 'No one would be in good shape out here overnight.

Keep him warm, layers, no hot baths, alcohol or direct heat on his limbs. Think you'll be okay?'

'Of course.' Olivia thought of Annie and their baby. 'You need to go home too.'

'Sure do. Just have to go back to headquarters first and sort everything out. Take care.' He grinned wryly, heading back through the snow to the vehicle.

'You too. Thank you.'

Olivia returned to the house, thanking the two other volunteers who were waiting with Tom in the sitting room. He was hunched on a green velvet sofa and the room wasn't very warm without the fire lit. She flew upstairs, grabbing blankets from the box on the landing and dashed into Tom's room for clothes. She had to rummage through drawers, feeling awkward for going through his belongings, but finally had enough for him to change into.

The volunteers gathered their blankets and left them alone as Tom thanked them tiredly. Olivia was oblivious and already helping him undress, tugging the soaking jacket off and then the two layers beneath over his head, replacing them with a T shirt and a thick hoodie. He was trying to smile in between bouts of shivering.

'Hell of a way to get me naked, Olivia, calling 999. You could've just asked.'

'You're not completely naked,' she told him briskly. She knelt to remove his trainers and socks, feeling the chill on his legs even through the running trousers, and dragged them off too. 'And I didn't call 999. But you do need to get those shorts off.' She paused, suddenly warm. 'Can you manage?'

'I hope so. Not sure how I feel about the alternative.'

She busied herself lighting the fire and turned around to find him trying to pull on cotton lounging trousers with trembling fingers. She helped him with those too, tugging on socks and making him lie back whilst she covered him with two blankets.

'I'm going to bring you a hot drink.'

The shivering wasn't so obvious when she returned with a mug of strong tea topped up with two spoons of sugar. 'Here.' Olivia passed Tom the mug, rearranging the blankets around him as he sat up.

'Thank you.'

She threw some more logs on the fire, satisfied the blaze was heating the room nicely now, and not directly on him. She watched him drink the tea, and made sure it was all gone before she took the mug away. He caught her free hand, already laying his head back onto the cushions she had plumped for him.

'Thank you. I've been such a fool, I'm really sorry. I've never needed rescuing before.'

She didn't know why she doubted that. 'That's okay.' His hand felt cool and she held it, remembering somewhere that you weren't supposed to rub hands or feet for hypothermia. 'Next time please take your phone.'

'Mmm.' He seemed drowsy now and she watched anxiously, wondering if he was only tired or if it was a symptom of something more serious. 'I still feel cold.'

When her daughter had been poorly as a child, she had loved to be held, cuddled and comforted; Olivia would bring Ellie into her bed and snuggle her through the night until she was better. There was another way Olivia could help Tom and keep an eye on him at the same time.

'Can you move over?' She pointed to the back of the sofa. 'Turn on your side.'

He did as she asked, shuffling across and she got onto the sofa and lay down behind him, pulling the blankets over both of them. She slid her arm around him, covering his cool hands with her small one.

'Spoons,' Tom said sleepily. 'This is nice.'

'Hush.' Her voice was a whisper as she snuggled up to him, tucking her legs into his bent knees. 'Don't talk, just rest. You are an idiot, by the way.'

'Mmm. I like this,' he said, his fingers squeezing hers. 'Like you're trying to wrap yourself around me.'

'I'm just trying to warm you.'

'Maybe we should both be naked now. Warmer that way.'

She swallowed, felt the tremor in her fingers. 'That's not going to help.'

'Mmm. Probably would.' Tom sighed. 'Not used to being held, cuddled.'

She brushed that one away. 'Not since you were a child maybe.'

'Not even then.' He was sleepier still. 'Was me who did the looking after. Don't leave me, please. Don't want you to go.'

Olivia felt her heart bump. That was totally unexpected, and she had no intention of moving or leaving him. She held him even more tightly than before, remembering doing the same for Ellie, her dad soothing her all those years ago and before that her mum, and she wondered if Tom really had had no one in his life to do that for him. Gradually she felt his shivering reduce and heard his breathing change. He was asleep. Olivia's eyes grew heavy too, and it wasn't many minutes more before she joined him, wrung out by the anxiety and the drama.

When she woke up hours later, she felt stiff and disorientated. She blinked, the lamp she had lit earlier brightening the room. The fire had dwindled to a glow and Tom was still asleep. She touched his hand, relieved it felt warm, and lifted the bottom of his hoodie to check his stomach. It too was fine and she carefully slid away, tucking the blankets tightly around him. A glance at her phone told her it was one a.m., and she didn't want to reply now to the text Annie had sent earlier that she had missed in case she accidentally woke her friend up.

Olivia quietly put more logs on the fire, poking it gently so they began to catch, and settled on the armchair opposite Tom. She wanted to go back to holding him but was frightened of waking him and disturbing the rest he so obviously needed. She covered herself with a spare blanket, resisting the impulse to check her inbox when sleep refused to find her quite so easily as before.

Daylight was stirring outside when she woke up again, creeping over to Tom on the sofa to check on him. He was on his back now, and his eyes opened just as she was sliding a hand beneath the blankets.

'Where did you get to?' he asked drowsily, covering a yawn with the free hand he lifted from the depths of his makeshift bed. 'I woke up and you weren't there.'

'I was just on the chair.' She removed her fingers from his. 'I didn't think we could stay like that all night.'

'Aren't you supposed to be warming me up?'

'I did.' She hoped she wasn't revealing how much she liked taking care of him. That was new. 'How are you feeling?'

'My head hurts.' Tom was blinking at her. 'I'm a bit cold still, like I might have come down with something.'

'Paracetamol and a hot drink. Stay there.'

Olivia made him a hot blackcurrant from some juice in the fridge, found paracetamol in her bag. She didn't have many and Tom would probably need more, so she would have to go out later. She re-laid the fire whilst he drank, his gaze full of apologies whenever hers wandered over to his, unable to stop checking on him.

'What about work?' He still sounded half asleep.

'I think you might need a day off from writing, Tom. You should probably rest.'

'I meant yours.' He pointed to the window, the curtains she had forgotten to draw last night still open. 'The snow's thawing. You should be able to get to your appointment.'

'Maybe.' Olivia expected the roads would be very wet, probably flooded in places. She had planned to go to Cumbria today, but she didn't like the thought of leaving Tom alone with no one to check on him. She knew Annie would do it in a heartbeat but neither did she want to drag Annie out in poor weather, not with the baby due in a month. 'I can rearrange it for later in the week.'

What was she saying? Olivia never rearranged anything that wasn't out of her own control, though she supposed she had the excuse of the poor weather again. She hoped her anxious vendor wouldn't mind and decided it was tough if they did; she was staying here.

'Would you like some breakfast?' She was starving and they'd both missed supper last night after all the drama.

'Maybe later.' Tom was pushing the blankets aside to sit up and she went to help. 'I'm okay, thanks. I need to go upstairs.'

'Don't have a shower or a bath yet,' she told him as he stood up carefully. 'It might still be a bit soon.'

He raised a hand as he limped slowly from the room, and Olivia remembered that he had apparently slipped and fallen last night. She hadn't asked about other injuries. Shaking off the thought, she picked up her phone to reply to Annie, thanking her and Jon again and letting them know that Tom didn't seem too bad.

Porridge seemed like the perfect choice and Olivia had a pan on the go when he reappeared, still in the clothes from last night and looking a bit grim. He settled at the table, and she left the pan to bring a blanket from the sitting room that she tucked around him.

'You must stay warm and I think we should check your temperature. If it goes up you'll have to take a layer off. There should be a thermometer somewhere.' She rummaged through a medicine box until she found one and he sat obediently whilst she checked.

'A fraction below normal, so that's okay.' She was back stirring the porridge again. 'It's better in the sitting room, the fire's still going. Go and get comfortable and I'll bring breakfast through to you.'

He went without a protest, which worried her slightly, and she ladled some maple syrup into the porridge and made another hot blackcurrant juice. That ought to be enough sugar for now; he didn't need to be bouncing off the walls, he needed rest. She carried the tray through to find him on the sofa, staring blankly through the windows.

'Is the paracetamol helping?' Olivia didn't want to sound too concerned but even in his quiet moments subdued wasn't a word she would use to describe him.

'I think so. I just feel so tired.'

'You need to give yourself permission just to rest, Tom. Don't fight it.' She gathered the blankets, ready to cover him again as he swung his legs onto the sofa.

'Like you do, you mean?'

'We're not talking about me. I didn't spend a couple of hours in the snow in wet clothes.'

'I owe you an apology. And Jon, having to call everyone out like that.'

Olivia placed the tray on Tom's lap, watched as he began to eat. 'It's what they do,' she told him, glad to see him tucking in. 'They're used to it.'

'Yeah, but I should've known better. They didn't need to be out there, searching for me in that. I'm sorry.' He hesitated, spoon halfway to his mouth. 'No one's ever taken care of me the way you did last night, Olivia. Wrapped themselves around me.'

'I hardly did a thing.' She was almost knocked sideways by the expression of pain on his face, felt her breath catch at the sight, the flash of vulnerability he'd revealed. 'Anyone would've done the same.'

'But without you I might've been out there all night. Might not have made it back.' He put the spoon down and pushed the tray aside. 'Sorry. Maybe later.'

'That's okay.' She took the tray away, left it on a coffee table, and settled on an armchair.

'Don't you believe me?'

'About what?'

'No one taking care of me before.'

'Of course I believe you. It was a surprise, that's all, not what I expected.' Olivia wasn't sure how to proceed, whether he wanted reminding of his muttered words before sleep had claimed him for the night. 'You don't have to share anything with me, Tom, your life is private.'

His attention on her was unwavering, incredulity in his voice. 'Are you seriously saying you haven't googled me to find out more?'

'I haven't, unbelievable as that sounds. Seeing as I'm sharing a house with the man himself, I thought I'd try the old-fashioned way to get to know you.'

'I'm not used to that.' Tom's shrug was half-hearted. 'Most people I meet have preconceived ideas if they've already heard of me. It can be harder to be yourself when others think they already know who you are.'

'They see the characters and not you?' Olivia had almost fallen into that trap herself when she'd learned who he was.

'Sometimes.'

'I must be one of the few, then. I listen to more podcasts and music than I watch television.'

'Lucky for me.' The suggestion of a smile was already gone, his hands clasped together and the seconds slid away until he spoke again. 'It was just my dad and me, growing up, never really knew my mum. She'd disappeared by the time I was six and I've hardly seen her since.'

Olivia felt her stomach dive at Tom's matter of fact comment and the automatic reminders it brought of Ellie's father and the similarity to her own situation. His family circumstances seemed hard to match to a man who looked as though every opportunity in life had been made available to him.

It hadn't been difficult to imagine or expect an ordinary family like hers, with parents who'd cared for him and had provided a home. Not the broken one he'd revealed. She was beginning to understand how his strength, intelligence and even his appearance had played their own part to bring him to this point, to present the man he was supposed to be to the world. She wanted to hold him again now, but where might that take them? She made herself sit still.

'My dad was diagnosed with Parkinson's disease when I was twelve. It was just us and he wasn't the most loving or tactile of dads, even though he tried. Not easy for him either. We were okay for a while, I learned to take care of him as best as I could. Neighbours helped when I wasn't around.' Tom's head dropped. 'When I was older.'

'Oh Tom, I'm so very sorry. How awful for you both.'

'I was used to it and I didn't know any other life. I had to look after him: he needed me. Drama was the thing that got me through and gave me other worlds to think about.' Tom's breath came out in a sigh, as though he had been holding himself in for a long time. 'Took me years to learn to live with the guilt for leaving him to go to drama school when I had the chance. He developed pneumonia and died when I was nineteen. I wasn't there.'

'Tom, you can't blame...'

'Myself for his being sick?' Tom's head was against the back of the sofa as he stared at her. 'Not for that, I don't. But it's still painful to remember how much I wanted to get away from home, to be an ordinary student having fun. Learning my craft. Not fretting about how he was or what I needed to do for him. Then he was gone and I couldn't do any more. I felt guilty then about being free of it, the constant worry.'

Olivia crossed to the sofa to sit next to Tom. She hadn't even realised she'd covered his hands with hers until she saw him watching the way her fingers were stroking his.

'Sometimes I feel like I've been playing a character half my life, pretending to be a version of myself. The one who hadn't left a sick parent behind to go off and live his life. I learned to be what people expected, to hide myself in plain sight behind a part when it suited me.'

He looked around the sitting room as though he were seeing it for the first time. 'It wasn't like that here, with your dad. We got on from the start and he knew my story, made me feel at home. I could be more like myself here. Just a writer, not the actor and everything that comes with it, or the characters. Just me. Sometimes I think I'm still finding out who that man really is now I haven't got a career to fall back on.'

'What about your marriage? Wasn't that like home too?'

'For a time. We were both busy chasing work that kept us apart. My ex-wife is a make-up artist and she was often on a different production.'

'Why are you telling me all this?' Olivia's pulse was hurrying. 'Don't you think it's going to make everything so much more complicated?'

'We've been complicated since the moment I found you on the landing on Friday night, wouldn't you say?' Tom's voice was gentle, matching his expression.

She nodded slowly. She hadn't let herself think of how he'd looked when she'd warmed him last night and taken care of him, had wanted to. Sometimes she would sense an ease between them and then it would flee in the glances they exchanged, politeness and the reserve covering what lay beneath.

'I still don't think we should do anything about it, Tom.' She inched away from him, wondering why it felt as though something she couldn't even name was already passing her by. Not trusting another stranger with her life was the resolve she needed to cling to, not the story or the plea in his eyes, the way she knew he wanted them to be more.

'Our lives are too different and we'll have to move on. We've both been through marriage and the mayhem of divorce and I like my independence. My dad needs me and I don't see enough of him as it is. It wouldn't be fair to expect someone else to settle for what's left.'

'I understand, Olivia. It makes sense and I have little to recommend me, as the saying goes.' Tom was wry as he freed his hand from hers. 'I hope we're still friends at least.'

Olivia's heart plummeted. 'Of course we are.' However much she liked him and was attracted to him, they were every bit as complicated as he had said. There simply wasn't room for each other in their lives and it was a truth she suddenly disliked intensely. Chasing off to Cumbria for work tomorrow had never seemed less appealing.

Chapter Eight

When Olivia walked into the kitchen early on Wednesday she was surprised to see Tom at the table, cradling a coffee and giving her that smile she still found so disarming. She sternly reminded herself that it was only yesterday they had both agreed to remain friends.

'You look much better.' She heard her relief as she found some granola, added yogurt, poured a coffee and held the cafetière up questioningly. The online shop had arrived yesterday, and she had been thankful to fill the shelves, especially if they had snow again and couldn't leave the village.

'Please.' Tom passed his cup across. 'I feel it. I slept better.' His eyes were telling her he'd missed having her beside him again and she felt her resolve wavering with a look like that. 'I'm thankful to have escaped without anything worse. Might give running a miss for a few days though, my ankle's a bit sore.'

'That sounds wise.' She noticed him taking in her navy dress, the heels she hadn't worn since she'd arrived in Thorndale. She liked the appreciation on his face even as he looked away, presumably remembering their discussion, that decision.

'You were right, yesterday, about resting and not writing. It helped.'

'Good, I'm so glad. How's the book going? Are you writing today?' Olivia settled at the table opposite him, trying not to shiver. The old range did its best, but she'd been wearing more layers these past few days.

'Don't think so. It's going fine but I'm at the stage when I need to regroup, make sure I'm heading in the right direction. I like to step back every now and again and take a look.'

'And how do you do that?'

'A long walk or a run. Time to think, clear my head. Different view.'

'Come with me.' She'd spoken the words before she even realised she'd thought of them. For a skilled nego- tiator she was certainly finding it difficult not to play her hand when she was around Tom. 'Today. Why not?'

'To Cumbria?' He sounded surprised as he lifted his cup.

'Sorry, probably not the best idea.' Olivia tried to find an excuse for him to back out. 'I'll be in the car half the day and I don't suppose not being alone is conducive to thinking about your plot.'

'Actually, spending the day with you is exactly what I'd like.' He drained the last of his coffee and reached for his phone nearby. 'When are you leaving?'

'Seriously?' It was too late to pretend she wasn't quite so pleased that he was coming with her.

'Were you joking?' Tom was on his feet and looked worried for a second.

'I hadn't planned to say it, but it wasn't a joke. I'd love you to come.' But she couldn't ignore the thought running through her mind, one she'd been pondering ever since she'd found out that he'd been an actor. 'What if you get recognised? Does it happen a lot?'

'Not as much as you'd think. Sometimes I can see people wondering but they don't always get it. Being noticed out of context with different hair and clothes can be helpful. And I haven't worn breeches for years.'

Olivia thought that was a shame but managed not to voice it.

Tom was at the door now, a suggestion of laughter following. 'Seeing as we've apparently had the wedding I can always pretend we're on our honeymoon and don't want to be disturbed.'

'In the wilds of Cumbria in December? Do you think your public would buy that?' she quipped. Her pulse was already quickening at the thought of a day with him, the house she was planning to view moving a little further back in her mind.

'I'm an actor, I reckon I can fake it. What about you?' He and his grin were gone before she replied, her words muttered to the empty kitchen.

'I'm not sure I'd have to.'

The roads were mostly clear as she drove them across the Dales and into Cumbria. It would be weeks, months even, before the hills gave up their snow topping, the whiteness reaching up to the greying skies. They chatted until eventually Tom fell asleep and she left him in peace, thinking of his brush with hypothermia only two days ago.

The house she was viewing was close to Penrith and within two hours they had arrived at the edge of the village beyond the town. Olivia had been here before and knew the amenities on offer. She drove to the house and pulled up at the end of a long drive. First impressions were everything and this one was magnificent.

She could see the large Victorian property set at the head of a sweeping lawn, lined with mature trees, far enough away from the house to allow light still to reach it. Tom woke up as she got out to take the first few images for her client, wanting to convey how it had felt to arrive at this property, what the long, tree-lined drive was suggesting lay at the end.

They had already agreed that he would go for a walk whilst she viewed the house and its gardens. Detailed measurements and a brochure for her waiting client would be put together by one of her colleagues, who would return this week if all went to plan and the sale was put in motion.

She could have invited Tom in, passed him off as a colleague, but she felt that it would be unprofessional and there was always the chance he might be recognised. Unlikely, but she wasn't going to take the risk. They'd talked about it on the way, and he'd told her that he always just said he was doing research if anyone ever spotted him, and people accepted it. She and Tom hadn't discussed what they would do after the viewing and Olivia was planning to drive back to Thorndale once the appointment was over.

She always carried a case in her car with practical boots, a winter coat, a change of clothes and some food. She'd been caught out a few times in the early days of finding properties, trapped somewhere remote on a winter's day with not much more than her suit and a smart coat to sustain her.

Looking at the snow lingering on the fells behind the house and the wet ground, she would need all her layers to explore this place once she'd been in the house. Tom joined her outside, already wrapped in a practical waterproof and walking boots. He pulled a beanie over his hair as he came to stand beside her. An evergreen magnolia tree was draped in Christmas lights on the lawn, glittering brightly against the winter's day.

'Beautiful.'

'Yes. I wouldn't fancy all those bathrooms to clean, though.'

'Me neither.' Tom checked the time, pulled on gloves. 'Ninety minutes? Sure that's enough?'

'Plenty. I just need to get a feel for it, see if it matches what my client's after and how they might upgrade it. They're looking for a project and this could be a really nice one. I'll text you when I'm done but take as long as you like. There's a cafe in the village, I'll head back there and…'

'Work? Relax with a coffee? Read a book?'

'Very funny. Work.' They'd already swapped numbers on the way here, Tom adding hers to his phone and texting her back. 'I'll have to write up some notes, although I record most of them whilst I'm walking round the property.'

Olivia was done in eighty minutes, calming the anxious vendors and promising to speak to her client later today about a potential purchase. She knew the house was perfect and the vendors were relieved that they weren't likely to be faced with weeks of viewings and uncertainty as they prepared to swap their period vicarage for an apartment in a country house development.

She'd texted Tom to let him know and had been in the cafe for about fifteen minutes when he arrived. She had a coffee beside her, had written up some of her notes and emailed the client to schedule an early evening call. Not for the first time she wondered what Tom made of her job, finding properties such as these when he had no permanent home of his own.

'You done?'

She looked up. Tom's skin was glowing from the walk, and he seemed re-energised from a couple of hours in the cold, the dark shadows under his eyes gone. 'Pretty much. Would you like a coffee before we go?'

'No thanks. How's the rest of your day looking?'

'Emails to respond to and I've scheduled a call for this evening about this house. I need to speak with Julian and a couple of colleagues but I can do that from the car. Why?' Olivia sounded suspicious.

'So other than that, you can more or less take the day off?'

'More or less. Why?'

Tom grinned. It was one of the things she was coming to appreciate most about his company: the laughter they shared. She was also realising how little she laughed normally, being mostly on her own. That was an unwelcome jolt, a different view of her life she hadn't really considered before.

'Because I've just discovered the most brilliant thing and seeing as you've more or less got the day off you could come with me and do it.' He glanced down at her feet. 'Change your boots, though. And definitely your coat.'

She swapped her boots and coat back at the car and they left it in the village, retracing Tom's steps. After fifteen minutes they arrived in a farmyard and instead of the sheep and cattle she was expecting, she was astonished to find the fields full of woolly alpacas.

'We're visiting an alpaca farm?'

'We're doing more than that, we're going walking with them.' He halted, his eyes tangled with hers and she felt her breath catch at the new excitement in his.

'Walking with alpacas? I didn't even know you could.'

105

'I saw it earlier and thought it would be fun. You up for it?'

'I think so. How hard can it be?'

They'd arrived just in time to join a group walk of three others, all women and friends who'd travelled together. Olivia was nervous when she approached the animal she was soon to get to know. He was called Stevie Wonder, a brown and white alpaca with a fluffy topknot flopping over his halter, and he seemed as suspicious of her as she was of him.

There was a safety talk from their enthusiastic leader, who was sporting a cheery Santa hat, and then they were off, walking in single file along a grassy track on the edge of a wood with Tom behind, and Stevie stomping beside Olivia. He was a bit skittish, planting his feet to stare from time to time and she lengthened her lead rope, until he stuck his head down into a patch of grass and she nearly lost him.

She looked back to see Tom laughing at her, his own little white alpaca much better behaved, and her attempt at a scowl turned into a grin. She started to get the hang of leading Stevie, forgetting about her phone until they were back in the yard three quarters of an hour later.

He seemed quite reluctant to leave her now and she stroked his woolly coat, content to stand with him for a few minutes. A young girl came to take the alpacas away and Olivia was quite sad to see Stevie go as he stomped off, his little legs heading happily for the feed she'd been told he was expecting. She pulled her phone from her bag, checking for messages, and was happy to see there were no new ones.

'Well? Did you enjoy a bit of time out?'

'I did, it was fun, although I did wonder if you'd lined up the naughty one just for me.' Olivia leaned into Tom as they left the yard, pushing his shoulder. 'Thank you.'

'Pleasure. That's what friends are for. He just needed a strong woman to lead him.'

'Good job he found one, then,' she murmured. She was enjoying Tom's company, playing truant from work for an hour, something that would have astonished her a week ago.

He pulled the beanie off now they were free of the yard, running a hand through his hair. She realised that the hat was another layer of disguise, another means of hiding the character she was sure people sometimes saw instead of the man, his words from yesterday morning coming back to her. They ate a quick lunch at the cafe, the only customers, before setting off back to Thorndale.

Tom was making notes as she drove, scribbling on the pad resting on one bended leg, chewing the top of his pen absently. 'Sorry, bit antisocial of me.'

'It's fine.' Olivia was quick to reassure him. 'I've been working too, and we both know you came for a change of scenery and a chance to think. I hope it's helped.'

'Not as much as I thought.'

He sounded frustrated and she was disappointed. She had enjoyed the day with him even more than she'd expected, appreciating how he understood that she too needed time to think, time to be quiet and work.

'I'm sorry. Can I help at all?'

'Not unless you know anything about Irish ferry timetables in November.'

'Nope, you got me there, sorry. Good old Google, I guess.' She voiced a thought that was bothering her. 'Why don't you write in the library in the house, Tom? It's so

107

cold and bleak in the dining room. Didn't my dad suggest the library?'

Tom flipped over a page on his notepad, stared at the blank lines. 'He did. But I didn't want to invade his privacy: it's such a personal room. He was always so at home there.'

'I think he'd love the thought of you in there, writing your bestseller.' Olivia was picturing her dad in the library, glasses at hand or on his head, piles of books at his feet. She blinked back a quick rush of hurt as she saw his new flat in her mind. How did he bear it, living there alone after the life he had shared with her mum in Thorndale, the friends he had around him?

'It's a bit early to suggest it'll be a bestseller.' Tom's laugh was wry. 'Next you'll be wanting to know what the book's about.'

'Ah.'

'Hasn't your dad ever told you that you should never ask a writer what their book is about? Terrifying question.'

'Don't change the subject. Just tell me.'

'Tell you what?' There was an innocence in Tom's question, a smile she guessed he was hiding by looking out of the window at the landscape flashing by.

'If you're planning to publish it then you're going to need an answer, don't you think, Tom?' She was gentler now, mischievous. 'As your wife wouldn't I know what you're writing?'

'Invoking marital status now, I see.'

'Of course. There's got to be some upsides to being married to a heartthrob even if his heyday was years ago.'

'You really know how to flatter me, don't you? I'd hate to see you try and put someone down.'

'Oh, I think you've probably had more than your share of flattery.' Olivia loved teasing him. 'Stop changing the subject.'

'It's a thriller,' Tom eventually replied. 'A body is discovered on an abandoned monastic island off the coast of Ireland. When a second one is found on another holy island five hundred miles away, my guy's brought in to help find the connection and the killer.'

'Who's your guy?'

'Niall Costello, a former Olympic marksman and bodyguard who works in counter-intelligence in the SDU, the Irish national security agency.'

'You're going to need that pitch,' she said, indulging the rush of happiness she felt now that Tom had shared the premise of his book with her. 'A lot. I think it sounds fantastic. When will it be out?'

His shoulders rose in a shrug. 'I have no idea.'

'The publishers haven't told you yet?'

'It's not that. I don't have a publisher, Olivia. Or an agent, or a publicist. When I've finished it, edited it enough to know I'm happy to send it out, I'll just have to submit like everyone else and hope for the best. Or maybe go straight to self-publish.'

'I hope you're not planning to use a pseudonym when you do publish or submit?'

'Why not?'

'Because you already have a profile that people recognise, Tom.' The traffic was heavier now as rain followed the thaw and she slowed the car as spray hit the windscreen time after time. 'You can use it.'

'I can't. I'm right back at the beginning.' There was a resignation in Tom's voice, a new flatness. 'No career to speak of any more.'

'What happened?' Olivia was glad to turn off the motorway, leaving the heavier traffic behind. She thought of him growing up taking care of his dad, the lack of support, her heart softening once again.

'Why don't you just check Google?'

'You'd seriously prefer me to do that?' She tried to keep the disappointment from her response. 'When we both know that not everything I'll discover online is the absolute truth.'

'Fine, Olivia.' The resignation was back and she was already regretting pushing him. 'Playing Harrington led to some great opportunities and my US agent was pressing me to do a pilot for a comedy series. I wanted to play a psychiatrist in a movie instead and the agent dropped me when I didn't get it and turned down the comedy because I didn't want to be tied down for more than a season. There's only so many times you can fail or say no when there's thirty other guys ready to jump in front of you.

'The parts were gradually drying up but I was focused on writing my first book, about an American family across five generations, and didn't really notice until my agent in London dropped me too. I handed the book in and signed up to produce and take the lead in a new play, thinking it would be good to let people know I was still there.' Tom sighed. 'Didn't quite work out that way. The play bombed, closed after two weeks and I haven't performed since. Then the book didn't sell well, and the publishers dropped me before I finished the second. Suddenly my career was pretty much over.'

'I'm so sorry.' Olivia wasn't sure what else to add, how to properly express her sadness for what he had experienced.

'Thanks, Olivia. Acting's such a tough business and you get used to the rejections, but the book was hard to take. I thought a writer is who I really am now.'

They weren't very far from Thorndale and she slowed to avoid the snow still lingering, piled up in drifts on the sides of the lanes. 'And you still want to write?'

'Yeah. Crazy, I know, given my previous experience. But I love it, I feel most like myself when I'm writing. Creating the characters, building their world and telling the story, and this is definitely my genre now.' He shrugged. 'In theory.'

'What about acting?'

'Think that's done for me. Not sure I'd go back.'

'You must be a fantastic actor, Tom,' she told him gently. The screen on her dashboard lit up with a call and she saw her assistant's name. Olivia didn't want to take it right now and risk snapping the thread of the thoughts Tom was sharing with her.

'I imagine characters like Harrington don't come around very often and it takes a brilliant performance to keep on resonating with people down the years. And your new book sounds wonderful and I'm sure it will be a success.' Her hand reached out, found his. 'As your friend I have every confidence in you and I'm not just saying that to make you feel better.'

'Maybe that's because you don't know me well, Olivia. I'm not a great bet.'

She didn't want to let his hand go and he stopped her when she tried, lifting it to kiss her fingers quickly. She knew he meant it as a thank you but it was impossible to halt the way her stomach plunged in desire, taking her straight back to that night in the pub. He released her and she tried to concentrate on the drive, ignoring thoughts of a voicemail she expected to follow that missed call.

'Promise me you won't write the book and then lock it up in a cloud somewhere, Tom, my dad would be horrified. He's always said that books are for reading. Sharing, talking about, disagreeing over, but above all reading. He wouldn't want you to write a book you don't want anyone to read.'

'I know, he's told me that too. I will think about it, writing in the library.' Tom's voice was casual now as he asked, 'So when you did that online shop did you order the ingredients for spaghetti carbonara?'

'What, spaghetti and carbonara?' She wasn't surprised that Tom had changed the subject after sharing some of the story of his career with her. 'Isn't that all you need?'

'Very funny. Do we have eggs, parmesan, spaghetti, bacon or pancetta?'

'"We"?' She tried not to love how that sounded. '"We" don't.'

'Then stop somewhere, I'll pick up the ingredients and show you how to make it.'

'I know how to make it. You pierce the film and put in the microwave for three minutes. Job done.'

Chapter Nine

Olivia's call with her client about the Penrith property took longer than the scheduled forty-five minutes and it was over an hour later when she finished. When her dad had been at home they would settle in the library, the fire blazing, content. But she and Tom seemed to gravitate to the kitchen, and she was beginning to think of it as the new hub of the house. She saw that he had set out ingredients and was writing on his notepad. He looked up as she walked in.

'All done?'

'Yes. I'm sorry if I kept you waiting.' She put her phone down on the table, reached into the fridge for the bottle of white he'd already opened and poured some into the second glass he'd left out for her. 'My client is happy to proceed so we'll be onto contracts and conveyancing soon.'

'Based on your visit today? They don't want to see it in person?'

She savoured a mouthful of Pinot Grigio before giving him an answer. 'They haven't got time. They're both professional athletes who want a private plot and the old coach house will be perfect for the gym they need since it's already been converted for another use.'

'They must really trust you, Olivia. Making that choice for them.'

'I suppose they do.' She caught Tom's gaze, held it. 'It's usually about the time clients don't have and what they can do to a property. They almost always bring in architects, designers, and create something different. And very often they move on. New club, new company, new country. They don't see it like home in the way most of us do.'

'Right.' Tom sounded brisk as he pointed to the range and the ingredients he had already prepared. 'Time for your cookery lesson.'

'You'll need more wine.' She refilled his glass and wondered if he had changed the subject on purpose when they had been talking of a home, one he didn't have. She hated the thought even more than when she had first heard it. 'This could test your patience.'

'We'll have to see.'

When they sat down to eat supper twenty minutes later Olivia knew for sure she was in trouble. Tom had been funny – and patient – as he explained how to make spaghetti carbonara, dropping into a different character once or twice and making her laugh. Thankfully not his most famous one, Harrington. That she would have found far too distracting, had he turned the full force of his power on her.

It was a shock to realise how much she liked having Tom here, sharing the simplest of chores the way they already did after so few days together. Thoughts of her taking care of him two nights ago – curling herself around him, trying to warm him – continued to pop, unprompted, into her head and it was an effort to shake them off. Her attraction to him hadn't changed and she could feel herself wanting to be with him, to see his eyes linger on her.

'This is amazing,' Olivia said hungrily, winding spaghetti around her fork and trying to find a way to eat it with more elegance. 'You do realise you're ruining me for microwave meals for ever?'

'That's not seriously all you live on?' Tom was staring at her, his expression unfathomable.

'No. Actually I have a confession to make.'

'Now you're going to tell me you're an accomplished cook who knows her way backwards around a kitchen?'

'Not quite.' She tilted her glass towards him, liking the smile hovering on his lips. 'I have all my meals delivered and I cook them myself. I only usually resort to the microwave when I'm desperate. When my daughter Ellie was small I batch-cooked everything and froze it. Busy working mum, see.'

'And you let me stand there, blathering on about egg yolks and when to add the water from the pasta? You're a fraud, Olivia Bradshaw.'

She ducked, the tea towel he'd lobbed sailing past her head, and savoured his pretend outrage and the teasing layered beneath it. 'I am not! I've just never made spaghetti carbonara from scratch before.'

'You can cook supper next time,' Tom told her. He'd almost finished eating and leaned back in his seat. 'I'll do lunch instead. No wonder you offered to make sandwiches or heat up soup. I'm going for the easy job tomorrow.'

'You'll soon change your mind,' she told him smoothly. 'If I cook, you wash up and you won't want to do that again when you've seen the state of the kitchen afterwards.' She stood up to clear their plates to the sink, filling the bowl with hot water. 'My cooking ability doesn't stretch that far.'

Tom joined her, drying the dishes she was washing. It was all so unfamiliar and yet so comfortable.

'Have you been divorced a long time, Olivia?'

It took her a couple of seconds to remember the answer, her previous marriage seeming very far in her past in this moment. She drew in a breath, let it out. 'Yes. My marriage was over pretty much before we'd even begun. I met Jared at a gig. He's a musician and we eloped six weeks later.'

'I wasn't expecting that.' Tom was staring at her, the cloth stilled in his hand. 'I didn't have you down as someone quite so impulsive.'

'I was younger and more reckless then.' She raised a shoulder. 'It lasted until I was seven months pregnant and Jared was gone before Ellie, our daughter, was born.'

Olivia held the hurt in, trying not to remember the fear, the worry about the days ahead and how she would cope on her own, the living she needed to make. The empty promises her ex had made to do better, the sporadic financial support and the flying visits. The disruption, the loneliness, the occasional frightening midnight dash to A&E with a poorly toddler.

'I'm sorry. It must've been very tough for you both.'

'It was.' She knew in that instant Tom recognised that their lives were mirrored in some way through their different experiences. 'But we got through it, so much more than that, and I have a wonderful daughter whom I'll always be incredibly thankful for, however feckless her father is. His career was taking off when we met, and he was already public property. You learn very quickly that you're already in the background of someone's life, with people looking straight past you to see him.' She paused. 'You must know what that's like, Tom.'

'Yes. Nicole, my ex-wife, felt it too sometimes, especially after the series came out. The attention, the demands. Somehow it changed us without us even realising. I don't think I changed because of it but people treat you differently when they think they know you. When they can't find the boundary between me and the character.'

'Exactly.' Olivia understood perfectly, feeling a glimmer of sympathy for Tom's ex-wife.

'What about since?' He hesitated. 'Has there been anyone else for you?'

'Beyond the crappy dates and the dodgy dinners? The no-shows and the effort of even bothering?' Olivia was weary but not bitter. 'Not seriously. I had a little girl to think of and I wasn't going to bring anyone into our lives that wouldn't stay or didn't fit. I learned my lesson well and I won't rush into something like that again. And I haven't really found anyone I'd like to see more than a couple of times.' Until now, but she wasn't going to admit that part to Tom.

It was a few moments before he offered a reply. 'Does Ellie still see her father?'

'Sometimes. Jared lives in Tobago and he sends her a ticket every six months or so. They get on. It could've been a lot worse and he's incredibly lucky to have her in his life at all. She has three half brothers and sisters scattered around and she sees them too from time to time. She's actually going to be with her dad this year for Christmas, with her boyfriend.'

'Not you?' Tom dried the last of the dishes, stacking them neatly on the worktop.

Olivia was trying not to love having him alongside her. 'No. She spent last year with me and the year before that in Australia, with Logan's family. It's only fair, I can't keep her all to myself, much as I'd like to, and we'll Zoom on the day.'

She wondered how Tom felt, listening to her talk of her daughter, her child, as she thought about him telling her that he hadn't had a family but had wanted one. She'd finished the washing-up and couldn't find a reason to linger, crossing instead to the fridge to see how much wine they had left.

'You're teaching me bad habits, I don't usually drink on a school night.' She lifted the bottle out. 'There's still another glass or so each in here. Would you like to finish it with me?'

'I would.'

'Probably not worth lighting the fire in the sitting room, even though it's warmer in there once it's going.'

'I remember.'

Her eyes caught Tom's and she was trapped there, sure he was having the same thoughts, remembering Monday night and how she had held him. She saw the alteration in his face, the desire that it be more for him, too, and her resolve to remain friends was fading dangerously with a look such as that aimed her way.

'I should probably catch up on work later.' She wrenched her eyes from his and pulled out a seat, pulse still hurrying. Her phone was on the table and she put her glasses on to toy with it, scrolling through messages without seeing them. 'I'm taking some annual leave soon so I ought to try and get ahead.'

'What, six-hour days instead of twelve?'

His flippant comment didn't make her laugh as she began to realise its truth. Even when she was on holiday she always checked in, kept an eye on her emails, told her assistant to call her if necessary.

'Sorry, I... That wasn't fair.'

'You have a point, Tom. Maybe this time I'll aim for three.' She turned her phone over and took her glasses back off. As long as Ellie and her dad were all right, everything else would have to wait until tomorrow. 'You must think my work very trivial.'

'Of course I don't. It's your job and you've clearly made a great success of your career. Almost no one gets to be a success just on luck alone.'

'I'm sensing a "but" coming.'

'Not from me. You're clearly dedicated to your clients and I hope they appreciate it, know how much of yourself you give them.'

'A few do, not all.' Olivia thought of the hours, the travel, the last-minute requests. She had intended to go a Pilates class yesterday afternoon and had missed it. Was it all worth it, really?

'How did you get here, Tom?' She raised her glass to the room, this house where neither of them was completely at home. Maybe they didn't know each other well enough for her to be asking that of him. She was aware of some of the choices he'd made and the disappointments that had followed but she didn't yet understand how it had brought him to her dad's door with nowhere else to go.

'You mean why am I effectively homeless?' There was resignation in his tone and she nodded. He joined her at the table, sipped more wine.

'My marriage was in trouble before Harrington came along, probably since we both wanted a family and eventually found out we couldn't have one because of me.' A flash of pain darted through his blue eyes. Olivia thought of Ellie and how much she loved her daughter, how many times she'd held her throughout the years, and she was saddened that Tom didn't know that same love for a child when he clearly wanted to.

'After the series came out, I spent more time in LA and we were living off what I'd already made and Nicole's career, until there wasn't much left. I kept assuming something else would come along and she tried to get me to see the reality: that it wasn't happening. I just buried it, ignored what I didn't want to hear.'

Tom paused, his look unflinching on Olivia. 'We'd bought a bigger house which I re-mortgaged to invest in my comeback play and lost it. We separated soon after, split what little was left. Eventually she met someone else and they wanted to try for a family and we divorced. Nicole's ten years younger than me and still had a chance.'

'Tom, I…'

'Don't, Olivia.' Tom held up his glass. 'If you were going to say something kind then please don't. I walked away with almost nothing, which was all I deserved. At least she's with someone who's really there for her. I've always been able to take care of myself and leave when I needed to.'

'I'm sorry.' Olivia saw the sympathy he blinked away. 'Is that when my dad offered to help you?'

'No, it was about a year after the divorce when he found out. We'd kept in touch but I didn't really tell anyone how it was for a long time. I stayed with friends whilst I worked out what to do next but there's only so many times you can impose, however good they are to me. I couldn't afford to rent anywhere in London without regular work but selfishly I wasn't quite ready to give up the arts completely.'

Tom finished his wine and put the empty glass on the table. 'I'd had the idea about the thriller and took myself off to Ireland to research it and rented a scruffy old cottage near the sea in Kerry. I was only planning to stay about three months, but it ended up being nearly nine. I did some bar work and shifts on boat tours in the summer, other bits of casual work.'

'Didn't anyone recognise you?'

'Occasionally, but I picked up the accent pretty quickly. That helped, it wasn't what people expected to hear if they thought they'd seen me somewhere else. A few locals found out and made up a story about me being a black sheep back to make amends with my family.' Tom smiled and Olivia's own followed.

'It was a tiny village miles from anything and you were soon put in your place if they thought you were getting above yourself. The people were great, just what I needed. A world away from LA and all that nonsense. Living there gave me time to think, and I decided I had one last chance at writing something decent and I was going to give it a go.

'Then your dad got in touch and learned I was writing again. I couldn't afford to keep the cottage over the winter without work and when he found out he offered me the house on the spot. Told me he was leaving soon and I could stay as long as I liked. The only condition he imposed was that I had to write; he wasn't going to let me get away with not finishing a draft. I'd been to see him to sort things out, that day I met you in the pub.'

'So had I.' Olivia wondered if everything between them might've been different if she'd bumped into Tom at her dad's flat. They'd have passed one another by, offered a polite nod and been on their way, strangers still – not sitting here in her dad's house, spilling stories of sorrow into the darkness. She only had to close her eyes to recall that night with Tom in her room. A shiver worked its way down her spine at the memory of their arms around one another, the intensity of their kiss. 'I'm glad Dad asked you to come.'

'Are you really?' There was a suggestion of humour in Tom's question. 'Because that's not what that atlas implied.'

'Good thing you switched the light on, then.' She gathered her phone and her glasses, offering him a smile she hoped didn't reveal all of the turmoil his story had sparked within her. 'I'm sorry, I've got work I need to do. See you tomorrow.'

'Night, Olivia. Sleep well.'

She wasn't at all sure she would now after hearing the softness in his reply.

—

Olivia's plans on Thursday changed again with the arrival of an email before she had even woken up. Another house had become available north of the Scottish borders and it made sense to see it after the Northumberland one. Given the vagaries of the weather she decided to stay at an inn close to the second property and travel back to Thorndale on Friday.

She preferred the Scottish property to the Northumberland one when she viewed it and informed her business partner accordingly. The house in Scotland, Victorian with some interesting features and a burn in the grounds, would suit a client who was moving from Surrey and wanted a country home within shouting distance of Edinburgh.

She didn't rush on Friday, calling in to see her dad on the way back to Thorndale. He was in good spirits and wanted to know exactly what she thought of Tom and how they were getting along. She told him the truth but was careful not to let him suspect that her feelings for Tom were changing, growing every day she spent with him. Hugh didn't seem too worried that she hadn't had time to do much about clearing the house yet.

They parted when he eventually told her to leave, concerned about her driving through the Dales on a night glittering with frost. She brushed away his concern, despite knowing she would be saying exactly the same had it been her speaking to Ellie. Olivia promised to Zoom on Sunday and pop in again next week.

Arriving back at the house, she was absurdly pleased to see the glow of a light in the library and that Tom had apparently taken her up on the offer to work in there. It was much more comfortable, and she couldn't have said why she liked the idea of his writing with her dad's old books around him. She had eaten a sandwich in the car on the way home and took a glass of water to bed without disturbing Tom.

She was up early on Saturday and surprised to see a light still on in the library. She knocked and stuck her head around the door when he called her to come in. 'Morning. Please tell me you haven't been writing all night?'

'Not quite.' Tom gave her a grin and Olivia decided she rather liked that first thing in her day. 'I came down at five, couldn't sleep. How was your trip?'

'Productive. The Scottish house will sell, the Northumberland one wasn't right.'

'Shame.'

'Yes. Coffee?'

'Please.'

She brought a cup back to the library and placed it on the desk. His thank you was a distracted one and she left him to it. As it was the weekend, she decided she ought to get on with some Christmas shopping, her phone upstairs. Ellie and Logan were due in a week and she still hadn't got their stockings sorted. Tom joined her about forty-five minutes later, finding her browsing on her laptop and halfway down another cup of coffee.

'Work?' He helped himself to more coffee, nodded at the laptop.

'Would it astonish you if I said no? I'm Christmas shopping. That day is coming round far too quickly for my liking.'

'Are you going to the Christmas market, then?'

Olivia looked at him blankly. 'What market?'

'The one outside your front door.' Tom checked his watch. 'The one that's already started, with all the festive stalls you'd expect in December. I'm heading over soon.'

'Shopping?' She wondered who for, pushed the thought away. It was not her business.

'No, I've offered to help with selling Christmas trees for the fell rescue, they have a space outside their headquarters on the green. I thought it was the least I could do after my escapade on Monday,' he finished wryly.

'Oh, I saw something about that on a flyer. That's nice of you.' Olivia thought that she might find a few stocking fillers at the market. Her dad only ever wanted books or socks, and she was certain he had enough of both. Surely she could find something else, there was bound to be—

'Why don't you come with me?'

'What?' She looked up, her finger poised on the mouse, ready to click 'checkout' on the gifts she had selected for her team in the office. If she were quick she'd get them on an overnight delivery. 'To the market? With you? Why?'

'Why not?' Tom finished his coffee and stood up, stretched in a way she found distracting as he lifted his arms above his head, tilting his neck sideways. She returned her attention to the laptop instead and completed her purchase.

'Selling trees will be fun. Plus you might pick up a few gifts, save buying everything online.'

'Standing around outside in the freezing cold, dragging Christmas trees about? Your idea of fun is a little odd, Tom. Mine usually starts with a good meal, a decent bottle of wine and ends with a great movie.' First bit of shopping done, Olivia tried to turn her mind to her inbox instead, the contract she needed to read. But a morning with Tom was far more appealing and she was wavering.

'Don't be such a wuss. Wrap up and let's go. I've got to be back by lunchtime anyway to open up the shop. Getting out and about might take your mind off work for a while.'

'I'll need a miracle to do that,' she muttered, following him upstairs to change. 'Not sure I've brought enough layers for selling Christmas trees on the green.'

They met in the hall soon after, Tom wrapped up in a grey waxed jacket, a thick scarf around his neck below the beanie covering his hair. Olivia went for the practical over stylish, helping herself to her dad's coat and woolly scarf again.

'Will you be warm enough?' She took in Tom's jacket, flushing as she saw his eyebrows raise.

'Worried about me?'

'Only a little. As your friend. I don't want you to get another chill.'

'I'm fine. Thanks. If I do get chilled will you warm me?' His grin was unabashed. 'Encourage me to take my clothes off again?'

'Definitely not. That's not a sight I could cope with twice in one week.' Or should be thinking about as much as she was.

'That good, huh?'

'Nope.' She threw him a look over her shoulder as she opened the front door. 'I might've had a sneaky glance at Harrington and I'm not convinced those breeches will still fit.'

'You cheeky...' Tom went to catch her and she was already darting ahead into the garden. 'I can see I'll have to prove you wrong.'

'Promise?'

'Maybe.'

They were still laughing as they set off and Olivia had to admit that Thorndale looked beautifully festive. Stalls were lined up on both sides of the green, with chairs and a covered marquee in the centre for enjoying mulled wine and the hot, seasonal food on offer. Cars were crawling along the high street and the brass band was back, accompanying some carol singers.

It was much smaller than the city markets Olivia was used to and she appreciated the village charm, the groups of people chatting together and taking their time to enjoy it all. It was an unpleasant jolt to realise that Ellie had been to the market with her grandad, but Olivia hadn't. Last year something had come up with a client and she'd gone racing off to sort it out, leaving her daughter and her dad to spend the weekend without her.

Sam Stewart was behind a stall selling handmade bags and Olivia promised to return later for a proper browse as she followed Tom to the fell rescue spot. It was already busy outside the barn headquarters. People were sizing up the different trees on offer, pulling them from their stands to stare critically or put them straight back.

She saw Annie and went inside to say hello. Tom was with Jon, shaking his hand and, Olivia guessed from the look on his face, apologising for having to call the team out on Monday night. Annie's bump seemed to have expanded again in the week since Olivia had seen her, and she admitted she was tired and not sleeping very well. But she brushed that away, wanting to know more about how Olivia was getting on, sharing a house with Tom.

'I bet your dad's enjoying creating a bit of mischief, Liv.'

'You know him well, Annie.' Olivia saw Tom laughing with Jon and looking ridiculously sexy, her resolve to remain friends wilting a little further at the sight. 'Tom's actually quite nice to share a house with, it could be worse. He cooks and he doesn't mind clearing up. And we're both busy.'

'We were at the vicarage for supper a couple of weeks ago and Tom was there too. He and Sam were as thick as thieves, chatting about drama and acting, and he had us falling about with some of his stories.'

'I can imagine.' Olivia could, all too easily. He was lovely company when he allowed himself to be.

'Sam's hoping he might take an interest in the arts consortium too.'

'Oh?' Olivia tried to tone down her surprise. 'Why?'

'You know what she's like, Liv.' Annie had one hand on her bump as she lowered herself carefully onto a chair. 'They're going to need someone to manage the events programme for the retreat and she's got this idea that he'd be perfect. I think she's been talking to your dad about it too, she took Esther to see him the other day.'

'You don't think Tom would seriously be interested, do you?' Olivia was watching him outside, supporting a tree with one hand and talking to a young couple who, by the look of them, were hanging onto his every word.

'Possibly, he did tell Sam he'd think about it. Sorry Liv, I'd better find Jon and get going. We've got a birthday lunch to go to. Don't know why I bothered sitting down.' Annie slowly stood up again. 'Would you like to come over for supper before the baby's here? It would be lovely to catch up before I'm otherwise fully occupied.'

'Why don't you come to me instead?' Olivia was horrified that she'd nearly said 'us', reminding herself sharply that she and Tom were definitely not an 'us'. 'Only if you have time and I wouldn't like you to go to any trouble, not with the baby so close.'

'I'd love that, thank you. I've got your number, shall we look at dates and message before we run out of time?'

'Perfect.'

They said goodbye and Annie disappeared to collect Jon. Olivia went outside into the cold, thinking she had better do something useful before Tom thought she really was a complete wuss.

Chapter Ten

It turned out that helping people choose Christmas trees was more fun than Olivia had been expecting. It was only when her hand went to her pocket about twenty minutes later did she realise that she had accidentally left her phone behind. She wondered anxiously about dashing back to the house to fetch it but was distracted by another new customer instead. Now that Annie and Jon had left, it was just her, Tom and two other volunteers.

Olivia couldn't miss how easily Tom chatted to people, most of whom seemed to have no idea that they might have seen him on television in something or other. He showed her how to slide the trees through a tube that gathered them into a net. The first time she tried to shove a tree through by herself she couldn't get the net cut cleanly and it ended up in a bit of a muddle until he came over to help her sort it out.

They were kept busy, her mind flitting to her phone and wondering how many emails or messages might be piling up now that she was here without it. Her annual leave was due to start any time and she never put an out of office on her email, there simply wasn't any point. She never really was out of office, not for her clients.

The smell of chestnuts roasting on the stall next door was proving a constant temptation. Olivia had never tried them and decided today would be a good time to start, checking she hadn't forgotten her purse too. A few people were wandering around dressed in Victorian costumes and collecting donations for the fell rescue. She had to admit that this was a lot more fun than juggling clients and contracts on a Saturday morning, especially when Tom caught her eye and winked.

There was a short lull in customers and she called across to him. 'If this was one of those Christmas TV movies, then after we'd finished at the tree lot we'd share hot chocolate, go home and bake cookies.'

'You're on.'

'What? I was joking.' She pointed to their surround-ings. 'Seeing as we're very obviously not in one of those movies. There isn't any snow left for a start, or giant candy canes lining the street. And you've got my dad's shop to open later.' Olivia tilted her head. 'Don't tell me you watch those movies? Have you actually been in one?'

'I will admit to having seen a few and no, I haven't been in one. Don't you think I'd be great? Playing the good guy and getting the girl at the end?'

'Nah.' She waved off a family with their tree, smiling at the excited children waiting to take it home. 'You'd be better off writing one.'

She went to pick up a tree that fallen over, not realising Tom was so close to her until he spoke. 'If I was writing a Christmas movie then the cookie baking might look a lot different.'

Olivia swallowed, taking her time with the tree. 'Oh? How might it look?'

'More mess. Fewer cookies at the end.'

'Right.' She'd finished with the tree and didn't want to turn around just yet to find those wicked blue eyes tangled with hers. Hearing his voice lowered like that was quite enough. 'I definitely wouldn't watch that.'

'Why not?'

'I'd want there to be cookies at the end. And all that clearing up and mess would stress me out if there was nothing left to eat.' She'd finished with the tree and couldn't put off turning around any longer, hoping for a customer to distract her. There were none that needed her help in this moment and she looked up, Tom's blue eyes locking with hers.

'Mince pies.'

'What are you talking about?' Olivia raised her eyebrows.

'When we bake. Let's do mince pies instead, they're nicer than cookies.'

'Tom, I was joking! We're not baking anything, that's what shops are for. If you're desperate for a mince pie then get some at The Courtyard, I've heard they're excellent.'

He looked disappointed now and she laughed. 'Next you'll be wanting to make a Christmas cake and dose it with sherry every day or whatever it is you're meant to do.'

'Feed.'

'Feed what? Are you hungry?' She was starting to lose the thread of this conversation, her mind still half on the cookies and the movie she'd suggested he write. She definitely would watch it, that was the problem, especially if he were in it. Forget the mince pies, maybe she could help with the research. She could spread the butter on…

'The cake. You feed it with sherry, you don't dose it. It's not sick.'

'What?' Olivia dragged her mind away from that particular daydream. 'Oh, right, the cake. Well, I saw a cookery programme once when I was in a hotel and the chef was sticking holes in a cake and dabbing it with something that was meant for drinking. And it wasn't even Christmas when I watched it.'

A couple was approaching them now, tugging a tree, and Tom sauntered off to go and help them. She followed and was quite proud of herself when she fed the tree through the tube, and it all came out in one tidy piece at the other end.

She noticed an older woman staring at Tom from the edge of what she was now thinking of as the tree lot. One glance at him told Olivia that he had noticed her too. The woman was nudging the man alongside her now and saying something that Olivia couldn't hear but guessed at all the same.

'They're coming over.' Tom straightened his beanie, tugged his scarf a little higher. 'Probably too late to make a run for it.'

'Gosh, you're very like Tom Bellingham,' the woman said enthusiastically, phone already in her hand. 'You're not really him, are you? I loved him as Harrington, I've watched it so many times. You're almost as handsome as him, though.' She followed this up with a giggle and Olivia saw Tom looking on patiently.

'He gets that a lot.' Olivia's lips were twitching as his surprised gaze dashed across to her. 'Don't you, Tom?'

'You are him!' The woman giggled again, sidling a little closer to Tom. 'Well that's a surprise. Fancy finding you here in Thorndale when all we thought we were going to see was trees and stalls, not my favourite actor. Fancy that, Bob.' She gave the man with her a nudge and he nodded, then added something to the conversation that Olivia missed.

'But what are you doing in Thorndale? You're not filming one of those Christmas movies, are you?' The woman's hopeful glance was darting around the market, presumably searching for a film crew that wasn't there before resting on Tom once again.

'Research.' Olivia hadn't known she was going to say that until she did. 'For his brilliant new crime novel.'

'A novel? Ooh that sounds exciting. Will it be on television? Will you be starring in it?'

'I er, no, I won't be playing the character.' Tom seemed relaxed but Olivia recognised the diffidence in his voice.

'I keep telling him he should consider it,' she said smoothly. 'What's not to like? Looks, charm, charisma. I think he'd make a great detective.'

'Exactly.' The woman was beaming now and clearly agreed with Olivia's opinion of Tom. 'Are you his…'

'Publicist.' It was Tom's turn to jump in and he gave Olivia his best smile, which she thought was doing a nice job if he was trying to shut her up on purpose. 'This is Livvy. She never misses an opportunity to tell people about my work. She's very strict about what I do, though. A bit fierce, even.' This was accompanied by a conspiratorial nod to the woman and Olivia was struggling not to laugh now that Tom was playing her at her own game.

'Oh!' The woman's look rushed from Olivia to Tom and back to Olivia. 'I was just hoping for a selfie. Would that be all right?'

'Of course. We always allow selfies with fans, don't we, Tom?' Olivia tugged his arm, arranging him into position as the woman darted to stand next to him, presumably before Olivia could change her mind. 'Shall I take it for you?'

She held up the phone, saw Tom's smile and the happy face of the woman at his side through the screen. 'Say Christmas cookies, you two.' Olivia clicked away for a few seconds. 'That was great. Here you go.'

She handed the phone back and leaned a little closer to the woman. 'Tom doesn't mention his new novel too often yet as he's still writing it, but as his publicist I always tell him its lovely when his real fans get to find out first what he's up to.'

'Oh definitely. It's very nice of you both to let me have the photo.' The woman was clearly delighted by her encounter with a bona fide ex-heartthrob, even if he was already edging away to pick up a fallen tree.

She thanked Olivia again and set off with a wave and her partner, her day made. Olivia's smile stayed in place long enough to hide herself behind the nearest tree before her gasp of laughter escaped. Tom joined her and she knew the glare he was giving her was false.

'Real fans,' he protested, shaking his head. 'Brilliant new crime novel? What did you think you were doing, Olivia?'

'As your publicist I would've thought it was obvious.' She was wiping her eyes now. 'Still, telling her I was your publicist was probably better than your wife.'

'True.' Tom's gaze was unfathomable now and Olivia hurried on.

'That might have taken a bit of explaining on your Wikipedia page.' She paused. 'Do you still have a Wikipedia page?'

'Of course I do. At least I think I do.'

'Anyway.' She dismissed that. 'Your lovely fan will now go and tell…'

'Next door's cat most likely.' Tom sounded flat and Olivia touched his arm, trying to make him understand.

'No, Tom, she won't. She will go and tell everyone she knows and a few she doesn't that she met her favourite actor today, had a photo with him and found out that he was writing a new novel. And if she's never read crime before in her life she'll read yours. Or buy it, anyway, and give it to someone who does.'

'She won't.'

'She will.' Olivia was staring at Tom. 'Don't you get it? You still have fans, however long ago you played that part or what they remember about it. And some of them will still be there when your book comes out. You were twinkling away in that photo like a Christmas tree. Crinkly eyes, lovely smile.'

'I was not.'

'Oh you so were, Tom. You know you were, and she loved it.' Olivia was still feeling merry. 'I've had an idea.'

'Not another one.' Tom groaned and she gave him a stern look. 'Does it have anything to do with Christmas movies or buying mince pies?'

'Definitely not. Has Dad said anything to you about Twitter?'

'No. Why do you ask?'

She heard the suspicion in Tom's voice, a quick evasiveness she was beginning to recognise. 'He used to love tweeting about authors and their books, following other booksellers and publishers. Then when the shop in town closed he more or less gave up but he's never deleted the account.' She was watching as Tom tied a coloured ribbon to a tree, indicating its price band. 'I wondered if he had started tweeting again now that you're opening the shop in the annexe for him.'

'Not to my knowledge. He knows I don't have any social media accounts and I wouldn't be interested.'

'Do you have a website?' Olivia asked. Tom sighed and she was aware she was pushing him. But they didn't have long; someone with a wallet in one hand and trying to carry a tree in the other was approaching. 'Don't you have any kind of online profile to connect with readers?'

'What readers? I don't have any of those either.' His mouth set into stubborn lines. 'What would I put on a website?'

'Tom, just about everyone has some form of social media. My company use it all the time, we employ one person whose only role is to manage our online presence. Make us look the best, keep us relevant to what's happening in the market. It's about connecting.'

'So? It's not the same.'

'Of course it is, it's just a way of reaching people. And eventually you're going to need to do that.'

'Stop, *Livvy*, please. I'm not interested.'

'Okay.' Olivia couldn't miss the emphasis he placed on Livvy, the role she had adopted as his publicist. She pasted a smile on her face as the customer neared them. 'Because your readers are just going to magically know you're there, to flock and buy your book like they did last time.'

She knew that was a bit harsh but she hoped to help him understand and think about connecting with potential readers. Accepting payment from their customer, she watched as Tom fed the tree through the tube. As the two other volunteers were dealing with the only family still choosing, she nipped next door and bought four bags of hot chestnuts. She gave two to the volunteers and went to stand beside Tom. The green was packed and she recognised Mrs Timms from the cafe at a stall selling brownies and other baked goodies.

'Here you go, try these.' Olivia gave Tom a bag of chestnuts. 'Sorry for saying what I did about your previous book.'

'That's okay. I wouldn't exactly call it a "flocking" but I did sell some.' His lips stretched into a sardonic smile. 'You haven't read it, then?'

'No, sorry. Should I do? I haven't seen "the series" either.'

'With fans like you, Olivia, I'm beginning to think I'm going to need all the social media I can get.'

'I'm not a fan.' She saw the amusement on Tom's face as he pulled out a chestnut, knew he enjoyed teasing her as much as she did him. 'I'm just someone unlucky enough to be sharing a house with you. I've seen you all bleary-eyed and sleepy when you come down for coffee in the morning, remember. Oh!'

'What now?'

'We should tweet that or post it on Instagram. You all rumpled and cute first thing, hair wet from the shower, sexy little smile. The author before he sits down to write.'

'Rumpled and cute? That's what you think I look like? I don't know whether to be flattered or horrified. And I don't have "a sexy little smile".'

'I've heard people say you do.' That was evasive enough; Olivia hadn't admitted she thought he did. She took a bite of the warm chestnut and spat it straight back into the bag again. 'Urgh, that's horrible!' Tom was still laughing as she pointed to a stall. 'See look, Mrs Timms is selling mince pies. I'll treat you if you like, it'll be cheaper than buying the ingredients.'

'No thanks. We're still making them.' Tom checked his watch. 'Our shift's over, got time for that hot chocolate?'

'Only if there's chilli in it.'

'Done. I want to hear more about how cute you think I am in the mornings.'

'That won't take long,' Olivia retorted. 'I was going to say rough but wasn't sure your ego could take it.'

'My ego is non-existent these days and wouldn't dare rear its head again now I've met you.'

Somehow they were bumping together as they walked and she liked it, liked having him at her side. Friends, she reminded herself firmly. They were friends.

'I need to check out a few stalls for presents. Come with me?'

'Sure. Long as the shop's open by one I'm fine.'

Olivia quickly found a handmade leather bookmark which her dad would love, and bought a different one for Logan, who still preferred to read books on paper instead of digitally like Ellie, something that thrilled her dad beyond measure. She bought organic soap, a hand-knitted sweater and a key ring for her dad, a beanie for Logan, and some vegan sugarplum lip balm and pepper-mint hand cream for Ellie. Olivia was filling a bag with her purchases less than fifteen minutes later and handing over cash to pay for a messenger bag from Sam's stall that her assistant would adore.

'You're like some kind of Christmas ninja now, racing from stall to stall, practically knocking people out of your way.' Tom had kept up with her and they halted as she put her purse away.

'That's not very flattering.' Olivia tried to glare but it was hard to maintain in the face of the amusement she saw in Tom's eyes. 'I haven't got time to window-shop all day and I'd still like that hot chocolate. It was freezing, selling Christmas trees, and now you know I'm not a wuss.'

'I never thought for one second you were a wuss, Olivia. You're many things and wuss would be right at the bottom.'

The Courtyard was predictably packed and they turned away, making the decision to go back to the house instead. Tom nipped off to pick up hot chocolate from a stall and Olivia bought two more of the incredible turkey sandwiches she'd had the night she'd arrived in Thorndale.

The brass band had returned from their break and she stood for a moment, peaceful, enjoying the music and the familiarity of the carols she had used to sing. The carol service at church was something she and Ellie had gone to every year with her dad, and Olivia realised she'd dropped that too, when Ellie had moved away.

Whenever Ellie hadn't been with her for the holidays then Olivia had hurried to Thorndale on Christmas Eve, her online grocery shop already delivered. She'd stay with her dad, happy to have a couple of days together, feet up, book in hand. Then she'd rush back to work, ready to tackle the New Year onslaught as clients decided a new house was just the resolution they needed.

Thoughts of work reminded her that her phone was still in the house and she bit her lip, wondering anxiously what she might have missed. The fun she'd had this morning was her first thought and she was surprisingly glad that she hadn't brought the phone after all.

Olivia wandered over to a stall selling handmade tree ornaments and bought a couple, wryly musing on why she was adding to the stuff that needed removing from the house, not chucking more away. Then Tom joined her and they took their goodies back home. She hung up her coat, dropped everything in the kitchen and raced up to her room to fetch her phone.

Five missed calls. A flare of panic raced across her skin as she checked them for anything to do with her dad. There were none, just a message from him telling her about someone he'd met in his residents' lounge who had been a writer. It seemed he could sniff out an author at fifty paces and she rolled her eyes, sending a quick reply.

The calls were all to do with work, three of them from her client in the States in the last hour and she felt it was a bit early, even for them. She played back the voicemails as she returned downstairs, listening to their concerns about the house they wanted and already composing a reply in her mind.

To her surprise, Tom was waiting for her to begin eating and she pointed to her phone in apology. He nodded, unwrapping his turkey sandwich and his eyes lit up. Olivia suppressed the simple joy that blossomed inside her at seeing him happy. Her hot chocolate was cooling, and she sipped from it as she reached the last of her voicemails and brought up her calendar to schedule another call for Monday afternoon.

She'd almost suggested taking the call later today but that would make it Saturday night and surely there ought to be some boundaries, a point where her professional and private lives didn't have to permanently overlap. She would have a solution for them on Monday, and probably one that would include the search for a new property if their concerns about planning permission for alterations were still to the fore. She sat down and glanced at the rest of her emails – nothing too urgent, they could wait for a while – then finally she took her glasses off.

'Sorry Tom, I didn't realise you were planning to wait for me.'

'Don't apologise. I didn't say so and I should've realised you'd have work to catch up on seeing as you left your phone behind. On purpose?'

'No, I actually forgot it, if you can believe that.'

'And there was me thinking you just didn't want any distractions whilst we were selling trees.'

Olivia wasn't about to confess that she was finding Tom much more of a distraction than clients or Christmas trees right now. 'It was more fun without my phone, I will admit. I know I would've been checking in and then all I would have thought about was work.'

'So you're admitting to having fun with me?'

'I didn't say you specifically. Just that the market and the morning was fun. But the selfie thing with your fan was definitely fun.'

Tom pulled a face. He'd finished eating and was watching Olivia as he sipped his hot chocolate. His face was unreadable and she assumed it must be all his drama experience that made it easy for him to shutter his thoughts from her. She unlocked her phone and opened up the Twitter app. She updated the password to her dad's old account and found a few new authors and booksellers to follow.

'So I had a thought about the shop and Twitter. Would you like to hear it?'

'Won't your dad want to know first?'

'No, he'd love the idea, he won't mind in the least. I wouldn't be surprised if he doesn't want the new password to send a few tweets of his own. He's a dab hand with his smartphone.'

'Are you really going to do this?' Tom's fingers were tapping a quick rhythm against his cup. 'What do you want to achieve by starting it up again? The shop will be shut again soon once the house is sold.'

'That's a good question.' Olivia softened her tone, made sure to sound composed and neutral to remove any threat he may be trying to perceive. 'I think it might generate more interest in the shop, maybe bring in extra customers. Sell some books. Maybe let them know about you being here, looking after it.' She paused. 'Does that concern you?'

'Some. It's not the recognition as such, I don't mind if a few people want selfies now and again.' He sighed, dragging a hand through his hair. 'It's more about what I'm doing here. Playing around in a shop, trying to write a book. Not really working. Some people will wonder. Maybe start looking.'

'What is it you're afraid of, Tom? Will you tell me? Help me understand?' She closed the app down, slid the phone away. The room seemed to be singing with silence and she wondered if she had gone too far.

Chapter Eleven

Tom's agitated hand was rubbing his jaw, his eyes burning into hers. 'I'm not sure you can understand when you haven't been where I have. Never experienced failure like I have.'

'Why would you assume you'll fail again? You just need to try, to—'

'It's not that simple, Olivia.' He slammed his cup down, spilling the dregs of his hot chocolate onto the table. 'You haven't been told no time and again when you've stood in front of a producer or a director, told that you're just not quite what they had in mind, sorry. Or that being so well known for one character makes it difficult for them to give you a chance at something else.

'How can you possibly understand what it's like to say no to something you're not sure is right for you and then be dropped by everyone around you because you did? As though your achievements amount to nothing because it's all about what comes next. The next big part, movie, drama, play, whatever.'

Tom lifted a hand and gestured at the room they occupied. 'You grew up with a family around you, standing at your side and supporting you when you needed it. And you take it all for granted.' He was blazing now, and Olivia was shocked by the words he was aiming at her. 'Your dad, this house, your home, maybe even your daughter. You have no time for you and barely any more for your dad, and he misses you. Do you ever think about that? My friendship with him is the closest I've come to having a proper father again, someone who understands me. That means the world to me and I'd do anything for him.'

Olivia shoved her chair back, feeling the stab of truth, the guilt she always carried as she stood up, wanting to get away from Tom and the words he was hurling at her. The reminder came again that maybe she could do more, *should* have done more for her dad – kept a better eye on him and been more present in his life. Was this what Tom really thought of her and her career? She was clutching the chair, heart racing.

'You want to know the real reason I gave up acting, Olivia? Why I don't do it any more?' There was a bitter irony in Tom's question. 'Because a couple of nights into that last play I discovered I couldn't speak properly, couldn't get my words out in the right order. I'd struggled with shyness as a kid, and it was only when I got into drama at school that I learned how to overcome it. I was lucky enough then to have a teacher who believed in me and pushed me to go further, and I made it to drama school and then a career. I thought it was behind me until the play came along.' Tom's eyes were shimmering with hurt. 'There you go. Tweet that.'

They were staring at one another and she was shaking, hating that her bottom lip was trembling as she fought to control her own tears. She hated that there was some truth about her life amidst the scorn that Tom had flung at her. And her dad, her lovely dad. She swallowed, refusing to allow more guilt to diminish her even further in this moment. She reached for her phone, calmly moving around the table. Tom was staring at her, a muscle twitching in his cheek, as though he couldn't quite believe what'd he actually said.

'I'm sorry for what you went through and how your career ended.' Olivia was thankful she was able to manage a level tone. She could've yelled, ranted, accused him of interfering where he had no business, as he had. 'And you're quite right, Tom, I know there are some changes I should make. You said before that you thought I was many things and I think the same of you. But I didn't have you down as someone clinging onto failure and using it as an excuse not to try again. Write your book. Or not. Like you said, who's going to notice if you don't?'

'Olivia.' Tom's hand was urgent on her arm as she tried to hurry past him, and she shook it off. 'Please, I...'

'Don't, Tom.' She turned to look at him from the doorway. 'How can I possibly understand your life when my own is obviously perfect?' She hurried out to run up the stairs, ignoring him as he falteringly called her name again before letting it fade away.

–

Someone was knocking loudly on the back door and Olivia couldn't imagine who it could be. She was in the spare bedroom, furiously sorting out piles of belongings and ignoring thoughts of work. Tom had disappeared after their fight almost an hour ago and she hadn't seen him since. She ran downstairs, marched through to the kitchen and opened the door, astonished to see two middle-aged men smiling brightly at her.

'Sorry to bother you,' one of them said. 'We saw the sign for the bookshop but it's closed. Are you opening the shop this afternoon?'

'Oh!' Olivia glanced at the kitchen clock. It was one thirty and Tom would normally have opened up by now. She wondered if he had forgotten or changed his mind after what had taken place between them. She was about to tell the two men that the shop was closed for the day and then decided not to.

'We are yes, I'm sorry about that.' She pointed to the annexe. 'If you wouldn't mind giving me a minute to find the keys I'll meet you there.'

'Are you sure? That's kind of you. We used to love visiting Bradshaw's when it was in town.'

Olivia shut the door as they ambled off. She found the keys and pulled on a coat. The heating should be on in the bookshop but without the fire it would probably still be cool. She made sure to bring her phone too so she could keep an eye on her emails. If Tom wasn't going to open the shop, then she would. Messing about in there was more appealing than creating piles to cart off for recycling and she had no desire to continue emptying her dad's home of its history.

She opened up the annexe and left the two men to browse. The little Christmas tree seemed sad without its lights and she switched it on, instantly making the room a little cheerier. It was chilly inside, despite the heating, and if she were actually planning to stay all afternoon then it would be better to light the fire; at this rate she'd be perished even with her coat on. There was a Bluetooth speaker on the desk; that must be Tom's too, she'd never seen it before. Now seemed as good a time as any to have a Christmas playlist going.

Business was bound to be hopelessly slow, even if Tom had left the old wooden sign at the front of the house to entice people in. If anyone else did find the shop then Olivia expected them to wander in, declare it quaint and hurry back out again without making a purchase. She rolled up newspaper and placed it in the hearth, added sticks, found the matches and lit the fire. Her two customers stayed for twenty minutes or so and then left, having paid for five books on railways and military history between them.

To her surprise she did have more potential customers within half an hour. A man and two women appeared, confirming they'd spotted the sign and thrilled with the effect of a real fire. Olivia offered a welcome and left them to explore, distracted by an existing client's email request for a new property in Lancashire. Before they left one of the women positioned herself at the desk and bought three books on politics and dropped some change in the fell rescue donation box.

Olivia realised that she was actually beginning to enjoy herself, the Christmas playlist a soothing backdrop to the quiet old room. She had pulled plenty of Saturday shifts in her dad's shop before now and this had a feeling of familiarity to it. When the door rattled again she looked up, expecting visitors. Tom stood on the threshold, and she felt her anxiety leap a level, matching the one she read in his uncertain face.

'I should take over.' He was still holding the door open. 'It's my responsibility, I'm sure you need to work.'

'There's no need to be sarcastic.' She was stung by his words. Was he really going to be pathetic enough to cling onto the remnants of their row and dredge it all up again? Use her work against her? 'I'm fine.'

'I wasn't being sarcastic, I promise. If you need to work then you should have the space to do it.' He hesitated. 'And I think we need to talk.'

'No, we don't.' Olivia was busy with her emails, happy to try and ignore him. Suddenly Christmas seemed a long way off as she thought of the days ahead with Tom in the house. 'You were perfectly clear. And could you shut the door, it's freezing and you're letting all the heat out.'

The door closed and as far as she was concerned he was on the wrong side of it. He crossed the shop to stand in front of the fire while she continued swiping at her screen.

'Olivia, please. At least let me apologise.'

'For what? Speaking the truth?'

'I want to say I'm sorry for bringing you into something that's really my problem.' Tom sighed. 'I should never have said those things about your family and your career, it simply wasn't fair. I can see how hard you work, and you've earned every single one of your considerable achievements.'

'Have I?' Suddenly Olivia's voice was small and she was appalled to hear a catch in it. 'When my clients have more of me than my own family does?'

'Hey.' Tom was at the desk now, reaching out to touch her free hand briefly. 'Don't. You do what you can and your dad's so proud of you.'

'He said that to you? But at what cost?' One shoulder rose in a shrug and Tom stepped away as another customer entered. It seemed a lifetime until she paid for a nice copy of *Wuthering Heights* and left.

'This is no place for a conversation,' he said as the door closed, leaving them surrounded by books and bedlam. 'I'm tempted to bring the sign in until we've talked.'

'Tom, we just have to do our best to get through this time until I leave. You've said all you need to. Thank you for apologising, I'm sorry too. Now just let me get on. I can't make you fight for something you don't want.'

'Fight for what? What don't I want?'

Olivia banged a hand on the desk, making her phone bounce. 'For your future. For your book, another chance at a career. You have a chance, here.' She'd almost said, 'with me' and was relieved that she hadn't actually gone quite so far, such words would have been impossible to take back. If friends were all they could be then she would still take it. She'd never met anyone before in her life – not even when she'd run off with a wild guitarist and married him – who'd made her want to care so much. Madness, but here she was.

'I don't think it's that simple any more, staying here.' Tom spoke slowly. 'Not for me.'

'What do you mean?' She whispered the words, waited to hear his reply.

His smile was rueful, then gone. 'Being your friend when really I want to be more. To trust you and for you to trust me. But maybe it's just me who feels that way?'

'Maybe it's not.' Olivia's gaze was clear on Tom's and she saw the rush of pleasure in his face before she carried on. 'But I don't have the time and you have to work too, you need a book you can sell at the end of all this. Let's just leave it at that. We can do this.'

'Can we?'

'We'll have to. Maybe if we'd met another time, another way.'

There was a moment when she knew they were both thinking about hugging and he stepped away, pushing his hands into his jeans pockets. 'Why don't you go back, I'll stay here.'

'Really, I'm fine.' She nodded to prove she meant it, swallowed down the disappointment of not acting on what she felt. 'Go and write. You've already missed a morning and I bet my dad wants a progress report.'

'He does.' Tom smiled in that way she found so lovely and which really didn't help her resolve to remain only friends. 'Thank you, are you sure?'

'Absolutely. Get out of my way, there's barely enough room in here for one shop assistant, never mind two. I'll be a brilliant bookseller; I bet I can shift loads of stock before five o'clock.'

'I doubt it. But I am curious to hear how you get on.' He was at the door, ready to open it. 'I'm about to introduce a hot new love interest for my character and I'm thinking of making her a bookseller who annoys the hell out of him.'

'You wouldn't!' Olivia really didn't know whether to be flattered or furious.

'Try me.'

Surely Tom wasn't thinking of her. Was he? 'I'm not a bookseller.'

'From where I'm standing you look a lot like one right now.' There was a moment as she waited to see if he would say more, but he didn't need to, she saw that same resolve wavering in the way he was staring at her.

'Then go and write it.' She chucked a book at him, ignoring the flutter in her stomach. The book slid harmlessly to the floor without touching him and he laughed. 'I want a progress report about what they're up to when I come back.'

'Can't do that, sorry.' Tom opened the door, stepped outside. 'You'll have to wait for the book to come out.'

'Maybe I can help you with the research.' She hadn't really meant to say that out loud and his eyes narrowed delectably.

'Whilst that's a welcome suggestion, you should know I have an excellent imagination.'

'And plenty of experience, no doubt,' she muttered as he headed back to the house, taking that cheeky grin with him. She was so flustered by thoughts of Tom's character and what he might be up to that she very nearly pressed send on an email to a client that she meant for Ellie, catching up about her daughter's visit next weekend. That wouldn't do, Olivia thought dryly, she couldn't have her clients thinking she had a social life of her own.

Two older men strolled in whilst she was still holding her phone and she noticed one of them pick up a copy of Truman Capote's *A Christmas Memory*, then put it down again. Soon he came to the desk, two American literary novels and a book on Victorian poetry in his hand. He pointed to the Capote book.

'That's a lovely copy you've got there,' he remarked. 'I have an illustrated 1989 one at home from my grandchildren but yours is a first edition from 1966. Is it for sale, I couldn't see a price?'

Olivia hadn't read the Capote book for years, remembering the joy and spirit she'd found in it, the age difference between a boy and an elderly woman somehow enhancing the feeling layered in the words, the fun and festivity, and their mutual love finding a home one with the other. It was a book that she'd always found charming, full of pathos as the two characters stuck together to create their own Christmas traditions, reminding her of doing something similar in different circumstances.

'Of course.' She brushed away a spark of unease. Much as she loved books and had spent a fair bit of time in her dad's shop over the years, she didn't have any real idea of their value if there was no price. She'd have to hope for the best, fairly sure it couldn't be worth hundreds of pounds if it weren't in the cabinet with the more expensive editions. She did know that anything of great worth was already in the library in the house.

She left the desk to pick up the book, making sure there was no signature or handwritten detail to increase its value. There wasn't and she breathed a sigh of relief. 'It's sixty pounds.'

It was a stab in the dark but her customer was already nodding, reaching for his wallet to pay for his purchases. Olivia was struck now by the terror of having sold it too cheaply. Too late if she had. He had a final look around as he and his companion prepared to leave, winding scarves back around necks against the chill outdoors.

'You have a lovely shop here, even if it is a little small. I remember Bradshaw's from its days on the high street. A loss to the town now it's closed.'

She thanked them, pleased that there were now a few less books to rehome. A quick stab of guilt followed as she realised there were also fewer for Tom to take on, given the gift of her dad's library. She was busier still as the afternoon wore on. Perhaps today was an unusually good day, with shoppers already in Thorndale for the Christmas market and full of festive cheer.

Mrs Timms made an appearance, asking after Hugh and telling Olivia she was planning to FaceTime him later and visit next Wednesday. A number of people Olivia also knew vaguely from the village popped in too, wanting to know how long the shop was staying open for. She couldn't reliably answer that one and offered the barest details about the arts consortium planning to take over the house.

There was less time than she'd expected for going through her emails, kept occupied instead working out prices, accepting payment and wrapping up books. She sent her dad a couple of images and he replied with a delight in what she was doing that made her gulp back the emotion his simple message had produced. It had been dark for over an hour by the time she locked up at five p.m. and dragged the sign away from the front of the house.

It was her turn to cook supper and she brought out a ready-made lasagne from the fridge and left it beside the range as she put a salad together. Tom probably wouldn't be impressed by her lack of proper cooking this evening but it would have to do. Maybe she could wow him with her skills in the kitchen some other time.

But she did make a mean espresso martini cocktail and so Olivia stirred instant coffee with hot water in a jug and left it to cool. Her dad usually kept a well-stocked drinks cupboard, a leftover from his days hosting guests, and she'd improvise if he didn't have exactly the right ingredients. The door to the library was still closed when she went to look, and she hesitated before knocking.

'Come in.'

She stuck her head inside the room. Tom was at the desk, still working. 'Hi. Am I disturbing you?'

'Yes. No.' He groaned, reaching a hand to his neck and rubbing as he shoved his chair back. 'You're not, I was about to stop. I really need to move and stretch.'

Olivia crossed the room to stand behind him, her hands light on his shoulders. 'May I?'

There was only the slightest pause until Tom lowered his dark head towards the desk, where a lamp illuminated his laptop screen. 'Please. Right now I'd stick pins in my neck if I thought it would help.'

'You're tense.' She smoothed her hands across his shoulders with more pressure. It would be better without his sweater in the way and she saw the outline of the T-shirt he wore underneath. 'It would be easier if you took this off,' she said casually, tugging gently at the neckline of the sweater. 'I promise I'm trained; I know what I'm doing.'

'Here we are again. Clothes coming off.' His voice was low and amused as he pulled the sweater over his head.

'Purely medicinal. Again.' She ignored the spike in her pulse, feeling the tension, the bunching in his muscles, before going to his neck and massaging gently.

'That feels amazing.' Tom tilted his head again to make it easier for her. 'When did you learn to do that?'

'I did a course about two years ago. One of those things I went along to with a friend but I haven't used it much since. I'm glad you're enjoying it because I have a confession to make.'

'Is it about supper? I knew it, you want me to cook again, don't you?'

'No. But I do have a ready-made lasagne and some salad.'

'Hell, Olivia, right now I'd cook every day for the rest of the month if it meant you could keep on doing this.' He groaned again and she was loving the new relaxation she could feel in him as she massaged, pressing into his shoulders. It would be better with almond oil to smooth over his skin and no top, but she certainly wasn't going to suggest that.

'Time to stop,' she said briskly. She hadn't meant to do anything other than soothe the tension he had been feeling but touching him had moved her thoughts elsewhere, to acting on the attraction they both still felt. 'That lasagne's not going to put itself in the oven, is it?' She stepped away, passed his sweater to him. 'How would you like a cocktail?'

'Almost as much as I liked you massaging my shoulders.' Their eyes met and his slid away first as he pulled the sweater back over his head. 'What are you making?'

'I'll let you know when I've investigated Dad's drinks cupboard.'

'I'll be right with you. Let me just reply to a couple of emails first.'

'It's Saturday night,' she said from the door. 'Please don't tell me you're working.'

'Pots and kettles come to mind,' he told her as he turned back to his laptop. 'Ten minutes, I promise.'

'Don't make me come and find you,' she teased, nearly kicking herself. What would he do if she did? She knew what she wanted to do and told herself firmly that friends was as good as it got, for both of them.

The drinks cupboard offered up all the usual random stuff she had expected, including Angostura bitters and bourbon, giving Olivia another idea. She added the bourbon and bitters with the cooled espresso, sugar syrup and ice in a cocktail shaker and was pouring their drink into two glasses when Tom joined her.

'Mmm, something smells delicious,' he said, looking across to the range. 'Reminds me of ready meals.'

'Would you like to drink this Old Fashioned or have me tip it over your head?' she asked him mildly, meeting him halfway.

'You remembered? From that night?'

She was thrilled that she had surprised him. 'Of course, I have an excellent memory. It's even got espresso in it.' They clinked glasses and she tried hers, liking the different flavours, feeling the bourbon warming her. 'Not bad.'

'It's a lot better than not bad.' Tom took in the table already set for two, the salad in its bowl. 'I'd offer to help but it looks like you've got everything under control. Piercing the film and all that.'

Chapter Twelve

They had to make more espresso for the martini that came next. Olivia preferred it to the Old Fashioned and then Tom mixed a Black Russian, adding a measure of Cointreau for a festive twist, and she loved that. The lasagne had long since gone and even she had had to admit that it hadn't been amazing.

Her phone was busier than normal with notifications, and she saw that a lot of them were from Twitter. She put her glasses on and clicked on the app, startled to see she had over fifty. Assuming it was a mistake, she began going through them and soon realised it wasn't. 'Oh, crap.'

'What is it?' He was clearing away the remains of their meal. 'Everything okay?'

'Yes. Sort of.' She was flicking through some of the notifications. 'Maybe you should see this.'

Tom came to stand beside her, looking over her shoulder. She liked having him there, his head close, arm brushing hers.

'Twitter.' Olivia lifted the phone to show him. 'Or more specifically, Twitter and one of our customers this afternoon. He bought a few books and he's tweeted and tagged the shop. Look.'

Tom was staring at her screen and she clicked on the customer's profile. She soon saw that he was an author of some renown, with a distinguished playwriting career still

157

flourishing and a knack for adapting the right television dramas. He had tweeted about his visit and included an image she had not noticed him taking, remarking that although the space was small, the choice of books was excellent.

The shop looked welcoming and festive, and some of his many followers had already retweeted it, resulting in the jump in interest and new followers. There were a few comments about her dad, some people remembering him from his days on the high street in town, and she sensed Tom stepping back.

'I wasn't expecting this,' Olivia told him quietly. 'I just logged back in this morning and reactivated Dad's account before you and I spoke. He was still sending the odd tweet and hadn't deleted it.'

Tom was leaning against the sink, hands pushed into his jeans pockets, brow creased in a frown.

'It doesn't mention you and I'm sorry to have raised the possibility, Tom.' Olivia put the phone down. 'I'll reply to the author, then I'll deactivate the account in the next day or so and let Dad know. After thirty days it won't be recoverable and the shop will be closed soon anyway.'

'What if you don't? Deactivate the account?'

Tom's question was a surprise. 'Then interest in what we're doing might keep growing and could bring more visitors. You know that.' She eyed him warily. 'Some of whom would probably recognise you and might put on social media that you're here. Wonder why.'

'I love how you're saying "we" after precisely one afternoon in the shop.'

'Hey, I've done my share of hours in the shop over the years, thanks very much. Way more than you.'

'Back to being a bookseller again, I see.' Tom's eyes narrowed and she laughed.

'I'm happy to share my experience of bookselling with you as long as it's crucial to your research.'

'Duly noted.' That low note in his voice was still there and this time it was Olivia who looked away first to fiddle with her phone. 'I did some thinking, after we spoke this morning.'

Her own smile was wry. '"Spoke" is an interesting term. It was more of a "shout" and I think you told me more than you ever meant to.'

'I've shared more with you than I have with anyone other than your dad in years, Olivia.' Tom shrugged. 'You Bradshaws seem to have that effect on me. And I'm sorry for shouting, it was crass.'

'You were upset, I understand. I'm sorry for suggesting something that's making you uncomfortable. I was just trying to help.'

'I know that.' He came to stand beside her again, his back to the table. 'I've already been recognised in the shop so it's probably on someone's social media anyway. Most people in the village know I'm here but they're not that interested, other than to chat. I'm not Colin Firth.'

'Well, you're younger than him for a start. I guess you're lucky that Sarah Holland is still living in Thorndale. Dad always said she was genuinely nice once you got past her trying to put everything she saw on Instagram.' Olivia was referring to a local resident who also happened to be a rising star in Hollywood and was currently away filming a Netflix series. 'What's on your Wikipedia page?'

'You mean about my background, the end of my acting career?'

Olivia nodded; she knew Tom would understand what she had been alluding to.

'A brief paragraph about being raised by my dad and getting bitten by the acting bug as a kid. Not too much about my early life, it goes on to my making it to drama school and then a career.'

'Have you ever spoken about it?'

'In interviews? Not much, but I've never tried to make it a secret, there wasn't any point.' Tom was rubbing his jaw distractedly.

'What about the play, when it closed?'

'It only happened once, when I couldn't speak, on what turned out to be the last night. The play wasn't doing well anyway, and the producers put out a statement saying that I'd been taken ill with a virus, couldn't continue and decided it was better to close.'

'How did you feel?' Olivia leant against him, didn't want to move away from his body beside hers.

'Relieved, angry, confused. I hoped to carry on but they weren't prepared to risk it, no one else involved wanted more failure attached to their names. I convinced myself after that that no one would cast me and I crept away, didn't want to try again.'

'So you could if you wanted to? Try again?'

'It's been too long.' Tom's voice was quiet and he turned to stare at her. 'I realise it's probably arrogant of me but I don't want to try and establish myself again now that I'm older.' He gave her a smile that was accepting, lifted his hands. 'Honestly? I just want to write.'

'What about closure?'

'You don't always get it the way you want. I've more or less come to terms with what happened, and I've tried to move on. Found myself stuck sharing a house with

160

someone who asks more questions than most interviewers I've had before.'

'Only because I care.' Olivia was glad she'd admitted it when she saw the happiness her words brought to his face. How his eyes crinkled in just the way she had teased him about earlier and his lips were pursed in a smile that was slightly rueful.

'That makes two of us, then.'

Her gaze was holding Tom's, an unspoken acknowledgement of the looks she noticed him giving her, how she loved watching him bring a meal together, the laughter they shared, the drinks they made for two. She knew he liked his coffee strong with a dash of milk, and when she drank tea he made it just the way she preferred, fit for the burliest of builders. How had they come to this in barely a week?

'If you want to tweet about the shop, Olivia, then I'm okay with that. I know you're right, what you said before about reaching people, if I have a book once I leave here. And it's your dad's shop and yours, not mine. Your decision to make.'

'Thank you for saying so but I'm not going to do anything that makes it difficult for you by bringing attention you don't want.'

'It's not like I've never been noticed before.' Tom raised a shoulder in a slight shrug. 'And there are worse places than a bookshop for a writer to be spending time. I can always say it's research and your dad's already known for running a retreat.'

'Tell me tomorrow just in case you change your mind. I'm not suggesting we tweet a picture of you in the shop in breeches and boots. That really would be taking it too far and dragging it all back to Harrington. Although,' Olivia mused with a smirk. 'Just imagine how it would look, all snowy and festive, and there you were, leaning against the wall, shirt half—'

She caught sight of Tom's own look of horror and stopped. She'd been getting far too carried away at the thought.

'I'm not doing that.' He pushed himself away from the table. 'Those days are definitely over, I had my share of photo shoots when I did the series.'

'I was kidding, you're so easy to tease.'

'I'm careful not to use Harrington as a means to everything else. It was good for a time and I've moved on.'

'I know that.' Her voice was softer. 'But there are moments when it won't do you any harm to have people remember. Like this morning, with the selfie and then mentioning your book.'

'Good, because if I ever wear breeches and boots again it won't be on camera.'

'Oh? Did you keep everything, then? Is that a promise, to wear them again?'

'Olivia, you've got to be one of the most persistent people I've ever met, and I know a few.'

'Probably not a bad trait for your publicist to have,' she said merrily. She glanced through the window into the night. 'Shall we go for a walk?'

'Now? It's nearly eleven o'clock.'

'Worried you'll turn into a pumpkin?'

'No,' Tom muttered, giving her a sharp glare belied by the twinkle she could see in his eye. 'More likely an ugly sister.'

'I think you'd make a lovely dame,' she said dreamily. 'Maybe you could write a new version of Cinderella. I haven't been to a pantomime in years.'

'Only if you promise to play the Fairy Godmother. It would suit you perfectly, flying around with a wand telling everyone what to do.'

'Can I choose my own costume? I'm thinking black.'

They were still laughing as he pulled her coat down from the stand and shrugged into his. They'd need scarves and hats too – it might not be snowing but Olivia had seen frost forming when she'd closed up the shop and the night was icy.

'We used to do this when Ellie was small and we came to spend Christmas here with my dad, go walking at night and look at all the lights. I haven't done it for years. I'm thinking it just might be time to start a new old tradition.'

'Let's go, then. I like the sound of a new old tradition.'

Thorndale late at night seemed to be shimmering in an extra layer of silence as they left the house and set off along the high street, walking slowly. The huge tree on the green glittered white, dropping shadows around it. Lights were draped outside houses and Christmas trees were blinking in windows with curtains not yet drawn; Olivia realised how magical it all seemed.

The fell rescue association was shut, thankfully, reminding her of last Monday and how she'd watched the volunteers setting off into the snow to search for Tom. It wasn't difficult to recall first the fear and then the relief when they had brought him safely back. The Christmas trees outside the barn were stacked up ready for tomorrow, and she wouldn't have been too surprised if Santa Claus and his reindeer had shot across the sky in a scarlet sleigh. Frost crunched beneath their feet;

their breath silvered shadows disappearing into the air. Someone walking a dog on the far side of the green raised a hand in greeting.

'Wow.' It seemed the most natural thing for Olivia to tuck her arm through Tom's.

'Pretty, isn't it?'

'Gorgeous. So quiet. I'd forgotten what being out of the city can look like at night. Those skies.'

'What other new old traditions might you rediscover whilst you're here?'

'That's a good question.' She felt a clench in her heart, thinking about when her mum had been alive and how afterwards her family had shrunk to just her and her dad, aunties and uncles far away, grandparents elderly or gone. It was always so much easier to remember how family felt when she was back in Thorndale, never closer to a real Christmas than when she was here. 'Singing carols, I used to love doing that. There's just something about those songs in the depths of winter.'

'Agreed. What else?'

'The smell of turkey roasting on Christmas Day. My dad always took care of it, and I'd come down in the morning to pancakes and we'd sit around the tree to open presents. A frosty walk on Boxing Day followed by a lazy afternoon in pyjamas with a good book. The smell of a real tree.'

'Sounds wonderful.'

'Yes. Usually it was.' Olivia heard the wistful note in her reply. 'How about you? Any traditions from your marriage?'

'Not really. Nicole and I usually ate out or spent it with her family. They were kind but it never quite felt like home.' Tom's voice was quiet and Olivia wrapped both

164

of her arms around his. 'My earliest Christmas memory is getting on a bus with my dad to spend it with my grandparents. Taking presents and having them look after us both. I liked that. We went every year but they died before my dad was really ill. Not much room for tradition then, I was just taking care of him and getting through school as best I could.' Tom sighed. 'You lost your mum too, though. I'm sorry.'

'Thank you.' Slowly they drifted to a halt and then they were hugging on the high street. His arms tightened around her as Olivia carried on. 'It was awful, we missed her so much and my dad was broken-hearted. But he and I helped each other and tried to do some things the same, though some had to be different. He adored the shop and his books, the people he knew. They looked after him too.'

Gradually she and Tom separated and they strolled on, Olivia's arm back through his. She could hear the hoot of an owl, and the post office and cafe appeared so different without the usual bustle of customers, the art gallery lit with light enough to frame the paintings and a sculpture of boxing hares in the window.

'May I ask how your writing went today?'

'I'm translating that as, "Tom, did you write the love scene today?"'

Olivia adored the amusement in his voice, the way he countered her question with a comment that drew them back to flirting again. 'Maybe.'

'Let's just say they're having an interesting evening.'

'And?'

Tom added nothing to her question and she tapped his arm with impatient fingers until he continued. 'And that's it. An interesting evening, like I said.'

'You're seriously going to make me wait for the book?'

'Yes. Patience. But I am thinking maybe there is a way we could trade?'

'Oh?' She heard his lowered tone, realised suddenly that maybe their own evening was getting more interesting. She was already smiling at the irony of strolling through a darkened village lit by Christmas lights and stars in the dead of night. She tried to think of her inbox instead and failed utterly at his next words.

'Maybe you could massage my shoulders when I'm done for the day, like you did before. In return I'll cook supper. That lasagne was so grim, I wouldn't have thought it beyond you to have chosen it on purpose.'

'Done,' Olivia said happily. 'And I was in a rush when I bought it so it wasn't exactly on purpose. I'll buy some almond oil. Although,' she crashed on, her face becoming warm despite the chilly air. 'Better not. You'd need to take your top off and you can't be doing that.'

'Can't I?' His voice was soft, like another caress on her skin, and she felt her heart bump.

'Stop it,' she muttered crossly. 'I might accidentally tweet it.'

His laughter followed as they walked in an easy silence, turning left and making their way slowly beyond the village, lights petering out and leaving them in darkness. There was a lane ahead leading to a footpath and they followed it, eventually drawing to a halt outside an old farmhouse, its cobbled front garden bordered by a stone wall decorated with an overgrown rose bare of its leaves. Four sash windows neatly divided the front of building, the top two tucked into the roof beneath wooden eaves.

'Let's have a closer look.' Tom dropped his arm so that Olivia's hand slid down too and he caught it, pulling her gently towards the house. There were no lights, signs of occupancy, barking dogs or parked cars.

'Tom, it might not be empty. We could be about to give someone the fright of their lives. And it's trespassing.'

'There's no one there, I'm certain. I've been running past it most days and I would have noticed by now. Plus it's for sale, so we won't be the only ones having a nosy.'

He pushed aside the metal gate and led the way to the front door. The path was covered with weeds bursting up between the uneven stones. Tom tried the door gently and Olivia would have been astounded had it yielded. Finally letting go of her, he leant in to stare through a downstairs window on their right, both hands around his face against the glass.

'I think this is the sitting room, there's another room on the opposite side and the kitchen's at the back. It's really rough, though, doesn't look like it's been updated in years.'

'Let me see.' She was alongside him now, her own hands to the glass and she could only make out an empty room, a carpet she was sure would be threadbare. A stone wall divided the house from the barn attached on its right and Tom placed a hand on the wall and swung his legs over it.

'Let's go around the back.' He held out an arm through the darkness.

'No thanks, your legs are longer than mine for getting over that wall, I'd probably go flying on the frost. I'll walk round.'

He waited for her, and behind the barn they found themselves in a scruffy concrete yard, lined by posts and rails and a farm gate, which separated it from a meadow. A wooden fence was having a go at dividing the house from the barn but half of it had fallen down, revealing an empty patio telling the same story of emptiness.

'I've been amusing myself when I'm out running, thinking of this place and who used to live in it. What their story might have been.'

Olivia followed Tom to shine the torch on her phone through another window. The back of the farmhouse looked even sadder and she felt sorry for it, trying to remember when it had last been occupied, and couldn't. There was nothing more to see now, the ripple of a stream somewhere nearby the only sound.

'I imagined a murder, a body boarded up, ghostly voices in the night.' Tom reached for her hand, tucking it through his arm again as they wandered back out to the darkened lane. 'Someone afraid to go to sleep.'

'Always the writer, hey?'

'Of course.'

'You didn't picture a nice family then, farming their land, raising their children, a few chickens scratching about, cattle in the barn.'

'I don't like chickens.'

'You prefer murder?'

'To write about? Yes. But I can picture how the house might look though, renovated. A new family, a new story.'

'Me too. And sorry to disappoint you, mine doesn't involve dead bodies.' Olivia was remembering the For Sale sign, her mind running through her clients. It was smaller than most of the properties she found, but even so there could be someone who might be interested. She decided to search online for the details tomorrow just in case.

'What would your story for the house be?'

It was a few moments before she could give Tom a reply. 'I'm really not sure. A new beginning, I guess, like you said. New people. A new kitchen and heating for a start, convert the barn and extend the house. It would be a nice project for someone. But we should probably head back before I freeze to death and you turn into that ugly sister.'

'As my fairy godmother, I hope you wouldn't let that happen.'

They strolled back towards the village, frost sparkling on the ground and clinging to plants, giving them a ghostly whiteness beneath the stars. Olivia liked her hand on his arm again as they walked to the opposite side of the green in the centre of the village. Just as she had that thought, Tom removed her hand and crossed the cobbles towards the trees bundled outside the fell rescue barn. He was rummaging through the collection, separating them as he pulled one from the other.

'Tom, what are you doing?' Her question was a horri-fied splutter as he lifted a tree to assess it.

'Isn't it obvious?' She heard, rather than saw, his grin. 'There's no tree back at the house and we should have one. The smell, remember?'

'We don't need a tree. And certainly not one that you've stolen.'

Tom came to stand in front of her, holding the tree triumphantly. 'I'm not stealing it. I'll leave a note and come back tomorrow with the money. It's a bit small but better than nothing. After all, what's a home at Christmas without a tree? New old traditions, remember?'

'Maybe, but I always take the decorations down on Boxing Day.'

'Boxing Day! Olivia Bradshaw, you're a disgrace. Don't you know there are twelve days of Christmas?'

'In theory, but that doesn't mean you need to surround yourself with wilting trees spilling needles everywhere. Anyway I'm not sure where Dad's put the decorations since we last had one, he might've even got rid of them.' As far as she was concerned Christmas was for people who had time to prepare and then enjoy it. 'There's so much stuff in the house and it'll probably be January before I can lay my hands on them.'

'They're in the shop, I've seen the boxes. I've started clearing out some of the books that aren't fit to sell, and he keeps reminding me to go through everything. That's when I found the Christmas decorations.'

'The shop? Why would he put them in there?'

'No idea.' Tom's head was bent as he scribbled a note from a pad he produced from his pocket and stuck it to another tree. 'I've signed it from Olivia so if anyone's seen us pinching a tree it'll be your neck on the line, not mine. I'm famous, remember. I can't have any scandal attached to my name.'

'You didn't!'

'No, of course I didn't, I just said it was Tom at the bookshop, they know where to find me. Let's go, it is perishing out here.'

'I'm not decorating it tonight,' Olivia warned him. 'I need my sleep first.'

'But not beauty sleep, though, do you?'

She liked that, she thought, helping to carry the tree between them as they crossed the green to the house. The library was still lit, its lights shining down onto the shallow front garden and offering a welcome to her and Tom that felt like home.

Chapter Thirteen

Olivia reached for her phone first thing in the morning as usual. She flicked a cursory glance over her emails and messages, more Twitter notifications, and replied to the message from her friend Gina, checking in about their brunch date in a couple of weeks. They messaged for a bit and when Gina had to disappear, Olivia searched for the farmhouse she had seen last night with Tom. She soon found it and read the agent's details with a practised eye. She knew about the attached small barn and learned there was planning permission for conversion already granted.

She hadn't expected the acre of land or that the stream she and Tom had heard was at the bottom of a tree-lined meadow. There was plenty of work to be done in the house and she saw some of its history revealed in the photos. An old story for sure, and a new one waiting to be written, just as he'd said. She saved the details on her phone, thinking over a couple of clients who could be interested. It was in a lovely location, beyond the village but not far, and it wouldn't be long before someone snapped it up.

They'd left the Christmas tree outside last night and when she walked into the kitchen, Tom had already brought it into the house and wedged it firmly inside a metal stand. She had to smile at the sight: Tom flat on the stone floor, tightening the ratchet that would keep the tree upright, spiny green branches poking in all directions.

'Morning.'

'Good thing I saw your feet,' he muttered, still on the floor. 'Otherwise I'd be thinking you're trying to scare the living daylights out of me again.'

'You're the one on the floor this time. And I can think of better ways to scare you.'

'Oh?' His voice was still muffled and Olivia saw him sliding out from underneath the branches.

'Baking. You have no idea what you've let yourself in for. Where did you find the tree stand, by the way?'

'In the shop.' He was upright again, smiling at her in a way that made her want to kiss him good morning. 'I'm guessing your dad might've had a tree in the shop at one time. Morning.'

There was a moment when it looked as though he might be having the same thought about kissing. Tiredness cast shadows around his eyes and she loved the way his gaze lingered on hers before moving away.

She helped herself to coffee and refilled his empty cup. She felt more tired than usual, wondering if her body was finding it harder to adjust, to settle into doing less now that she was meant to be winding down to annual leave. Her mind was working at a speed that was fractionally slower than the normal pace, her work not at the forefront of her focus in these hours with Tom.

'Have you thought any more about Twitter?' Olivia passed his cup across the table. 'We're still getting notifications from yesterday. It's fine if you don't want to carry on.'

'Thanks. Actually I have and I hope you might find it interesting.'

'I'm all ears.'

'Let me move the tree out of the way first.' He looked at her. 'Where do you want it?'

'Between the windows in the sitting room.' Her smile was sad. 'It always went there.'

'Then that's where we'll put it.' Tom disappeared in a flurry of branches, leaving green needles scattered in his wake and she pulled a face that was also merry. And so the clear-up had begun.

She took her coffee and followed, watching as he set the tree in place. 'Have you paid for it yet?' She bit back the question she wanted to ask, about whether he could afford it.

'I went first thing, someone was already there and had seen the note. So you're off the hook, Olivia, no one is going to come pounding on the door and chasing us down for stealing a Christmas tree.'

'Good.' She paused. 'Want to split the cost? It seems only fair.'

Tom still had his back to her as he turned the tree until he was satisfied its best view was facing them. 'Can it be my treat, to the house for Christmas? And you and your dad, obviously.'

'If you're sure?'

'I am. It already smells gorgeous.' He stepped away from the tree, and she liked the triumph she saw on his face. 'What do you think?'

'Beautiful, if a little bare.'

'If your plans for work aren't too heavy today then we could decorate it later. If you'd like to. I am hoping not to have to do it all alone.'

'I've already checked my inbox and there's nothing that can't wait until tomorrow. Seeing as it's a Sunday and all.'

Olivia winked. 'I guess if you ever write that Christmas movie you'll need to know your way around decorating a tree, it's always crucial to the plot. So technically this is work for you.'

'Movie or pantomime? Which would you like me to write first?'

'Oh the movie, definitely. Look at how much research you've already done: tree lots, Christmas market, hot chocolate, starlit walks, petty theft.'

'It was not theft, I've already paid for it. Temporarily borrowed maybe, I could've always taken it back. And the starlit walk was your idea as I recall.'

'I just wanted a walk, I didn't know there would be stars as well.'

Tom gave her a look that suggested he didn't believe a word of it, and they were both laughing again. She loved how easily they did that and tried to remember a time when she had laughed with someone else quite like they did, but couldn't.

'So what were you going to suggest about Twitter?' Olivia dropped onto the sofa, watching as he chose an armchair nearby.

'What do you think about creating a hashtag for sharing Christmas books that the shop recommends? Old classics, family favourites? We've got less than two weeks to Christmas now and I was thinking we could maybe change the book every other day? We could call it Bradshaw's Books at Christmas. Plus hashtag, of course.'

She could already see the tweets, the interest, the charm. 'Tom, that's a brilliant idea. We could ask my dad for personal recommendations, he would adore that.' Olivia paused, thinking over the practicalities. 'What about you? If we do start getting more visitors, then your cover could be well and truly blown.'

Tom shrugged. 'I'll cope. Twinkly eyes, cute smile, remember? For the selfies.' He winked as she tried to pull a disgusted face. 'I thought I might even do a recommendation of my own. Maybe you could too? Given all that bookselling experience you keep telling me about. Honestly, it's like you're trying to get me to write you into my book.'

He ducked as a cushion flew past his head and she was still laughing as she got up. 'I'm sure I can always use a bit more experience in that field. I'm going to fetch my phone before you change your mind, I might just have had a marvellous idea for our first choice.'

Olivia had to search on the shelves in the library for a few minutes for the book she wanted and returned to the sitting room when she'd found it, Tom coming to sit alongside her. She logged into the shop's Twitter profile, messaging her dad first to let him know what she and Tom were doing.

For the banner she uploaded an image of the shop's interior as reorganised by Tom, since there was no inviting window display. It came out well enough, making the shop look comfortable and appealing, if a little crammed. For the profile she went with one of her own snowy images of the building from last weekend, giving it an extra seasonal charm. *Bradshaw's Books* also looked good and she chose the words of the bio carefully:

> Sometimes it isn't only books that need a new home, it can be bookshops too. Welcome to Bradshaw's Books, no longer on the High St but here in Thorndale and still matching

books to people who love them. Visitors welcome.

Olivia knew exactly what she was going to tweet first. She typed the words, an image of a blustery winter's day from the gallery on her phone to accompany it, and pressed the blue button:

> For #BradshawsBooksAtChristmas we're going to feature different Xmas books between now & the big day. For our first we've chosen #AChristmasMemory by Truman Capote. Is it the weather for fruitcake yet? We'd love to know what you think!

'There you go. Done.' She felt a moment of alarm but Tom was nodding.

'Nice. Really charming, it's a great first choice.'

'So have you got one for our second?'

'Let's ask your dad, let him choose.'

'Good plan. I was thinking I would Zoom him later so we could do it then. So, tree decorating or baking mince pies first?' Olivia shook her head. 'I can't believe I'm actually saying that, I think you've corrupted me.'

'I certainly hope so.' Tom was doing that thing with his smile and she refused to look away, knowing he was trying to distract her on purpose, and then they were both laughing again.

'Have we even got the right stuff? I doubt my dad has much call for plain flour: Mrs Timms does all his baking for him.'

'I bought the ingredients yesterday so that sorry attempt at an excuse is gone.'

'What about writing, then?'

'Did two thousand words before you even left your bed. And no, Olivia, I'm not telling you what my characters got up to last night.'

'You literally do have an answer for everything, don't you?'

'I wish I did.' Tom's eyes on hers were wretched for a second and she wavered at the softness in his tone. 'Guess we'd better make a start. Then we can eat the mince pies whilst we're decorating the tree.'

'More movie research?'

'Absolutely.'

'I love your optimism: you're assuming we don't burn the baking. I've never really trusted that oven.'

–

Thirty minutes later it was clear they weren't going to need the oven, trustworthy or not. The kitchen was in utter chaos and Olivia was fervently hoping that she would not be the one who would have to clear up. Tom had known where to find the baking trays and they'd put on a pair of aprons she'd found which proved to be pointless.

It had started when she'd accidentally spilled flour whilst measuring it into a bowl. He'd accused her of being clumsy, pretending to be exasperated, and she'd dipped her finger in the flour, unable to resist smearing it on his nose. He'd retaliated by swiping a blob of butter on her cheek and she'd followed that up with a flick of mincemeat from the jar he'd bought yesterday. It had missed and landed on the floor.

Tom had then dropped his hand in the flour and run it through her hair. She'd shrieked in protest as some of it had fluttered down onto her face, making her sneeze. He hadn't managed to duck in time to completely avoid the handful she flung at him, and she'd been delighted when some of it had clung to the darkening stubble he hadn't yet removed.

The last of the flour had somehow ended up on the floor and the butter had softened into a clump full of fingerprints. He'd smeared some on the end of her nose and she'd squealed furiously, had tried to fling another blob and missed again when he caught her hand and held it above her head.

There was no butter or flour left now and the jar of mincemeat had fallen over and leaked onto the table, a steady trickle widening into a gooey puddle. They'd given up the fight and were sitting side by side on the floor, backs against a cupboard and staring at the mess all around them.

'Shop-bought ones it is, then. I told you we should've done that in the first place.' Olivia shook her head and stopped abruptly when another cloud of flour fluttered down. She didn't dare touch her hair for fear of what else she might find, she was sure there was butter in there somewhere. She wasn't sure either how she was going to make it upstairs for a shower without leaving a trail of havoc and flour in her wake. 'I am definitely not attempting mince pies again if this is your idea of baking.'

'I did warn you yesterday. More mess, less baking. Although I was aiming to have something edible to eat at the end.' Tom ran a hand through his hair and pulled a face at what he felt there. That second chunk of mince-meat had been her best shot and she was proud of it. 'You're absolutely right, though, you're a nightmare in the kitchen, not safe to be let loose. Microwave meals, useless at baking, horribly messy.'

'I am not. I made you a wicked cocktail last night and provided supper, even if it did come out of a packet. And you started all this.' Olivia gestured to the state of the room.

'I did not start it.' Tom's eyes were lazy on hers and she felt that jump in her pulse again. 'You stuck your hand in the flour first as I recall.'

'We'd never be in this mess if you hadn't suggested baking, so it is all your fault.' She was triumphant, happy to have found a reply to counter his truthful one. 'And I'm pulling rank. You're clearing up.' She edged away from him, trying not to make her escape too obvious. She really wanted that shower now.

'Not alone, I'm not.' He caught her leg and slowly tugged her back. 'Don't you dare leave me in here with this.'

Olivia was past caring about the chaos on her clothes and the dust in her hair. She had flour on her face and she could feel butter stuck to her skin. She gave in to Tom's grasp, one she knew he was keeping deliberately casual, allowing her to escape if she chose.

'Maybe you could put this in your book,' she gasped, her leg resting on his now, his hand light on her calf. 'Is there much call for baking in thrillers?'

'Or not baking, you mean.' His stare was weighted with a desire mirrored in hers. 'I wouldn't write a scene like this. Costello's more of a "don't get involved" kind of a guy. Avoids intimacy. Too many complications.'

'Oh?' Her breath caught again. 'Are you saying we're involved, then? Complicated?'

'We're definitely complicated, Olivia.' Tom gently lifted her leg from his and she saw the flash of sorrow in his face as he stood up, offering her a hand. 'I'm trying not to get involved. Come on, shower. You go first. I'll clear up.'

'Not a chance.' She let him pull her upright, attempting to attach relief to the disappointment that their fooling around was over. 'Nice of you to offer but it did take two of us.'

—

When Olivia came down from her shower there was a box of mince pies sitting on the table and she laughed. Tom was upstairs showering now too, and she hoped no one had recognised him when he'd run out to buy them in such a state. She went into the sitting room to lay the fire and light it. He stuck his head around the door a bit later and she noticed at once he had shaved.

'The decorations are in the shop, I won't be long.'

'I'll come and help.'

'No, I'm fine. It's cold, you stay there.'

She'd made them a coffee and added whisky to it by the time he dropped four plastic boxes on the floor. Suddenly nervous of what she might find and the memories of home it might trigger that she had filed away, she took the lid off the nearest box, pulling away a tangle of tinsel. Tom helped her empty the box and Olivia set aside the things she didn't want to keep: broken ornaments, baubles that were cracked, a reindeer without a head.

'Some of this stuff is mine, I can't blame it all on Dad. Look.' She was holding up a hand-stitched garland in red and green, the letters spelling Merry Christmas. 'Ellie made this when she was still in primary school, it must have got mixed up with some of our things when our house was sold, after she left for university. Christmas decorations hold so many memories, as though you're relearning their stories every time you open a box. I remember her rushing home with this, so excited to hang it the minute she came through the door.'

'You'll miss her, not being with you for Christmas.'

Tom was devouring a mince pie, making Olivia smile as she sipped her coffee. There was a wistfulness in his tone and she thought of his own marriage, the children he'd wanted and didn't have, and her heart ached for him in a way she really wasn't used to.

'I will.' Sorrow lingered in her tone and she strove to sound brighter. 'But she'll be with family and she'll love it, both her and her dad. Her other grandparents are there. Much as I'd like to keep her close, I want her to fly, find her way.'

Olivia picked up a strip of silver wire bent into the shape of a miniature Christmas tree and she stood it on a coffee table, liking how it looked on top of a couple of old hardbacks that hadn't found their way back to the library. She unearthed the nativity figures given to Ellie by her Caribbean grandparents to mark her first Christmas and arranged them on the mantelpiece.

Olivia was sensing the thread between her and Tom altering, drawing them closer. She felt more connected to him in a week than with anyone else ever before and she had to think of her career, of the New Year and settling her dad into a different life. Not their laughter, their teasing, the unspoken desire and everything they'd already shared. They would move on separately into the future. Home for the holidays in Thorndale would be the beginning and the end for them.

Tom had made headway with the lights, and he stood up to plug them in. She held her breath, half expecting a flash and a flurry of smoke, but the lights flickered obediently into life and she saw his grin. Her own smile was more troubled, caught up in thoughts of where he would go after Christmas, what he would do when the book was written. She watched as he wound the lights around the tree, his hands deft and sure. She turned her attention to the next box and pulled out some decorations, trying to stifle a gasp.

'Are you okay?' Tom paused with the lights, looking at her with concern.

'My mum made this.' Olivia lifted a row of white sheep, all wearing different tiny hats, the scratch of tears suddenly threatening. 'Knitted every one of them herself. Wow.' Despite the quick shock of grief pressing against her chest, Olivia couldn't help feeling a warm sense of wonder. 'She was a really talented crafter and she made a new decoration for the tree every year. I was obsessed with animals and I'd asked her to make me some sheep. Look at their little hats, and their faces are tiny Christmas jumpers.'

'They're lovely.' Tom had left the lights to crouch down next to her. 'Are you happy for them to go on the tree? I understand if you'd rather not.'

'No, they definitely should be up there. She would absolutely love that they still had a place in our lives all these years later.' Olivia sniffed, reaching into the box to find a miniature ship in a bottle, turning it over in her hands.

'She made this for Dad. He collected them and she wanted him to have his own tiny one for the tree. Christmas was her favourite time of year and she adored finding ways to represent our lives in her decorations. I haven't seen these in forever. I didn't really question it, but Dad must have found it too sad to put them up once I'd left home.'

'She must have been very special, Olivia.' Tom touched her arm. 'Your dad talks about her sometimes and I always got the impression that he adored her.'

'He did.' Olivia swallowed. 'He really must like you, Tom. Trust you. He hardly ever talks about Mum with anyone.' She put the ship in its bottle down, lifted out another bauble. 'This is a miniature of his shop, it was his absolute favourite.' Tom took it from her, let it spin carefully in his hand. 'You can even see the window display and his name above the door.'

She leant back against the sofa, gulping back a rush of sadness as a tear escaped. 'Suddenly it's like I'm a kid again and she's still part of our lives. Christmas was perfect then, just the three of us, and somehow you think it'll be like that forever. Then everything changes and you realise life's just not fair.'

'She's still a part of your life, in everything she gave you.' Tom settled on the floor beside her. 'The bauble of the shop is so perfect, I'd recognise it anywhere. That yellow paint.'

Olivia huffed a sad little laugh. 'Dad chose the colour, said it made the shop stand out and everyone knew he was there.'

'They certainly did, it was distinctive.'

'Do you think it was a mistake, him closing it?' Her voice was suddenly small. 'I know he still misses it.'

'He accepted it, Olivia, if that's what you mean. He knew he couldn't be there six days a week and it was time to let go. He couldn't keep it for ever.'

She didn't reply at once. 'It's like you said. That I'm never really there for him and I don't give him enough of my time.'

'Olivia, what I said was…'

'No, don't, Tom.' She held up a hand, dropped it down. 'I know there was some truth in it. I was always busy with Ellie and my career, and left him to get on with his life, alone. We popped in when we could, flying visits to the shop, but he must've been so lonely.'

'I'm not sure he was, not really, after the conversations we had.' Tom squeezed Olivia's fingers, let go. 'He enjoyed being in town, part of the festival, having people here. Even before I met you he told me about his wonderful daughter, how proud of her he was.'

'He did?'

'He absolutely did. He loves your independence, how you just see something and go for it, whether it was your marriage, your career or making a home for Ellie. He told me you were an unstoppable force and lived life on your own terms, just as your mum had wanted for you.'

That did make Olivia cry then and she brushed at the tears trickling down her face, appreciating his thoughtfulness when Tom stood and busied himself with the lights on the tree to let her have a moment. She got up too, gathered some of the decorations and he held out a hand.

'May I?'

'Please.' She couldn't prevent a smile when he chose the homemade miniature of her dad's shop and hung that first, giving her a wink.

'What do you think?'

'Perfect. Not sure we need any more.'

'I know the tree is small but that's taking it a bit far. We definitely do need a few more.'

They carried on, each decoration they hung a memento of her life as gradually the tree filled up. They didn't need conversation now; there was an ease to the quietness as they worked together, and Olivia liked it. Liked having him there, sharing the task.

'So you'll be with us for Christmas, then.' She made sure it wasn't a question. 'You might be amazed to know that a roast dinner is my speciality.'

'Olivia, I'm not going to presume,' Tom said softly. 'It's a time for family.'

'And friends, and goodwill to everyone.' She hadn't expected the fierceness in her tone. 'Don't even think about it unless you'd rather be with someone else. That's different.'

'Almost everyone I'd like to spend Christmas with is already here.' He shrugged helplessly as she caught his gaze.

'Good, because someone's got to clear up after me and my dad's not great at standing for ages.'

'Shouldn't take long.' Tom hung another decoration on the tree and they stood back to admire their work. 'I've never seen anyone pierce the film on a Christmas dinner before.' Olivia had already picked up a mince pie and he caught her wrist, holding it gently. 'Don't start that again,' he warned. 'Sometimes I think it would be easier to share the house with a bunch of students.'

'Good job you'll get your chance, then,' she told him smoothly, falling into the playfulness he was suggesting. 'Ellie and Logan are coming up at the weekend and they're messier than me.'

'How is that even possible?'

'You'll find out.'

Chapter Fourteen

The Zoom call Olivia had with her dad later also included Tom, and Hugh was so excited about Tom's Christmas hashtag idea that Olivia was almost ready to cry again. Thorndale seemed to be having a very strange effect on her and she'd be lying if she said she wasn't enjoying it. The book Hugh chose to come next was one she'd never read before, more familiar as she was with Dickens' famous festive classic, *A Christmas Carol*.

Nevertheless, Tom found the 1848 first edition hardcover exactly where her dad had said it would be, buried in a box with other Dickens works in the annexe. New and old Twitter followers were already speculating on what the shop's next choice for the hashtag might be, and their friendly author chap from Saturday had retweeted Olivia's *A Christmas Memory* tweet, creating yet more interest.

-

On Monday Olivia went into the office in Manchester to distribute her Christmas gifts amongst her colleagues. Most of her presents had been delivered to the house and after sharing another cocktail with Tom last night, she'd spent the evening wrapping everything. Between her online purchases and her finds at the Christmas market on Saturday, she was pretty much there with her family shopping.

She had a lovely catch-up with friends in the office, swapping gifts and plans for the holidays. She also met with her business partner Julian to prepare for her annual leave, and there were a couple of viewings she passed on to colleagues. There was one client who couldn't wait and when she checked their availability, she ended up having to schedule an online meeting with them just before Christmas Day.

Her client in the States had decided to press on with the purchase of the farmhouse she'd found them, and she was glad. She didn't fancy another difficult search with Ellie's visit and then Christmas so close. Afterwards Olivia wandered around the city, thoughts of a gift for Tom filling her head as she browsed. She had something in mind and she bought it, hoping he would like her choice even as she wondered if she would be brave enough to give it to him.

Back in Thorndale she cooked supper for them and afterwards Tom disappeared into the library to continue writing. From the energy and exuberance he was giving off, she sensed his work was going well and she took a hot drink into him before heading up for bed. He thanked her distractedly, and she banked up the fire and left it burning, the irony of her taking care of him again not lost on her after all her years of independence.

On Tuesday Olivia sent the tweet she had already prepared:

> For our second #BradshawsBooksAt-Christmas Hugh Bradshaw has personally chosen #TheHauntedManAndTheGhosts-Bargain by Charles Dickens. So great to see you joining with us – do get in touch

to share what you like about it or if you're
discovering it for the first time

A start on clearing more of the house was a priority after
that and she left her phone in her room, not wanting to
be distracted by either Twitter or her clients. She headed
back into the spare bedroom that had always been Ellie's.

Quite a bit of the furniture was included in the house
sale as there was much her dad couldn't keep and Olivia
was ruthless with clutter. She carted the piles downstairs
that she'd made the other day and loaded up her car for a
charity shop run. It wasn't the most practical vehicle for
the job but it would have to do. When she'd finished,
and after a thorough clean and a new, floral duvet cover
on the bed, the room did appear brighter, a welcome
dent in the otherwise monumental task.

The following evening, she had already arranged for
Annie and Jon to join her and Tom for supper. He had
offered to cook, with eyebrows raised in suspicion when
Olivia thanked him and refused. She planned to make a
mushroom risotto; it was a dish she was familiar with and
perfectly happy to produce. She nipped into town, left
her stuff at the charity shop and had an hour with her
dad before doing the shopping for the evening and the
weekend coming up with two active and hungry young
adults.

Her phone was as busy as ever with notifications when
she arrived back, and she decided to nip over to the cafe
to collect a late lunch for her and Tom. Waiting in the
queue, she unlocked her phone and gasped as she read
Annie's text.

So sorry, Liv, change of plan. My waters have broken and we're on our way to hospital. Looks like you might be right about that Christmas baby! News when we can x

Olivia fired off a text in reply, sending love and prayers. Thoughts of a new baby had her mind racing back to Ellie's birth and the emergency caesarean section she'd had to have. She hoped all would be well for Annie and Jon and their first child.

Sam was hurrying down the high street with Esther in a pushchair and Olivia stopped to chat with her, their talk all about Annie and the possible early birth. Sam was concerned about the baby coming at thirty-seven weeks and she and Olivia promised to share any news with one another as soon as they had it. Her dad would want to know too but that could wait until Olivia had more to say; she didn't want to worry him. He was very fond of Annie, and Olivia knew he had already gifted a first edition of nursery rhymes for the baby.

Back at the house she took Tom's lunch into the library and he thanked her, eyes reddened and tired. She was checking her phone more than ever now, although it was far too soon to hear from Annie or Sam. If all seemed well then it was possible that Annie might just be kept in hospital for monitoring rather than inducing the baby immediately.

Olivia had forgotten about the Zoom call that her dad had asked her to sit in with the arts consortium who were purchasing the house until he sent her a text telling her the meeting had begun. She jumped in with apologies but there wasn't a great deal she could add. The finance was in order, a board appointed and all agreed to proceed as necessary.

She kept checking her dad for signs of disappointment but he was enthused, offering his advice and support however he could once the programme was underway next year. There were lots of events being planned and she was sure that her dad had Tom in mind when he suggested that the consortium might like to consider a live-in programme director for the writers' retreat planned for the house.

The thought of Tom being in Thorndale on a more permanent basis was something that pleased Olivia, even though she had no idea how he felt about it. The literary festival was expanding too and searching for a couple of new roles, but she ignored her dad's pointed stare in her direction.

In the evening there was a text from Sam, who was in touch with Jon. Annie's waters were confirmed to have broken and the baby was going to be induced tonight. Olivia felt that flutter of alarm again as she thanked Sam. She knew from her own experience that induction could take time and the baby might not arrive quite yet.

There was still no sign of Tom, so she took supper into him in the library. The room was cool and she saw the fire had gone out. He was fast asleep with his head on his arm on the desk. His manuscript was open on the screen and she checked to make sure that AutoSave was enabled. She fetched a blanket from the sitting room to cover him, then went back into the kitchen to eat her meal alone.

A message from Sam arrived after midnight to say that Annie was in the early stages of labour and doing well. It was ages after that before Olivia fell asleep again and she heard Tom coming up, quietly crossing the landing to his own room and closing the door, reminding her of that first night here with him. How much had changed between them since then in such a short time, she mused.

She messaged Ellie in the morning, checking in about her and Logan's train on Friday and what time she needed to collect them from the station. Olivia couldn't wait to see them, ignoring the thought of Ellie being far away for Christmas. It was lunchtime before Olivia heard from Sam again and she grabbed her phone impatiently. She opened the message in a rush and shrieked in delighted relief.

> Baby Beresford safely here after an emergency section. Small but perfect, both doing really well. They have a daughter!

Sam had included every emoji possible, and Olivia replied at once with a few of her own, thrilled and thankful. Babies always made her cry and she wiped away a few tears. She wanted to message Annie and Jon too, but decided to leave it for a few hours. Olivia was sure they would be both elated and exhausted, and there would be time later on to offer her congratulations.

'What is it?' Tom sounded alarmed as he hurried into the kitchen. 'I heard you from the library, are you alright? Is it your dad? Ellie?'

'What? No, we're fine. It's Sam, she's messaged me to say that Annie's had a baby girl and they're doing well, even though she's a few weeks early. Isn't it wonderful?'

'Fantastic, they must be delighted.' He sank down into a chair, covering a yawn with a hand that couldn't completely hide the stubble gradually giving way to the beginnings of a beard. 'Sorry, long couple of days.'

'Don't worry, I know you've been burning the midnight oil.' Olivia wanted to tell him she'd missed him, sharing supper and chatting together in the evenings, but she held back, even though it was true. She liked the way the house felt with him here – more of a home.

'What time's Ellie due in tomorrow?'

'Around five if there are no delays.'

'Okay.' Tom rubbed a hand across eyes pressed shut. 'I'll make myself as scarce as possible, I don't want to be in the way over the weekend.'

'You what?' This wasn't in Olivia's plans at all. 'Tom, you don't have to do that.'

'But it's your one chance to spend time with Ellie before Christmas. Your family time.'

He didn't need to add 'not mine', Olivia could see it in his eyes now they'd opened. He got up to pour two glasses of water, gave one to her and drained his own, his back to her.

'Are you worried we'll disturb you?'

He put the empty glass down before replying, staring out of the window. 'Of course not. I'll write in my room, I don't want to take over the library with family here.'

'If you want to write and keep to your room then of course that's your decision and completely fine.' Olivia went to stand beside him. 'But if you're doing it because you think I don't want you around then you'd be wrong.' She leaned against him, didn't want to move away. 'I'd love you to meet them both and spend time with us, and Ellie's already looking forward to it.'

'She is?' Tom hadn't moved either. 'What have you told her, about me?'

'Just that her grandad's got me sharing the house with a friend of his.'

'That's it?'

'Pretty much; she'll have googled you anyway. What, you'd prefer I'd said you were this handsome and charming actor who loads of people used to have a crush on?' Olivia pushed against him and he was laughing as he steadied himself. 'You're certainly a handful but I didn't mention that.'

'So you think I'm handsome but past it? Thanks. I think.' The look he gave her was knowing, his eyebrows raised. 'I'd better go and open the shop, it's almost one.'

'Would you like me to do that for you?' Olivia had a contract to go over and a meeting to set up with a potential new client but she could do that in the shop. 'Judging by the hours you've pulled this week your writing's either going really well or very badly and I suspect it's the former. Want more time?'

'Are you sure?' Tom turned to her and she saw the new softness in his eyes. 'That's really good of you.'

'I know. I need to keep up with Twitter anyway and upload another book for the hashtag, the followers are still growing. I'll choose this one and you can do the next if you like,' she said. 'I'm hoping doing the shop for you might get me on your good side. We're going to need supper for four tomorrow night.'

'You devious...' Tom made a grab for her but Olivia was already gone, snatching up her phone and hurrying out of the room, his laughter following.

–

You might have seen the movie but have you read the book? For our third #BradshawsBooksAtChristmas choice we're going with #TheGreatestGift by Philip Van Doren Stern. Join us?

–

The train on Friday night was miraculously just fifteen minutes late and Olivia was only mildly perished as she went over the notifications from Twitter while she waited in the station. Followers old and new were commenting and retweeting the latest book, adding it to threads about *It's a Wonderful Life*. Yesterday afternoon had been busier than expected in the shop and a few customers had mentioned following the Christmas hashtag online.

She was still pondering Twitter when the train lumbered in and she saw Logan jump from the carriage and Ellie follow, throwing their two bags down to him. Olivia watched her daughter, swallowing back the blast of recognition never more apparent than after a separation. This always happened.

Ellie was so like her father and Olivia had a moment to take in the gangly limbs she was able to organise into something elegant, just like him, and the laid-back manner belying a fiercely competitive nature. She was just as beautiful too, long dark hair gathered over one shoulder, and Olivia blinked at the sight.

Then she was running to Ellie, everything else fading away in the joy of holding her girl again. They wrapped their arms around one another and hugged tightly. 'Ellie, you look amazing, so well. I was worried you've been too busy to eat properly.'

'Oh Mum.' Ellie pulled back, the laughter in her face still glowing, brightening eyes that were almost a shade of amber. 'I'm fine, we both are, we're perfectly capable. You taught me, remember?'

Logan was beside Ellie now with their bags and Olivia let go of her daughter to hug him too. She would've picked him out for an Aussie surfer anywhere, from the messy blonde hair escaping from his beanie and vibrant blue eyes to the skin just clinging on to the last of his summer tan. She always pictured him at home on a beach or in the sea, and her heart jolted at the reminder that he and Ellie would be doing exactly that in a few days, far from her and Thorndale.

'Ellie said it would be colder up here but she didn't tell me it would be this bad.' Logan shivered as he picked up the two bags and slung them over one shoulder, reaching for Ellie's hand as they headed for the car park.

'We'll get a fire going when we get back,' Olivia told Logan, who nodded gratefully. 'You'll soon thaw out in the house with a drink.'

'So how's Tom then, Mum?' Ellie was giving Olivia a sideways look. 'Grandad said you're getting along like a house on fire.'

'Oh did he?' Olivia was glad it was dark as she felt her face flush. She'd have to have a sharp word with her dad; Ellie never missed a thing. 'You know what your grandad's like: always exaggerating.'

'Maybe.' Ellie gave her a nudge that had Olivia rolling her eyes.

Ellie and Logan caught Olivia up on some of their news as she drove them back to Thorndale. The moment they were out of the car Logan was capturing images of the pretty stone cottages, bustling river and flickering Christmas tree on his phone to send to his family in Australia, Ellie skipping with excitement next to him.

Lights were lit in the library and sitting room as Olivia approached the house and she couldn't help the shimmer of happiness at the thought of Tom already there, waiting to meet more of her family. To her surprise she could see the cheerful glow of a fire in both rooms as she unlocked the front door.

'We're back.' Olivia pushed the door aside and Logan joined them as Ellie dropped their bags in the hall. Something smelled amazing and Olivia allowed herself to indulge the happiness that had now become a full-on glow inside her.

She couldn't remember the last time she had come back to a home that felt as magnificent as her dad's did in this moment, and it was impossible not to love the comfort it brought her. Darkness and the cold night were beyond the closed doors now; in here all was welcome, warmth and light. Tom appeared in the hall from the kitchen and their eyes met for a long moment as he walked to meet them, hand outstretched to Ellie. The once-famous smile was in place, a pleasure on his face that was completely natural.

'How do you do, Ellie? I'm Tom.'

'Hi Tom, it's great to meet you.' Ellie and he were shaking hands now and Olivia felt her daughter's look dart over to her before going back to Tom with a grin. 'I'm Ellie, but then I guess you know that.'

'I do, I've heard nothing but wonderful things about you from your mum and your grandad.' Tom was still smiling as he turned to Logan and the two men shook hands as they introduced themselves.

'That's nice, apparently only my grandad is prone to exaggeration.' Ellie slipped her arm around Olivia's shoulders, and she recognised the mischief in Ellie's reply. 'And Mum told me you were lovely. Didn't you, Mum?'

There was an innocence in Ellie's tone now that made Olivia want to invoke whatever scrap of maternal control she still had – which was zero – and send Ellie to her room this minute. And possibly make her stay there until it was time to leave for university again.

'Ellie, I said nothing of the sort.' Olivia batted the comment away. 'I might have mentioned that he was a lovely cook, that's all. Something does smell delicious, Tom, I hope you haven't gone to too much trouble.' She gave Ellie a look. 'Why don't you two take your bags upstairs and join us for a drink when you're ready?'

'We'd love to join you both.' Ellie and Logan picked up their stuff and bounded upstairs, leaving coats and hats draped over the stairs, a phone charger on the sideboard with two discarded gloves and a scarf, and a half-empty water bottle.

Olivia hoped she'd imagined the emphasis Ellie had placed on *both*. That left her and Tom in the hall staring at one another, and the smile was still hovering on his lips as Olivia went to take off her coat. Somehow she seemed to get her arms and her scarf in a tangle and he was there to pull the coat off and hang it on the stand. She felt about five years old until she caught sight of him in the small mirror.

'I'll take lovely,' he said softly, standing behind her. 'And in return I won't tell Ellie that you nearly kneecapped me with an atlas, insisted I took off my clothes, wrecked the kitchen not baking mince pies and encouraged me to steal a Christmas tree. I think you're an awfully bad influence.'

'Oh, I'm a bad influence?' Olivia was giving him a glare that was at odds with the laughter already bubbling. He smelled heavenly, and she loved how his short hair was all rumpled. But not cute, definitely not cute. Sexy for sure, and the stubble had gone, leaving him looking fresh and delectable. 'The tree and the baking were your ideas, I just went along with them. The undressing was essential. And quite frankly your Christmas movie would be absolutely nowhere without my assistance with your research.'

'True.'

Olivia could hear Ellie and Logan moving about upstairs. She sidestepped Tom and the way he was making it difficult to remember what she was meant to be doing. 'I'd better go and pour drinks. See what state you've left the kitchen in.'

'You'd hardly know I was there, I've already done most of the clearing up.'

'Actually, maybe I did say you were lovely to Ellie.' Olivia threw him a glance as she walked down the hall, his chuckle following. 'Maybe I wasn't just referring to your cooking.'

Olivia had poured beer for both Logan and Ellie and red wine for her and Tom by the time the young couple joined them. She couldn't miss Ellie's speculative look on her as she and Tom moved easily around the room without hindering the other. Ellie helped her lay the table whilst Tom put the finishing touches to the meal he had prepared for them.

He and Logan were chatting about Australia and the little town where Logan was from, which Tom had apparently visited when he'd toured there years ago with a theatre company. The atmosphere between the four of them was already so much easier than it could have been. That it would happen for one weekend only was an unpleasant thought Olivia didn't want to linger on tonight.

Tom had cooked chunky sausages filled with black pudding and treacle and they were perfect for a winter's night, with plenty of parsnip and potato mash, thick onion gravy and a nod to the season with sprouts he'd sautéed in bacon. Olivia tried not to watch him too obviously, her glass of wine in hand. She could feel Ellie's eyes on her occasionally and knew she would have some explaining to do if she wasn't careful.

The meal was amazing and they all fell on it ravenously, Ellie and Logan having two helpings of everything and constantly hungry it seemed to Olivia. She'd provided the dessert and took the jokes in good spirit when everyone, including Tom, teased her about the marmalade and whisky bread and butter pudding she had picked up from The Courtyard instead of making something herself. She caught Tom's eye at one point and guessed from the way he was trying to hide a smile that he too was thinking of their failed attempts at mince pie baking.

Olivia cleared up whilst everyone else stayed at the table, and it wasn't long before Ellie and Logan wanted to go and explore the village. Olivia promised to have hot drinks ready for their return and they were back within an hour, cold, with skin flushed from the chill, and laughing. She made everyone a hot toddy and it was late when they all finally headed up to bed.

Chapter Fifteen

'So Mum, anything to tell me?'

It was just after nine and Ellie was sharing with break-fast with Olivia in the kitchen. Logan was still in bed and Tom was already writing, politely refusing their request that he join them so the two women could have some time alone.

'You said he was lovely but you forgot to mention he was such a fox. I saw the way you two were looking at each other last night.'

Hastily, Olivia tried to shush Ellie before her clear voice reached Tom in the library. 'It's not like that, Ellie. He's a friend of your grandad's and yes, I'd say we've become friends too. But that's it.'

'Seriously? You're not going to do anything about it?'

'About what?' Olivia stood up to fetch more coffee, hoping she sounded casual enough.

'About the way you are together! You two look happier here, pottering about the kitchen, than some couples who've been living in the same house for years.'

'That's only because Tom's doing most of the cooking and he enjoys it, so it makes sense he'd be comfortable in here. And pottering, Ellie, really? You make us sound ancient.'

'Whatever.' Ellie jumped up to put more bread in the toaster. 'You're not getting any younger Mum, and he's really nice. It would make a change from swiping through profiles for a date.'

'I don't...'

'Swipe through profiles? Maybe it's time you started again.'

'Ellie.' Olivia tried to keep the exasperation from her voice. 'I simply don't have time. You know how busy I am with work and then there's this place to sort out. And your grandad to keep an eye on.'

'Excuses. You can have a life of your own, you know, Mum.' Ellie had buttered the toast and was at the door, giving Olivia a cheeky grin. 'Ask yourself how often nice people you actually like spending time with come around. Plus you're crap in the kitchen so I wouldn't be knocking Tom back if I were you.'

'Yes, well, I'm not you,' Olivia muttered as her daughter hurried upstairs, taking the toast to Logan. 'And I wasn't always crap in the kitchen.'

Sometimes she wished she still did have Ellie's easy confidence and assurance that life would mostly work itself out to its best advantage. She'd done all she could to create a family life for Ellie, encouraged the relationship with her father, such as it was, and hadn't allowed anyone else close enough to disrupt their lives, to zoom in and then fly out again. Olivia couldn't regret that; she'd rather have been on her own all these years and established a career than have someone take Ellie to heart only to leave them both again.

It was time to change the Twitter Christmas book so Olivia knocked gently on the library door. Her dad had asked Tom to choose and she hoped he wouldn't mind the interruption. When Tom called for her to come in, she opened the door and immediately felt the chill of the room, though she was warmed the moment he smiled at her.

'Hey.'

'Hi. Sorry, is this a good moment to talk about the Christmas hashtag? We could do with updating Twitter before the shop opens.'

'Sure. My killer can wait.' Tom pushed his chair back from the desk and Olivia went to the window seat, drawing her cardigan more closely around her. 'I've got my suggestion if you want to hear it.'

'Of course, I'd love it. Only if you're happy, though.'

'I am, really. What do you think about Tolkien's *Letters from Father Christmas*?'

'I don't know much about it, to be honest. But it sounds perfect from the title.'

'Tolkien wrote letters to his children every December pretending to be from Father Christmas and it was published posthumously. It's a small book and really charming, which fits with our previous choices. I had a copy when I was a kid, but I don't know where it went.' Tom paused, nostalgic for a second. 'I think my favourite letter is when Tolkien wrote about the reindeers escaping and the North Polar Bear turning on two years' worth of Northern Lights all in one go.'

'It sounds fantastic.' Olivia had never read it. 'What do you want me to say?'

'About me?'

'Yes.'

'Guest bookseller? Writer in residence? Friend of your dad's? What do you think? As my publicist.' Tom shrugged.

'As your publicist I'd be saying full-on Tom Bellingham choosing Christmas books in the little shop where he's based himself to write.' She paused. 'As your friend, I'd say let's decide on something you're comfortable with and leave it at that. Friend of my dad's sounds good.'

'How about, "Today's book was chosen by Tom, friend of Hugh, a writer and a reader"? That way I'm not hiding but I'm not shouting about it either.'

'Perfect. I'll show you before I tweet it.' Olivia got up, conscious of not wanting to keep Tom from his work any longer. 'Any idea where I might lay my hands on a copy? I'd like to have a look, find something to say about it.' She gestured to the bookshelves around the room, stacked high and reaching to the ceiling. 'Might be quicker than me having to go searching.'

'Actually I found one in the shop and I've been reading it. New old traditions and all that. It takes me back to being that kid again, remembering the magic of Christmas.'

If she had been nearer, Olivia would have touched him, placed a hand on his shoulder to show him she understood the mix of emotions he was feeling, reflecting on a time that was equal parts bitter and sweet.

Tom turned back to his laptop, and she knew it was time to leave him. 'It's beside my bed if you want to see it.'

'You don't mind? I can wait.'

'No, go ahead.' His reply now was distracted, quick. 'I'm fairly certain I haven't left anything lying around I wouldn't want you to find.'

'Sure? I'm easily shocked.'

'I doubt that. The night you rescued me comes to mind.'

She heard his chuckle as she left the room to run up the stairs, bumping into Logan halfway. Ever since Olivia

203

had first met him, she'd always thought he'd perfected the student art of seeming as though he'd been awake all through the night and had slept the day away. He gave her a sleepy grin as they exchanged greetings. Ellie had persuaded him to go for a walk and he was already wearing a hat and clutching a thick jumper.

She almost knocked on Tom's door, stopping herself at the last moment. The room was tidy and she noticed a pile of paperbacks beside the neatly made double bed. This was her dad's best guest room, with its floral wallpaper, carpet decorated with a swirly pattern and the sash window that always used to stick.

Tom's navy sweater was slung across an armchair, a couple of pairs of shoes close by, and she looked over the books, searching for the Tolkien one. She soon found it and left the room, closing the door quietly. Ellie appeared on the landing and her face split into a wide grin as she spotted Olivia.

'Seriously, Mum? That was quick work, we only spoke like, fifteen minutes ago.'

'Don't be ridiculous.' Olivia didn't mean to sound huffy, and she waved the book in her hand. 'I needed a copy of this, and Tom said I would find it in his room. I've never been in there before. I mean, at the same time as Tom. In his room.'

'Whatever.' Ellie ignored that reply as well. 'Me and Logan are going out, we'll be back for lunch. Tom mentioned something about you making it?'

'Oh, did he?' Olivia was smiling as they crossed the landing. 'So it's a good thing I've already bought soup and fresh sourdough from The Courtyard.'

'Then we'd like to help in the shop for a bit this afternoon.' Ellie was already running down the stairs. 'Tom said he would be opening up and that Logan and I were welcome to hang around.'

'You and Tom seem to have everything sorted.' They were in the hall now and Logan appeared, clutching another piece of toast and trying to get his coat on with one hand. 'Is there anything else I need to know?'

'We're still eating in the pub tonight, right?' Ellie gave Olivia a quizzical look and Olivia nodded. 'Good, 'cause I've booked a table for four. Tom said he'd like to come.' She grinned as Logan joined her and opened the front door. 'It's a date, Mum, you can thank me later.'

Olivia didn't know whether to laugh or be cross at being so completely outmanoeuvred by her twenty-two-year-old daughter. She'd planned to invite Tom to join them this evening anyway, she didn't like to think of him sitting alone in the house if he didn't want to.

But Ellie had obviously got there first and now it felt more like a double date than dinner with family and a friend, and that was absurd. But she was still wondering about what she might wear when Tom joined her in the kitchen a little later to make coffee. He poured a cup for her too and she thanked him.

'Come and look at this.' She held up her phone and Tom came to stand next to her. 'The tweet.'

She'd borrowed a small figure of Father Christmas from the tree in the sitting room, found a fountain pen and a sheet of writing paper, taken some images of them on a coffee table and chosen the one she liked the best:

Our fourth #BradshawsBooksAtChristmas is Tolkien's #LettersToFatherChristmas chosen by Tom, a reader, writer and a friend of Hugh. Let us know what you think of the North Polar Bear and his antics…

'Perfect, thank you. Love the imagery.' Tom touched her shoulder before disappearing back to the library with his coffee.

Lunch was a success, mainly thanks to the easy conversations the four of them already seemed to be sharing, and the spicy chorizo soup which Olivia served with chunks of sourdough laden with creamy salted butter. Logan couldn't get enough, and he and Ellie teased each other about his lack of cooking skills, reminding Olivia of her and Tom.

Ellie's words from this morning were still in her mind as Tom cleared up, waving away Ellie's offer to help. The two students seemed to leave a trail of belongings wherever they went, from coats and hats to phone chargers and boots and bags, making Olivia smile. Yet another thing that made the house feel lived in.

Afterwards Tom crossed the garden to open the annexe and Olivia didn't know what to do with herself, which was a shock. Her clients seemed to be taking her at her word, that she really was on annual leave, and her inbox wasn't piled as high as it normally would be, even without the services of an out of office message.

She'd only had two calls that couldn't wait from her assistant, and her client in the States had finally signed the contracts on their new home, which was a relief all round. Someone else in the company would now take over, smoothing their path as plans were prepared to ship the contents of their house from the USA to northern England.

Olivia supposed she should be emptying cupboards and loading the car with more stuff to be recycled, but she really couldn't be bothered. Christmas Day was only a week or so away and she was seriously thinking that the clearance would have to wait until the New Year, and she'd deal with everything then. She was supposed to be on holiday after all, and the house sale wouldn't be final for a number of weeks yet.

So instead she wandered down to the bookshop, which felt a little full with two potential customers plonked on the chairs, hardbacks in hand, and Ellie and Logan sorting through books that Tom had suggested needed dumping. The Christmas playlist was offering up *Carols from King's* and the tree on the floor twinkled a greeting. Olivia thought it all looked wonderful, including Tom in her approval. He was standing behind the desk, going through a pile of books on poetry, and he held one up when he saw her.

'Ever read this?'

She took it, her fingers brushing his. 'Not for years.' It was a Christmas anthology of children's poems in hardcover. 'My dad used to read it to me when I was little.'

'Maybe consider it for the hashtag, then?'

'Good idea, I'll take it back to the house when I go.'

'So what are you doing here?' Tom was flicking through another book on the desk. His question sounded innocent enough but she heard the slightly lowered tone, saw the flash of his eyes on hers. 'Still checking out what it takes to be a bookseller?'

'I might be.' She glanced across the shop in case Ellie caught her staring at Tom. Her daughter needed no further encouragement to matchmake. 'Perhaps my own experience in that field is a bit lacking.'

'I'll be opening up again next week if you're free. For more experience.'

'Are you still talking about bookselling?' Olivia saw the quick pursing of his lips that told her he liked their teasing, the bantering they always seemed to share.

'In theory.'

Two more people arrived, and it was all getting a bit of a squeeze so Olivia left them to it and went back to the house. She began to clear some of the chaos from her own room, sorting through old books and stuff she didn't want to keep. Gina messaged in the middle of it all and Olivia was happy to stop and chat.

She told Gina about Tom staying in the house and her friend was agog, wanting to know more about him and what he was like to live with. Gina was another who could spot a potential date at fifty paces, and she'd be haring over even sooner to meet Tom if Olivia so much as hinted that there might be something between them. She laughed when Gina sent her a gif of Tom from his days as Harrington with a mischievous message, and she couldn't resist the temptation to save it.

Later Olivia wished she had a bit more of Ellie's carefree attitude as she changed for the evening, trying not to feel as though she were dressing for a date. She chose a long-sleeved cardigan to wear on its own as a top, with skinny navy jeans tucked into her favourite brown leather boots. It was more or less what she'd already been planning for tonight and she definitely didn't want to appear as though she'd made a special effort.

She applied her usual foundation and a stroke of blusher on her pale skin. Eyeliner as well as mascara was her only nod to the evening being slightly more special than her usual nights in with Tom, and she finished with a matte lipstick she didn't often wear, in a shade below plum. Ellie was always trying to persuade her to try more reds but tonight wasn't the time to begin experimenting with something new.

The two men were waiting in the hall when Ellie and Olivia walked downstairs. Olivia felt caught in Tom's gaze, liked being the focus of his attention and saw the swift glint of approval he didn't need to voice.

The four of them walked around the top of the green to the pub in time for their booking at seven. Ellie and Logan settled at a corner table whilst Olivia went to the bar with Tom. She hadn't been in the pub for ages and looked around with interest. Off-white walls were dotted with landscape prints, interspersed with more modern art, and she recognised one of the artists' work from the paintings her dad had in his sitting room. Functional tables were scattered across stone-flagged floors between the bar and a slightly more formal room on the opposite side of the central door.

Not for this building the modern sophistication of the pub with Tom from a few weeks ago, but it was comfortable and had a reputation for great food. The roaring fire was offering welcome and warmth from the sharp winter night outside, and Olivia could already see Logan huddled as close to it as he could get.

Their drinks collected, Olivia and Tom returned to the table. Somehow she ended up sitting on the comfortable bench along the wall with Ellie next to her, leaving the two men opposite, and Ellie and Logan were already holding hands across the table. Menus were handed around and Logan couldn't resist a full Christmas dinner with all the trimmings, quite different to the fish and steak he usually enjoyed with his family back at home in Australia on Christmas Eve. Ellie opted to join him as neither were planning to eat turkey once they were in Tobago.

They were relishing Logan's stories of growing up with a dad who flew helicopter tours and a mum who was a stand-up comedian. The four of them swapped tales of travelling, and Olivia smiled at Ellie's passion and her love of the sea.

The young couple were interested to hear of Tom's time as an actor and he kept them amused with stories of some of the people he had met and worked with over the years. He was also interested in their respective studies and plans for future careers, hearing about Logan's wish to consult in renewable marine energy and Ellie planning to base herself in the West Indies to begin a career in marine biology and oceanography.

University life suited her bright and beautiful daughter and Olivia was so pleased to see how happy Ellie and Logan still were together. When they all eventually got up to leave, after Christmas pudding and coffee, it was almost eleven and a sharp frost, though sadly not the snow Logan had longed for, gleamed outside.

Ellie didn't need much persuading from Logan to go for a late-night walk and Olivia exchanged a smile with Tom as she remembered doing the same thing a week ago. Logan tugged his hat lower and tightened his scarf, still muttering about the cold. Ellie never seemed to feel it, darting in front of him with her coat unbuttoned.

The young couple promised to make the hot drinks this time when they returned, if the 'older' ones could stay awake that long. Olivia watched them heading along the green, feet crunching in the frost, and they turned into a lane out of sight as Tom unlocked the house.

'It's been a really lovely evening, thank you for joining us.' It was more pleasant inside the house and Olivia pulled the door shut, leaving it unlocked. 'I think Ellie and Logan really liked your company and appreciated your interest in them.'

Tom was hanging up his coat and Olivia wondered about lighting the sitting room fire or if it was too late to bother.

'I think it's me who should be thanking you, Olivia.' He was standing nearby and touched her hand. 'It was kind of you to include me.'

'We all wanted you there, Tom.' Her voice was just as low, allowing herself to reveal the pleasure his company had brought. 'I'm glad you enjoyed it.'

'Ellie is delightful and it's obvious where she gets her mischievous nature from. I have a feeling we were being properly set up.'

'She does make me laugh, bless her.' Olivia headed into the kitchen, aware of Tom behind her. 'It's as though she thinks we're not capable of deciding whether we can take ourselves on a date without her interfering. Especially when we have all this time alone in the house.'

'I think we're good at avoiding the issue.'

'What issue would that be?' Olivia was investigating the drinks cupboard, checking to see if there was enough brandy left to add a splash to the cider Ellie was planning to mull. She straightened, a bottle in her hand, to find Tom staring at her with an expression suddenly serious.

'How we feel about one another.'

She put the bottle of brandy down, suddenly edgy. 'Friends, like we said. Maybe good friends and I love how we laugh together.' She picked the brandy up again, her voice tremulous. 'It's only been a fortnight, Tom. I've done this before and I won't make the same mistake again. I won't let myself rush into something mad and be the one left behind.'

'Is it fair to judge what we might be against what happened before?' Tom was running an agitated hand through his hair. 'What if it's more than friends, Olivia? What if I can see the days and weeks running away into next year and I don't want to go, to stop doing this.'

'This?' she whispered the word, put the bottle down again. 'Sharing a house, you mean? Isn't that all we're doing?'

'We're back, Logan was freezing!' The front door banged shut and then Ellie crashed into the kitchen, Logan right behind her as she looked from Tom to Olivia. 'Hope we're not interrupting anything?'

'Of course not,' Olivia said casually. She picked up the bottle, tempted to neck a mouthful. 'I've found the brandy.'

Chapter Sixteen

Tom headed out for a run on Sunday morning, leaving Olivia time with Ellie and Logan to exchange Christmas gifts. Later Olivia planned to cook brunch before the three of them visited her dad in his flat and then Ellie and Logan would catch the train back down to university in Plymouth.

Annie had replied to Olivia's message of congratulations for her and Jon's baby daughter, sending a picture of an adorable bundle snugged in Jon's arms beneath his huge beaming smile. They were hopefully coming home early next week and Annie had already invited Olivia to pop in and meet the baby.

Olivia, Ellie and Logan settled down in the sitting room to exchange stockings, the Christmas tree that she and Tom had decorated flickering nearby. The tree had not gone unremarked upon last night by Ellie as she'd raised knowing eyebrows at Olivia and examined the decorations she, too, hadn't seen for years. The four of them had sat up and talked long into the night with their mulled cider.

Ellie was thrilled with her stocking, filled with goodies and a bottle of the perfume she adored. As always Olivia had included a nod to her childhood and her grandad's world, this time with a copy of *The Secret Garden* she had found in the bookshop. She had been giving Ellie books all her life, adding to a collection that was divided between this house and Olivia's apartment. Logan never seemed to have enough hats and he was chuffed with the one that Olivia had put in his stocking, along with the bookmark she had found him from the Christmas market.

Tom was back in time for the four of them to enjoy a lazy brunch before Ellie and Logan had to say goodbye. Tom shook Logan's hand and he seemed slightly taken aback when Ellie reached up to hug him. Olivia had no idea what words Ellie was busy imparting to him but they made him smile, whatever they were. Olivia had invited him to join her on the visit to her dad but he'd declined, telling her it was family time.

Olivia drove Ellie and Logan to the retirement flats and as always Hugh was overjoyed to see them. It made Olivia want to cry as she saw his pride in his granddaughter, joining in her excitement over her travels with Logan. They stayed for an hour and then it was time to head for the station and Olivia couldn't dismiss the knot in her stomach at the thought of Ellie being away again for Christmas.

Before they left, Olivia tried to persuade her dad one last time to join her at the carol service in Thorndale this evening. He refused again, telling her firmly that she didn't need to be driving him home again afterwards in the dark. She had no other choice but to accept his decision, hiding her disappointment that he wasn't going to be there. He'd made plans to have supper with another resident instead and she was glad that he was finding new company he enjoyed.

She shared a hug with Logan in the station car park and he tactfully left them alone so she and Ellie could say goodbye. Both women had tears hovering now and Olivia held her daughter tightly, smiling at Ellie's insistence that she really liked Tom and what was her mum going to do about it? *Very likely nothing* was Olivia's silent answer to that, and she made Ellie promise to send pictures of the celebration Ellie's paternal grandparents were planning to hold.

They arranged to Zoom on Christmas Day and then Ellie was gone, running to join Logan on the platform and jump on the train before it left them behind. Tomorrow they would fly out to Tobago and Olivia waved until the train was out of sight, swallowing back her gloom. She drove back to Thorndale through the gathering darkness, warmed by thought of Tom already being in the house. She was still thinking over his comment from last night, when they'd returned from the pub, wondering whether there could actually be more for them after Christmas had passed and the season had lost its sparkle.

He was in the library working, the door closed, and she was just able to freshen up before it was time to leave for the carol service. She thought about knocking to let Tom know and decided not to, not wanting to disturb him unnecessarily. To her surprise the door flew open as she was putting her coat back on and Tom burst into the hall.

'Hey.' He grinned at her, reached for his coat too. 'Did Ellie and Logan get away okay?'

'Yes, fine thanks, just in time. Ellie will let me know when they're back.'

'Good.' Tom was winding a scarf around his neck. 'How was your dad?'

'So happy to see them. Stubborn, still refusing to come to the carol service. I can't remember the last time he missed it.' Olivia was staring at Tom. 'Where are you going?'

'Same as you, I imagine.'

'The carol service? Why?'

'Also the same as you. I think I'll enjoy it and it's another of those new old traditions we talked about.'

Tom held the door open and followed her outside. He offered her his arm and she tucked her hand into the crook of his elbow. Groups of people were already making their way to church and she and Tom slipped in amongst them. Lights glowed in and outside houses and someone – Olivia guessed Charlie – had managed to fix a huge star to the top of the church tower and it was doing a marvellous job of lighting the way.

'Sam will be disappointed not to have my dad there,' Olivia remarked. 'He usually does a reading at the service and she's got me instead.'

'You'll be great. I have every confidence in you.'

'Thanks for that.' Olivia liked how Tom found her hand to squeeze it. 'Any tips?'

'Don't forget your lines.'

There was a droll note in Tom's voice and for a second she didn't know whether to laugh, her mind arrowing back to his pained recollection of forgetting his own onstage. He decided for her, leaning into her with a wink. Relief flooded through Olivia, understanding that he felt comfortable enough to joke with her about something that weighed heavy on his heart. They weren't far from the church now and she could already see candles flickering in the stained-glass windows.

'I should be fine, there'll be a bible to read from. It might even be large print if I'm lucky.'

'Shame.'

'Oh?'

'I like you in glasses. It's sexy.'

'Stop trying to distract me.' Olivia nudged him with her elbow as they strolled inside and found seats. 'I don't need to be thinking about you thinking about me whilst I'm reading.'

The church was lit by more candles and filled with vases of gleaming holly, winter flowering jasmine and viburnum nestling with Christmas box and adding a layer of scent. The brass brand was back, already playing carols, and a small choir was busily shuffling music. It was beautiful, seasonal and special, and Olivia recognised quite a few people she had once known better than she did now.

Some stopped by to ask after her dad, and she couldn't miss how attention lingered on Tom. Only one or two tried to draw him into conversation and she introduced him as her dad's friend. Tom was polite and patient, and she saw also how curious eyes went to her, at his side, trying to measure their friendship and whether he really was who they thought he might be.

It was a glimpse into his world, a reminder of the one she had briefly shared with Jared. She thought about the attention Tom had lived with for much of his career, especially since he had played his most famous role. Just then Sam came over with Esther, who was excited and doing her best to escape from Sam's arms. Olivia wished that Ellie, Logan and her dad were here with her, sharing this last Sunday evening before Christmas Day. Sam pulled out her phone, clinging on to Esther with one arm, to find the latest photos and news about Annie and Jon's baby, who looked gorgeous.

Charlie welcomed everyone as the service began and the brass band launched into 'O Little Town of Bethlehem'. Olivia felt a rush of affection for the season, the familiarity of all she had used to love doing with her family. It felt wonderful to sing again and she felt a thrill when Tom's baritone voice joined with hers to rise and fall on the differing notes.

Carol followed reading throughout the service and when it was Olivia's turn, she took her time to read the verses from Luke's gospel about the visit of the angel Gabriel and his foretelling of the birth of Jesus. They sang 'Hark the Herald Angels Sing' straight after, and Tom reached for her hand as she retook her place at his side, letting her know with his gesture that he thought she'd read well.

Somehow they didn't quite manage to let go until they stood for the next carol. Eventually Charlie led the final prayers and invited everyone to sing carols outside beneath the star at the top of the church. Most people braved the chill, huddling together as the children took off in search of treats in the hall next door.

Singing outdoors in the darkness felt even more special and Olivia's hand found Tom's again, slipping her fingers through his. Such a simple gesture and one she sensed was moving them to something more than the friends they already were. The carols were over far too soon, and she looked at him, catching his gaze softening on hers.

'Do you want to go home?' She couldn't explain why she'd said home to Tom when her dad's place had long been his and his alone. 'Back to the house, I mean. There are a few people eyeing you and if we hang around I think you might be swallowed up. There's already some speculation on Twitter as to who "Tom" might be and Mrs Timms looks ready to elbow everyone out of the way to get to you.'

'Home sounds good.' Tom shook Olivia's arm gently, tightening his hold on her fingers. 'I'm getting hungry and it really must be your turn to cook supper.'

'Will soup do? There's some left over from lunch yesterday.'

'I guess it'll have to.' He was grinning. 'Come on, let's go, Mrs Timms definitely means business. I think she's got designs on me.'

'For what?' Olivia was choking back laughter as they said good night to the people around them and hurried back on to the darkened lane.

'She mentioned something the other day when I popped into the cafe about an amateur dramatics production she's involved in. I didn't get any further, I made my excuses and escaped.'

'Is she trying to persuade you to take the lead?'

'Doubt it, I wouldn't put it past her to cast me in the chorus.'

The house felt welcoming, the light in the library still on when they let themselves back in. Olivia glanced at her phone, but it was too soon for Ellie and Logan to be back in Plymouth. They didn't check in on each other that much, but Olivia did like to know that Ellie had arrived safely whenever she was travelling.

She and Tom settled in the sitting room after finishing off the soup and some cheese from yesterday. Olivia had wondered if he would go back to writing and was pleased when he joined her. He was carrying a book as he dropped onto the sofa opposite her chair and pulled off his boots.

'Is that Tolkien you're reading?' She pointed to his hand.

'No.' Tom lifted the book to show her. 'It's *A Christmas Carol*. I read it every year and I'm a bit late starting this time.' He stretched out on the sofa, resting his head on a cushion. 'I thought I might read it to you if you like?'

'Out loud?' Olivia didn't manage to disguise her surprise.

'That's generally the idea if we're going to do it together. It's not compulsory.' He shifted his glance to the phone still in her hand. 'Only if you want to hear it. I thought maybe you'd like a distraction, after leaving Ellie at the station and not seeing her for Christmas.'

Oh, she didn't need thoughtfulness. Not on top of those dark good looks, blue eyes softened with a new tenderness and that clever, sharp mind seeming able to read hers at times. He was much easier to dismiss when they had been avoiding one another, keeping to the pretence that they were merely friends.

'I'd love that.' Olivia put the phone on the floor. 'I was just checking to see if there was anything from her but it's too soon.'

'What about work? Your clients?'

'Are you being sarcastic? It's the last Sunday evening before Christmas!'

'Of course I wasn't. I don't want to keep you from something you feel you ought to be doing.'

'You're definitely not doing that. Please, read. I can't think of anywhere else I'd rather be right now.'

Surprised to find that was the truth, Olivia snuggled into her armchair. She had a moment to wonder whether she ought to have brought them drinks but Tom had already started and now she didn't want to leave. His voice was one of the things she had been most attracted by when they had first met, and she found it utterly delightful to be read to.

220

She listened, his reading soothing, melodic, as he began by saying that there was no doubt of Marley being dead and of Scrooge knowing it. She hadn't been read to since she was a child and as Tom carried on, she found the experience deeply moving and powerfully intoxicating. Her eyes felt heavy and she was cosy, comfortable, tucked into her chair beside the fire on a winter's night, the Christmas tree flickering between the scarlet curtains drawn against the dark.

'Hey.' Olivia started as she felt a gentle hand on her shoulder, blinking to see Tom crouched before her. 'Sorry to wake you.'

'I wasn't asleep.' She tried to drag her thoughts into some kind of order and forgot all of them as she saw the playfulness in his gaze.

'You definitely were. I'm sure I've put some audiences off in the past, but I've never had one fall asleep on me quite so blatantly before.'

'I wasn't! I mean, I didn't plan to.' She covered her face with a hand, peeping at him from between her fingers. 'Did I really?'

'You really did.' Tom straightened up and she was sorry and relieved all at once, he looked delicious and very close. 'I'll forgive you because you were so peaceful, curled up on the chair and snuffling, like Piglet. I've never seen you that relaxed.'

He had been so near, she would only have had to lift a hand to reach his face, tilt her own forward to find his lips. She wanted to touch him, to trace her thanks onto his skin and follow it up with more. Olivia blinked back the thought in her sleepy confusion, sure her desire was already written on her face. Where would it take them if they acted on this attraction, always there no matter how hard they ignored it. Where would they both be, come January and the New Year, the old life?

'I was not snuffling! You're seriously comparing me to Piglet?'

'Just the snuffling. It was cute.'

'If I did fall asleep – and I'm not admitting I did – it was because your reading was so lovely.'

'You sure?' Tom stretched out on the sofa again, the book on the floor. ''Cause I was going to suggest that we carry on tomorrow but if you're just going to be snoring your head off every time I start then there's not much point. We only got as far as decreasing the surplus population before you were away.'

'Maybe I should be reading to you? See if I can put you to sleep.'

'You're on. Your turn tomorrow and then I'll do the next night. Let's see if we can finish it before Christmas, five staves. I'll complete the first one tonight, as long as you don't fall asleep on me again.'

'What will happen if I do?' Olivia swallowed as he shifted to stare at her.

'Fall asleep and I'll show you.'

'What about your book? Wouldn't you rather be writing in the evenings?' Changing the subject seemed safer.

'I'm almost there.' There was a note of triumph in Tom's reply that had her sitting up straight. 'Final chapter this week and then I start editing, trying to layer it.'

'Tom, that's brilliant! I'm so pleased. Wow. Congratulations.'

'I haven't finished it yet,' he warned, but Olivia could see the happiness that his achievement and her words had brought. 'But I think it's going to be okay. I think.'

'Is anyone going to read it before you submit?' The answer followed the question and they both spoke at the same time.

'My dad.'

'Your dad.' Tom laughed. 'He's already read the first five chapters.'

'And?'

Tom pursed his lips, trying to disguise his delight. 'He liked them.'

'And now the truth.' She was still staring at Tom, wanting him to succeed, wanting to him hear say that he knew, and her dad knew, that his book was good, better than good. 'Come on!'

'He loved it.' Tom held up a hand. 'I know he's maybe too close to me to be properly objective but he's tough, Olivia, and I know he won't pull his punches. He won't try and make me feel better for the sake of it. He won't let me waste my time.'

'I know that. So you're going to submit?'

'I am. Soon as I can get the first three chapters edited.'

'Perfect. What did Dad actually say?' Tom was still hesitating, and she pushed on. 'Come on, as your publicist you know I won't stop until I've got something I can use.'

'He said he'd set fire to his books in the shop himself if I didn't have a go.'

'That good, hey?' Olivia was enjoying Tom's relaxation, the delight he was trying to shrug off and that she already knew meant the world to him. 'I want a signed copy. I might even read it.'

Chapter Seventeen

'You've had another mad idea, haven't you?' Tom was making coffee for both of them when Olivia came down for breakfast.

'Why would you think that?'

She was already smiling as she found some yoghurt and added granola. She felt ready for a bacon sandwich but it would keep for another time. She'd stayed awake last night long enough for Tom to finish reading the first stave of *A Christmas Carol*. She'd loved every moment and wished she could make it as wonderful for him when it was her turn to read this evening.

'You've got that glint in your eye again.' He poured her a coffee and added milk, pushing the cup across the table. 'And the answer's yes.'

'To what? You don't even know what I'm going to say.' Olivia cradled the cup in her hands, enjoying his amused expression. 'For all you know you might just have agreed to wear breeches again. In fact, even if that wasn't my idea, it might be now you've said yes to anything.'

'Publicly or privately?' There was a husky note in his voice as he sat down opposite her.

'Let's start with privately. Just in case they don't fit.'

'Oh they fit, Olivia. I know they do. Now tell me your real idea.'

'Okay.' She adored how rumpled, and yes, sexy, he looked first thing. It was a shock to realise how empty, sterile even, her apartment in Manchester would seem once she was back there alone after the holidays. Not a home, not like this. Not without Tom there. 'Let me just check out Twitter and reply to some stuff first. And we need book five for the hashtag today.'

'Ask your dad to choose this time?'

'That's what I was thinking too. There's quite a lot of interest in this "mystery" friend of his now. A few people are speculating that it's you as some are saying they've seen you here.'

Tom shrugged. 'I'm okay with that.' His look became more serious. 'I take it your dad's told you that Christmas Eve will be the last time we open the shop?'

'He has.' A month ago Olivia wouldn't have minded in the least and now the thought made her feel sad. Yet another thing changing and one she was no longer sure she liked, even though it was inevitable with the house being sold.

'So why don't we open it every day this week? A last hurrah, so to speak. Five more afternoons.'

'Tom, that's a great idea, I love it. But do you have the time?'

'I do.' He sounded perfectly clear. 'What about you?' He grinned. 'I think I should have some help and you need the experience.'

'I definitely do. And I'd like to help.' Her clients could wait unless it was absolutely urgent; there was just one more to meet with before Christmas Day. She'd much rather be pretending to be a bookseller with Tom right now and that was new for her.

'Come on then, let's hear it. Your mad idea.'

'It ties in perfectly with opening the shop every afternoon.' Olivia was excited about what they might do for her dad and his shop. For Tom. 'I was thinking, why don't we open the house for a couple of hours on Christmas Eve? Dad's coming to stay over for Christmas Day and given his history with the festival and having guests, I thought it could be a lovely way for him to catch up with some friends and say goodbye to the shop.'

'I think that's perfect, Olivia. And I'm sure your dad will too, I can just see him in here or the library, guests all around him.' Tom was wistful, and Olivia was sure he was thinking of the times he had stayed before. 'You don't think it's too much, having people on Christmas Eve? Do you think anyone will actually come?'

'They will if we tweet it but it might be better not to, we don't want to be swamped. I was just thinking of villagers, any friends he wanted to invite. The very last customers.'

'We could even have a go at recreating some of his recipes.' Tom's eyes were gleaming now and it was Olivia's turn to be doubtful.

'Maybe a couple, we don't want to give guests any dodgy combinations right before Christmas.'

'True.' He was stroking a hand over a jaw roughened by an overnight shadow, and she wished she were the one doing it instead. 'I've got a suggestion for the final book too. How about *The Night Before Christmas*? It's a lovely poem and my dad always used to read it to me when I was small.' Tom swallowed. 'Maybe another of our new old traditions?'

'I think that would be wonderful.' Olivia had finished her breakfast and was behind where he sat at the table before she knew it. She'd recognised the anguish when he'd mentioned his father, saw the quick glint of sorrow usually hidden away. Her arms went around Tom's shoulders and his hands covered hers on him, her cheek against the side of his head. 'I'm sorry about your dad.'

'I know. Thank you.' Tom was still, other than his fingers stroking hers.

'You don't have to choose that book. You can have anything.'

'I think I do, I want to. Feels right somehow.'

'Okay.' Olivia was ignoring the instinct to touch her lips to his forehead, follow the shape of his face to his mouth. 'Are you going to trust me with the food for this party?'

'No. Yes. I don't know. How do you expect me to answer that when you're holding me like this?'

'Why do you think I did it?' She'd already let go before his splutter of laughter followed. 'I'll take that as a yes.'

'We'll do it together. If you think I'm letting you loose in this kitchen the night before Christmas then you're crazy.'

'We'll have to go shopping, it'll be too late to get an online order in now. I could ask The Courtyard if they can help too.' Olivia was elated at the opportunity to do this with Tom. For her dad, for the community that had supported him. For Tom, and even for her. 'Wait until you see my supermarket ninja skills, I can be in and out in a flash.'

'Not surprising when you're only visiting the ready-meals aisle. This time will be different.'

'It will. We're buying the mince pies for a start.' Olivia heard Tom's quick laugh as she collected her phone and handbag. 'I've got to go to The Courtyard now anyway to pick up a gift for Annie and Jon's baby before I go and see them. I'll ask whilst I'm there about food.'

'Good idea. Give Annie and Jon my best, it must be a wonderfully exciting time for them.'

Olivia nodded and saw the way Tom pursed his lips. She felt that clench around her heart again at the thought of him going back to a life lived alone, wanting something different for him. Perhaps for both of them.

'I don't mean to presume but would you like their gift to come from both of us?' she asked hesitantly. 'It's just some baby clothes and a new parents pamper set, when they ever get the time. Of course, I understand if you weren't planning to do anything or would rather do it yourself. It's from Dad and I anyway, and we could include you. If you'd like that.'

Tom said nothing at first and she was worried she'd gone too far, had tried to make him feel he was part of something he didn't want or a place he didn't belong.

'I'd love that, Olivia, if you're sure?' His voice caught for a second. 'Annie and Jon have been really good to me since I met them, and then there was that night.' Tom's smile was already returning and she couldn't help her own.

'Of course I'm sure. And I don't expect you to...'

Tom held up a hand. 'We can fight about that later.'

'Promise?'

'Absolutely. Whatever I need to do to make you agree to my terms.' He was already heading for the door too. 'Can't stand around here arguing with you, I've got a final chapter to write.' He blew her a kiss, which seemed to take them both by surprise, and she was still smiling as she left the house.

The food studio at The Courtyard was able to supply some vegetarian canapés and Olivia thanked them gratefully for the last-minute request. She and Tom would need to sort out a proper menu and she texted him from the car before she set off to suggest doing that this evening. He agreed and his cheeky reply was still making her grin when she arrived in town. She bought packs of napkins, plates and cutlery that they could recycle afterwards and settled in a cafe for a while to go through her inbox.

Emails dealt with, she made her way to the maternity unit in the hospital, carrying her gifts. She was sure that Annie and Jon would be inundated with visitors but Annie had been insistent that she come, and Olivia really did want to see the baby before she returned to Manchester on Boxing Day. A helpful nurse pointed the way to a small ward and Olivia quietly made her way in. She spotted Annie in the far corner at once, her auburn curls identifying her, wound into a knot on top of her head. Jon was seated beside her, and he had their daughter in his arms.

Olivia crept nearer, desperate not to wake the baby if she was asleep. There were more visitors clustered around other beds too, the sound of soft chatter filling the ward. She reached down to give Annie a gentle hug. 'Congratulations, we're all so thrilled for you. My dad and Tom send their best. You look wonderful, Annie. Barely even tired.'

'I can assure you I am. Thank you, Liv.' Annie glanced at Jon, who was beaming at her with utter devotion. 'I'm so glad you're here, come and say hello to Hannah Grace.'

'I'm not staying long, you three need your peace.' Olivia stepped around the bed, gave Jon a quick kiss on the cheek. She recognised the peculiar blend of elation and tiredness on his face, knowing that sleep would have been in short supply these past few days. 'Congratulations, Jon.

This one will have you wrapped around her little finger in a flash.'

'She already does. They both do, they're amazing.'

Olivia couldn't miss the wonder in his voice as she bent down to peek at the tiny bundle in his arms. Jon pulled back the blanket to reveal more of a small round face, lashes sweeping down onto pale skin, and a head dusted with red brown hair. She was fast asleep, one tiny finger hooked around Jon's much larger one.

'Oh, Annie, Jon, she's beautiful.' Olivia gulped back the rush of emotion at the sight of the little baby. 'You both must be so happy and relieved to have Hannah here safely after that excitement.'

Olivia saw the adoring look that passed between Annie and Jon. 'We are, absolutely. She's a little small but otherwise healthy and they're keeping a close eye on her. She was only in the neonatal unit for the first night.'

Olivia placed the gift bag on the table close to the bed. 'These are for you, and Hannah, obviously. For when you get home.'

'Thank you, how kind.' Annie looked from the bag back to Olivia. 'Everyone's been so lovely, I can't wait to bring her home – hopefully on Wednesday. There've been a few little hiccups with feeding her but we're definitely getting there now. Jon's dad and step-mum are flying back from their holiday this evening and they so excited to meet her.'

Olivia glanced at Jon, smiling as she saw that if his eyes weren't on Annie, they were on their daughter, still sleeping peacefully in his arms. Olivia refused Annie's offer to draw up a chair as a woman she recognised as Elizabeth Howard from Thorndale arrived in the ward, clutching flowers and beaming. Olivia excused herself and left, not wanting to take up too much of their time.

—

The house was silent when Olivia arrived, carting in her bags of shopping. She briefly wondered if suggesting a party for her dad on Christmas Eve really was a moment of madness, but she was excited by the plans she and Tom were making for him. Tom didn't emerge from library, and she decided not to disturb him, aware that he was writing his final chapter.

The thought made her feel miserable despite her happiness in his achievement, mulling over what he plans he might make for the new year, where he might go next. With his book finished, he would have less of a reason to stay here. She put the shopping away and sat down to upload book five to the Twitter hashtag. Her dad had replied to her earlier message with another selection, and she flicked through the copy he had directed her to:

> For #BradshawsBooksAtChristmas fifth choice Hugh wanted to share Nancy Mitford's #ChristmasPudding with you. Christmas in the Cotswolds anyone? Poor old Fotheringay, not the book he thought!

After the bookshop had closed for the day Tom headed back into the library and the evening was moving on when he reappeared. Olivia was going over the details of a property on her laptop in the sitting room. He was unshaven with red-rimmed eyes, but she recognised the jubilation in his expression as he stuck his head around the door.

'Well?' She drew out the word, saving the details of the property and putting her laptop aside.

He nodded slowly. 'Yep. One hundred and twenty-two thousand words. More to add but that's the draft.'

'Congratulations.' Olivia was on her feet and hugging Tom almost before she'd realised, holding him tightly. He lifted her off her feet, spinning her around in the hall until they were both laughing. 'I'm so happy for you.'

'Thanks, Olivia.' He set her down, grinning, and followed her into the sitting room. 'It feels amazing, although this could be the point when my thinking the manuscript is utter rubbish starts kicking in.'

'Maybe leave it alone for a while and then go back.' She reached for her laptop, keeping her next words casual on purpose. 'You do know there's no reason to rush off and leave. The house, I mean. Just making sure you haven't forgotten that my dad said you can stay as long as you like. Until the sale is finalised anyway.'

'I know, it's very good of him.' Tom sank down onto the sofa, tipped his head back and yawned. 'Good of you both.'

'Not me.' Olivia refreshed the browser and found the property but her attention was on Tom, enjoying watching him. 'I haven't got anything to complain about. I'm sharing with someone who was apparently voted the fourth sexiest man in breeches back in the day and it turns out he can cook too. Why would I want you to go?'

'Good to know I have my uses.' His eyes remained closed but she saw his smile.

'We should celebrate.'

'Celebrate what?'

'You finishing your draft, that's what.'

'I'll settle for another of your amazing cocktails and a quiet night being read *A Christmas Carol* to by you.' He opened his eyes. 'How does that sound?'

'Pretty darn perfect, I'd say.' She glanced at the property on her screen. 'But first I have a tiny bit of work to finish and then we should plan this party for my dad properly.'

'No problem. You do your work and I'll sort supper. We can chat whilst we're eating.'

'You sure? You're not too tired to cook?'

'No.' Tom threw her a wink as he stood up. 'Don't think it'll exhaust me to pierce the film on one of those meals in the fridge.'

'I'm so happy to have converted you.' Olivia was merry as he headed out of the room. 'Welcome to the club.'

–

Tom didn't have his phone glued to his hand quite like Olivia usually did and it was lying on the kitchen table the following morning. They'd gone to bed late after sharing cocktails to celebrate him finishing the first draft. Olivia had read aloud the second stave of *A Christmas Carol* and thoroughly enjoyed it.

She had been nervous to begin with, reading to an actor of such experience and success after not having read aloud since Ellie was small. Olivia had faltered a couple of times and he'd offered encouragement, told her how great she sounded and that he appreciated being able to just listen, to enjoy the text. Tom had been stretched out on the sofa the whole time and they'd teased one another about his being asleep, though she knew he was anything but.

He had nipped down to the shop to bring more milk just now and her attention was caught by a message on his phone that she saw was from her dad. She didn't mean to read it, but the first two words were unmistakeable.

> Happy birthday, Tom. Sending you all my best, Hugh

The message had Olivia hurriedly searching for Tom's Wikipedia page on her own phone and she soon saw that her dad was right. Today was Tom's birthday and her mind darted ahead to the day she had planned. There was some unavoidable work she needed to do before Christmas, then she'd intended to go shopping this morning and help Tom in the shop later.

Interest in their Twitter Christmas reading choices was still growing, and they'd already had a decent number of visitors yesterday, all of whom had bought books. Tom had told her last night that he'd been recognised again, and Olivia managed to get out of him that people were interested to hear of his writing and had appreciated the chance to chat with him.

He was soon back and putting the milk in the fridge. Olivia saw him glance at his phone as she pretended to be busy with hers and he picked it up, sliding it casually into a pocket. She'd already had an idea about how they might celebrate his birthday and it meant that she would need to shop on her own. She made an excuse to do with work and hurried off to change.

Having settled in town in a little sushi restaurant, she caught up with business emails. Everything seemed to be running well and her assistant had copied her in on some correspondence that Olivia needed to be aware of. They'd had notice of a few properties possibly coming up for sale and she made appointments to view them straight after New Year. She always preferred to see a property in person if possible, before it came onto the open market.

Tom was in the shop when she returned to Thorndale and she did her best to hide some of the ingredients she'd bought in the fridge, adding in a couple of large boxes of canapés that were for the gathering on Christmas Eve. She joined him in the shop but it was fairly quiet, so she excused herself and returned to the house after an hour or so.

She knew Tom was planning to close up at five p.m. and she wanted to be ready, hoping he would not mind what she was doing for him. This evening could be another friendly one like those that had gone before, or it could change their relationship into something quite different.

In the sitting room Olivia gathered everything she wanted for later and returned to the kitchen to prepare ingredients. She just had time to shower and change into a high-necked dress – navy with a simple floral pattern, an asymmetrical skirt and a small cut-out on the back that lifted it from the ordinary into something more chic.

She was in the kitchen whisking olive oil with mustard powder and egg yolks to make mayonnaise when Tom rushed in, shoulders hunched against the cold, and he shut the back door with a sharp bang. He was barely inside the room before he stopped dead.

'What's all this?' His look raced from her, standing at the range, to the table set for two, candles already lit, a playlist going. 'Sorry, I think I must be in the wrong house. This looks amazing, should I go out and come back in again? Will I hear the ping of the microwave if I do?'

'Ha ha.' Olivia propped the whisk on the bowl and walked towards him. Saw him taking in her altered appearance, the dress, her heels, and she felt the anticipation of what she was doing for him dance across her skin, nerves fluttering in her stomach. What if he didn't like it? Hated it?

In front of him now, she didn't hesitate, finding enough assurance for both of them. She kissed his cheek, rested a hand on his shoulder.

'Happy birthday.' She drew back, feeling the imprint of the shadow of his stubble on her skin. 'I thought it was my turn to cook something nice for you. Let me pour you a drink.'

Olivia saw his astonishment shift into a delighted recognition of what she was doing for him, and already knew her surprise was a success from the gleam in his eyes. She turned, about to fill the glasses she had left ready.

'Thank you.' Tom gently caught her hand, delaying her. 'How did you know it was my birthday?'

'As your wife and publicist, I would've thought it was obvious.' Her hand was still wrapped inside his. 'Actually I have to confess my dad texted you and I was there when the message popped up on your phone. I didn't mean to read it on purpose, I just saw those first words.'

'I'm glad you did. What are you piercing the film on for us tonight?' Tom's amused gaze was wandering round the room, searching for the ready meal they both knew he wouldn't find.

'You're going to have find a new joke to flog to death after tonight. Would you like that drink or not?' Olivia shook his hand lightly, reminding him they were still fixed together.

'Can you give me ten minutes or so? You look wonderful and I'd like to change. I look like a scruffy writer who's spent the day shifting old books around.'

'Of course.' She finally freed her hand from his. 'I'll be down here, slaving over a hot stove. Good start, by the way. The compliment.'

'Just don't set fire to anything whilst I'm gone. Then I'd love that drink.'

'And then you say that.'

Chapter Eighteen

Olivia was still smiling as she finished the mayonnaise she was preparing and when Tom re-joined her, she poured two glasses of champagne and passed him one.

'Cheers.'

'Are we celebrating?'

'Of course we are.' She clinked her glass against his. 'It's your birthday and birthdays should always be special.'

She took in his outfit, appreciating how the white shirt with its pattern of tiny blue spots printed onto the cotton highlighted his eyes. His hair was still damp from a shower he must have taken at lightning speed. Pretty cold too if she knew anything about the hot water system in this house. An awareness of the change in atmosphere in the kitchen – the room in which they'd spent so much time together – thrummed through her. The candles she had stuffed in empty wine bottles were flickering gently, the air heavy with an intimacy they had shared only once before.

'It's been a while since I celebrated mine. I've forgotten how, I suppose.'

'Then I'm even more glad that we're having a party tonight.'

'A party?' Tom's glance shot around the room again. 'What kind of party? Who else have you invited?'

'The surprise kind.' At least, Olivia was aiming for surprise, remembering his comment from their snowball fight about never having been much into games. A childhood spent caring for a sick parent must have put paid to much of that. She hoped he wouldn't find her plans upsetting or boring. 'I'm not telling you anything else and don't go into the sitting room until we've eaten. And it's just us.'

'I like the sound of that.' Tom brought his glass of champagne over to her at the range. She already had ingredients prepared: fries ready to go in, mussels cleaned and closed, white wine measured for the dish and parsley chopped. 'What are you making?'

'Checking up on me?'

'No.' He was behind her, his head peeking over her shoulder, glass in one hand. 'Just curious.'

'You could stand beside me.' She was distracted now, breathing in the ginger and cinnamon cologne on his skin, the one he'd worn once before. The minutes he'd spent upstairs hadn't allowed for shaving and she felt the brush of his stubble against her cheek again. 'Not behind.'

'I could.' He didn't move. His mouth was dangerously close to her ear and she felt his breath fluttering across her neck. 'Which would you prefer?'

This was the moment, the decision they had been building up to these past weeks, had been good at avoiding. They'd tried to keep things uncomplicated when they'd always been anything but, since that very first evening when they'd flirted their way through a time they would never have shared had it not been for the storm. Olivia also knew that planning a party such as this for Tom's birthday – with champagne, candles and the food she had chosen to make him – was a step into something much less simple and one they both wanted to take.

She turned around. Saw his eyes narrow, watching hers moving to his mouth, to the lips which had captured hers once before and knew already how to arouse her. She heard the change in his breathing, the way hers shortened to match it. But she wasn't going to rush this, to make it something and maybe nothing, over before the evening had barely begun. She reached up to cup his face with her hand, smoothing the roughened skin as his lips widened into a lazy smile.

'I can't cook whilst you're standing right there.' She moved her thumb to his mouth, traced the outline of his lips, saw the pulse pounding in his throat. 'Go away.'

'What if I don't want to.' His voice was low and she heard the unevenness in it, knew he liked what they were doing as much as she did. 'I'm not used to putting myself in someone else's hands and I'm beginning to discover how much fun it can be. Maybe you need some help?'

'Actually, yes.' Olivia turned around, ignoring him on purpose, acutely aware of him placing the glass on the worktop. He rested his hands on her shoulders before sliding them unhurriedly down her back to her waist, drawing her against him with an ease that felt intimate and tender all at once. 'If you want to eat then you could let go of me. Because you doing this is definitely not helping. With the meal at least.'

She was finding it nearly impossible now to remember the recipe she wanted to cook for him, especially when his reply was a brief kiss he dropped on her neck below her ear. He leant against the table to watch, glass back in hand, eyes intense and urgent whenever they found hers. Despite their teasing, she was a perfectly competent cook, and they were sitting down with candlelight and *moules-frites* within twenty minutes.

Tom topped up their champagne, reaching for her hand across the table and lifting it to kiss her fingers. 'Thank you. This birthday is turning out to be unforgettable.'

'I hope for all the right reasons.'

'Oh, I think so.'

Olivia held up her glass to him. 'Here's to surprise parties, rediscovering birthdays and you, Tom. And your book. May it fly off every shelf it ever sits on.'

'That's something to hope for.' He was staring at her and she saw the emotion hovering in his eyes, the wonder of what she was doing for him. 'And you, Liv, for this. For thinking of me.' His gaze swept over the table, the champagne, the candles, before landing back on hers, and she laughed. 'What?'

'You called me Liv. Only my family and a few friends call me that.'

'It's how I think of you.' Tom was still holding her hand. 'Olivia suits you but Liv is softer, more like the real you.'

'Softer?' She slipped her hand free. Much as she liked holding his, drinking champagne and eating were trickier with just the one. She loved watching Tom tuck into the meal she had prepared for him, discarding mussel shells into a bowl. 'Don't let anyone else hear you saying that or my reputation as a tough career woman will be gone in a second.'

'You're only tough when you need to be.' He dunked a few fries in the mayonnaise, held them out to her. 'And if I'd known you could cook like this I'd never have gone near the kitchen.'

'Why do you think I didn't let on,' Olivia replied smoothly as she took them. 'I'm not just a pretty face.'

'That's the last thing I would have used to describe you.'

'Thanks a lot!' She chucked one of her fries at him and it landed on the floor, just missing his shirt.

'I meant, *Olivia*' – she smiled at the emphasis Tom placed on her name – 'that you're one of the smartest and most striking people I've ever met.'

'You think?' She didn't bother trying to dismiss the pleasure his comment brought. 'You were an actor for years, think of all those fabulous co-stars you must have had. And I like it when you call me Liv.'

'Good, because I want to carry on.'

'Does that mean I can call you Harrington?'

'Depends on whether you want me to answer or not.'

'Not. I don't always need you to be talking, even though I do love your voice.' Oh, she'd said that out loud and she laughed, swallowing a fizzing mouthful of champagne that made her blink.

'You do?' Tom was pleased and Olivia's pulse leapt again at the look in his eyes. 'Good, because it's my turn to read to you tonight. Stave three of *A Christmas Carol* or had you forgotten?'

'Of course I haven't.' They'd finished eating and she stood up, waved away Tom's offer of help as she dumped their plates in the sink. 'But first we have more of your party to enjoy.'

'Oh? That sounds interesting. If that was our main course, what do you have for dessert?'

'Wait and see. Give me a few minutes and then join me in the sitting room? And no washing-up, this time it will have to keep until tomorrow.'

'I'll refill our glasses.'

'Perfect.'

Olivia had already lit the fire in the sitting room so it was lovely and cosy, the lights on the Christmas tree shimmering between the two windows. Tom had joined her by the time she had spread everything she wanted on the floor. She kicked her heels off, surrounded by battered old boxes she'd unearthed from a cupboard.

'Games?' He dropped down beside her. 'Seriously?'

'Absolutely, I thought they'd be fun. But only if you want to.' She pointed to the boxes. 'Which one would you like to play first? Operation, Cluedo or Buckaroo?'

Tom's reply came with a shrug, a shake of his head. 'I've never played any of them before.'

'Really?' Olivia's hand found his and held it. 'We don't have to if you'd rather not.' She paused. 'I was just trying to give you some fun.'

'I know that.' He shuffled up until his arm was against hers. 'It's brilliant, it really is. Maybe you should choose for us? And obviously let me win as it's my birthday.'

'Buckaroo, then.' She started to unpack the game from its box. 'It's easy, we just take it in turns to load the donkey until he bucks everything off. But there's no way I'm going to let you win because it's your birthday. I've played loads of times before, so I'm bound to be better than you.'

'You think?' Tom's voice lowered as he moved away.

'Definitely.'

She wasn't. He beat her three times in a row until she was protesting and accusing him of cheating, a claim she could not back up when he demanded evidence. She reached for Operation instead and he was winning until their fourth go, finally making a mistake that set off the buzzer. Olivia yelled with excitement, knocking the box over in the process.

'We haven't finished yet, I'm going to thrash you at Cluedo.' She was triumphant as she gathered the pieces of the game before they were lost and put them away.

'Oh, now this you're definitely not. I might not have played before but as you have pointed out previously, I'm about to be a bestselling novelist and solving murders is my speciality.'

'We'll see about that.'

She set the game up, a newer version enabling them to play with just two instead of the usual three players required. She won and when Tom demanded a rematch, she won that one as well and he accused her of cheating and trying to ruin his career before it even got underway. They had to agree to disagree and packed the games away, devouring the macarons Olivia had bought for dessert, laughing over her decision not to produce a pudding she had made from scratch.

Her phone was nearby and she reached for it when she saw a message flash up on the screen. She'd turned her email notifications off for tonight. 'Sorry, bad habit, I know. Just catching up with Ellie, I keep forgetting she's four hours behind us.'

'How are they doing? Tobago must be a wonderful place to spend Christmas.'

'They're great, let me show you.' Olivia slid across the floor to settle beside Tom. 'Her dad's already taken them out hiking in the rainforest and they're going diving on Christmas Eve. Perfect for Ellie, she'll never want to come home.'

'Are you okay, Liv? Not missing her too much?'

Olivia relished the solid feel of Tom beside her, the warmth of his body against hers. 'I'm fine, thank you. I suppose I'm used to it.' His arm was in the way and he lifted it, tucking it around her to draw her close as she swiped through the images Ellie had sent. Olivia felt his fingers lightly stroking her shoulder, all the more distracting for his gentleness and understanding.

She put the phone down. She had one final surprise and reached around the sofa to bring it from its hiding place, passing him the gift-wrapped box. 'Happy birthday. Again.'

'You got me a gift?' Tom took the box, and she was delighted she had managed to surprise him once more.

'Yes. It's not very original, I'm afraid; I didn't have much time. Had I really been your wife I would've been much better prepared but considering I only found out about your birthday this morning I think I'm not doing too badly.'

'I think you're doing perfectly.' Tom shrugged; his thanks caught somewhere amongst his amazement. He undid the box and lifted out a bottle of bourbon, staring at it appreciatively. 'Thank you, it's a favourite.'

'For your Old Fashioneds. I did think about giving you the espresso but just coffee as a gift seemed a bit mean.'

'It's wonderful and very thoughtful of you to bother.'

'My pleasure. It was either that or the Grinch socks I saw today, and I was so tempted by the socks.'

Tom leant across, silencing her with a light kiss he placed on her mouth. 'Shame,' he murmured against her lips. 'I might've even have worn them for you.'

'With what?'

He drew back and she missed him the moment he moved. 'Anything you like.'

'Oh, now I'm really wishing I'd bought them.' Olivia felt as if she was bubbling over with the fun they were having, the expectation hovering between them.

'Maybe you can give me them for Christmas.'

Her thoughts darted ahead, to bringing her dad home here for the last time. To thoughts of leaving Thorndale and returning to her silent, city apartment, and Tom moving somewhere else. She already knew she was going to miss him. After that first evening in the pub she had never expected to see him again, and yet he had found a way into her heart and this home in a way she wouldn't have believed possible in such a short time.

'What would you really like for Christmas, Tom?'

'More of this might be nice.' He lifted a hand, indicating their almost empty champagne glasses, the fire, the twinkling Christmas tree and the games not yet put away, the gift-wrapped bottle of bourbon. 'More time with you.'

'I can't wrap that up for you and put it under a tree.' Olivia's eyes were clinging to his, trying not to tell him everything she felt, not yet.

'Pity,' he murmured. He stretched out a leg, touching his foot against hers. 'I'd so enjoy unwrapping you.'

'I'm starting to realise how good you are with words. Who knew?' She moved so that her foot was on his leg, sliding to his knee, aware of him watching.

'Thanks for that. Next you'll be telling me I could make a career out of it.' He pointed to the copy of *A Christmas Carol* she'd left on the sofa last night. 'Shall we?'

'I'd love to.'

Tom stood up and she joined him on the sofa, aware that he was in no rush either to hurry their evening into something different, happy to draw out the anticipation for as long as possible. He shifted until she was nestled in the crook of his arm, the book in his right hand, her feet curled beneath her.

'Are you sure you won't fall asleep?'

'Certain.' She was far too aware of him against her for that. His head tucked on top of hers as he began to read about the second of the spirits and Scrooge waking in the middle of a snore, which made her smile and Tom chuckle.

When he had finished reading about Scrooge's vision of a phantom coming towards him, they were still sitting in the same position and Olivia moved first, leaning into Tom as she stretched. 'That was beautiful. Thank you.' Her hand was still covering his and she lifted it, bringing it to her mouth to kiss his fingers, letting her lips linger for a moment against his skin. 'You really do have the most gorgeous voice.'

'So you keep telling me. Thank you.'

'I can't help it if I find you attractive, can I?'

'Not just the voice, then?'

'Well, it's probably your best feature. Argh!' She wriggled away as his hand shot to her ribs, trying to tickle her.

'What, so you haven't noticed my devastating charm and handsome looks before? I got that from a review.'

'No, sorry. Are you sure it was yours?' Olivia turned around until she was facing him, kneeling on the sofa. 'You're not bad looking, I'll give you that, but as for the charm...'

Tom pulled her onto his lap and she was laughing until she saw the intensity of his look, scattering her senses as her pulse leapt. He tilted his head, his mouth close to hers as he held her shoulders.

'Liv, it's never really been just friends for me, much as I tried to make it stay that way.' His words were quiet, loaded with uncertainty and truthfulness. She had seen it time and again these past weeks, his eyes confessing one thing whilst his words had teased her, laughed with her, told her something else.

'Me neither. I thought I could keep it that way too.' Her breath caught at the expression of longing on his face.

They'd both tried to hold onto sense and instead had found the beginnings of a life together, sharing this house day by day. She had tried not to let him in, to make a place for him in the life she had thought she preferred to live alone, and it was too late, now, for that. He was already a part of her world and Olivia wasn't sure she wanted to go back to the one she didn't share with him.

'So. What happens next?'

She inched nearer to brush her lips across his cheek, whisper against his ear. 'You're the novelist, you work it out.'

'I told you, I wouldn't write a scene quite like this. My detective's doing his best not to get involved with his bookseller but she's really getting under his skin.'

'I want to hear more about that.' Her lips had reached Tom's mouth now and she felt his hands tightening on her, holding her close. 'How exactly?'

'I'm not telling you.'

Olivia let her fingers drift across his shoulder, tracing the shape of the muscles she felt beneath his shirt. 'Show me then?'

Tom's hand went to her neck and he pulled her in for the kiss they had both been waiting for. It was better than before. This time there was understanding and deeper feeling, as well as that same explosion of passion finding them again. She was on his lap, her hands roaming across his chest. She felt herself falling into the sensation of being held by him, their breathing in between urgent kisses rapid and rough.

Her fingers were undoing the buttons on his shirt and he helped her to tug it off, tossing it to the sofa. Her gaze fell to take in his firm chest, dark hair scattered with grey reaching to his flat stomach and disappearing beneath the waistband of his jeans. He was watching her looking at him and she took her time, slowly reaching out to touch him until his hands went impatiently to her back, tugging her against him.

'Should we take this upstairs?' Olivia heard the catch in her voice as he reached around her shoulders for the zip on her dress. She felt him smile against her neck, his mouth teasing as he kissed his way to her ear to murmur against it.

'Definitely. This sofa is way too uncomfortable for a second night.'

Reluctantly she untangled herself from him and stood up hurriedly, offering her hand. He took it, kissing her again as he walked her backwards to the hall. He let her go as they reached the staircase, the zip on her dress already down. She held the dress together for a second, and then let it slide from her shoulders, his eyes following as it reached the carpet. She stepped away from the gathering of navy material at her feet, leaving her in lilac and lace, his gaze roaming back up her body to pause at her mouth.

'I've been thinking about taking that off you all evening.' Tom surprised her as he scooped her into his arms and set off up the stairs. 'You're stunning.'

'So are you.' Olivia couldn't keep herself from touching him, exploring his chest, tracing a line of kisses across his shoulder. 'My room or yours?'

'Not the landing? I still haven't forgotten about you lying in wait for me that night.' There was laughter in his voice even as his heated gaze scorched her. 'Both.'

Chapter Nineteen

Olivia had darted downstairs for her phone during the early hours whilst Tom was asleep, always mindful of Ellie and her travels. She'd left it beside the bed and answered without thinking when it rang in the morning. He had disappeared, promising to return with breakfast, and Olivia was already missing him. She had never woken in this room before and she stared at the unfamiliar view, the corniced ceilings, floral wallpaper and the faded curtains closed against a view of the garden.

'So it had better be a good one. Your excuse.' Gina sounded sharp and disgruntled down the line.

'What?' Olivia was still feeling dreamy, and she shifted the phone to check the time. Ten thirty! How had she slept so long? She had no more words as her friend's clear voice resounded in her ear.

'For missing our Christmas brunch. Because I'm guessing that's what you're doing as I'm sitting here in The Courtyard, all nice and cosy, and you're, well, where exactly? Not here, obviously. I'm thinking it's work?'

'I'm so sorry, Gina, I had no idea it was this time already.' Olivia yawned, it swiftly turning into a laugh as Gina hurried on.

'Are you where I think you are, Ms Bradshaw? You sound as though you've just woken up. Have you and that gorgeous man finally sorted yourselves out? Really?'

The gorgeous man himself appeared in the bedroom, barefoot and carrying a tray, wearing his unbuttoned shirt above jeans. Olivia drank in the sight, noticing the way Tom was looking at her as he put the tray down beside the bed. He leaned over to kiss her and she tried to bat him away, stifling a giggle she hoped Gina wouldn't hear as the duvet slipped from her shoulders.

'You are!' Gina was managing to sound both astonished and delighted, and her throaty chuckle quickly followed. 'Well don't drag yourself away on my account. It's only forty miles or so that I've driven to see you.'

'I'm so sorry.' Olivia thought rapidly. 'Can you give me half an hour or so, please? And then I'll be over, I promise.'

'Of course. Now we've got a whole new topic to talk about. I'll order you a large drink, you're going to need it.'

Olivia swiftly ended the call now that Tom had discarded the shirt and jeans and was back in bed with her. She couldn't stay, couldn't let her friend down a second time and she laughingly tried to evade his hands as he reached for her.

'Morning. You look beautiful.'

She wasn't trying too hard to escape at all now and gave up entirely when his hand brushed the hair from her face, and he dropped a kiss on her mouth.

'Thank you.' She felt it too, basking in the gentleness in his face and the glint in his eyes. Her hand cupped his cheek and she ran her fingers over the roughness she found there, loving being able to touch him like this. 'I'm sure I've got stubble rash.'

'Not from where I'm sitting. But we could try again.'

'I can't, I'm blaming you entirely for making me forget the brunch I should be having right now with Gina.'

Olivia still couldn't believe she had neglected her friend, her body filled with an easy languor that was new.

'Oh, so now it's my fault?' Tom's expression was roguish as he leant back against the pillows, hands behind his head, the duvet around his waist. 'You were in no hurry to leave, as I recall.'

'Totally your fault, I would've been up hours ago if you hadn't...' She was half out of the bed as he made a playful lunge for her. 'I've got to go, I need to have a shower. I am sorry about breakfast.' She looked at the tempting tray of goodies he had brought them, none as enticing as him in this moment. 'I'm so hungry.'

'Still?'

She was smiling as she pulled on Tom's shirt. Her dress must be at the bottom of the stairs where she had left it. 'Well...'

'Should I join you in the shower?'

She crossed the room, brushing her lips across his mouth and relishing the look in his eyes as they held hers, his hand light on her face. 'No. I think we both know that ancient contraption isn't made for two. And you'd only distract me again.'

'Enjoy your brunch. I'll be in the shop and if you're still hungry afterwards I can probably help with that.'

Olivia darted from the room before temptation proved too difficult to resist. She was out of the house and hugging Gina twenty-five minutes later, a grin plastered on her face that wasn't only due to seeing her best friend again. They separated to sit down. The Courtyard restaurant and studios were packed with Christmas shoppers, cheery seasonal music adding to the festive atmosphere.

'I'm so sorry to have kept you waiting.'

'It's fine.' Gina was staring at Olivia with an expression full of amusement. 'I was glad to get out of the house and we both know it's most unlike you to forget an appointment. So. What's going on?'

It hit Olivia then, the tumult of emotions running through her after the freezing dash down the lane, in the quite literally cold light of day. Happiness tinged with anxiety, fear that she was repeating a past mistake. 'I'm really not sure.' She took a gulp of the promised Bloody Mary already waiting. 'We're friends, Gina, and we get on really well. Then last night, things changed.'

'Changed how? Apart from the obvious, of course. That I don't need to hear.'

'It was Tom's birthday. I gave him a little party and we went from there.' Olivia thought of his life, the details he had shared and trusted her with. 'He's not really used to celebrating birthdays and we both enjoyed it.'

'So what are you going to do about it, Liv? I haven't seen you this lit up since forever. Even Jared didn't make you this dewy-eyed and forgetful, and you were crazy about him.'

'I have absolutely no idea.' Olivia knew she sounded dejected. A waiter was at the table to take their order, collecting menus and promising to return with water. 'It's just so complicated.'

'Why?' Gina sounded perfectly reasonable as she started on her non-alcoholic Christmas cocktail. 'You like each other, you're both single, you're both here.'

'I have to get the house cleared, make sure Dad's settled, go back to Manchester and Tom will have to find somewhere…'

'Find somewhere what? Go on.' Gina was getting impatient.

'Find somewhere to live,' Olivia finished tamely. 'He'll probably be going back to London in the new year.'

'So? It's only a couple of hours from Manchester to London. And does it have to be London? You told me he was writing again, surely he can do that from anywhere? Even your apartment.' Gina tilted her glass to Olivia. 'Why are you creating problems where they don't exist? Or is there something you're not telling me?'

Olivia took a second mouthful of her drink, waving at Sam Stewart, who was over on another table sharing coffee with a friend who also had a child on her lap.

'Come on. What are you not saying?'

Olivia felt the euphoria of last night already disappearing, the reality of her and Tom's separate circumstances pressing in. Her head was starting to ache, the champagne, lack of sleep and the anxiety chasing away the bliss, leaving dread in its wake. 'I'm worried I'm doing it again,' she mumbled. 'Leaping in with both feet, falling for someone who's going to walk right out of my life and leave me behind. I barely know Tom, not really.'

'Liv, you don't know he's going to walk out. Why would you assume it's an end and not a beginning?' Gina paused while the waiter placed a bottle of water and glasses on the table, thanking him. 'You're older and wiser now, it wouldn't be fair to judge Tom against Jared.'

'Older yes, I don't feel much wiser right now.'

'Look, lots of us had a Jared in our lives, someone we were crazy about who made the world shine a bit brighter for a while, and you've told me before you never really expected it to last. You married him on a whim and at least you have Ellie. This isn't the same. Or at least, it doesn't have to be.'

'What if Tom tells me it's a mistake, Gina?' Olivia swallowed the sudden lump in her throat as she felt the fear running across her skin like a shiver. 'I don't want to go through all that again. Dating someone and not getting involved is fine, especially with my workload, but this could be so much worse. The upheaval, the effort. The end.'

Gina was sympathetic. 'It's only natural you'd want to be cautious. I haven't forgotten what it was like for you with Jared, him off living his life and you left at home to pick up the pieces and keep the show on the road.'

'Yeah.' Olivia pulled a face at the irony of Gina's remark. 'So he literally could be on the road. Just not the one I was on with Ellie.'

'Sorry.' Gina rolled her eyes. 'Poor choice of words but you know what I mean.'

'Jared and I were always heading in different directions and in too much of a rush at the start to see it. I thought I'd cured myself of being impulsive, especially where relationships are concerned. And now it feels like it might be happening again.'

'You're not really saying you don't want to see Tom again after Christmas, are you?' Gina couldn't disguise her surprise. 'Give yourselves a chance, Liv. Take a look in the mirror. You're glowing and we both know how rarely something like this comes along. Even forgetting all the fame stuff, which doesn't seem to be a big problem.'

'It could be.' Olivia sighed. 'It's not as though we're really going anywhere, we're almost always in the house on our own. It's pretence, a pause in our regular lives.'

'What is?'

'Staying at my dad's. We're playing at house; normal life doesn't look like this for either of us. I've been trying to encourage him to be a bit more open about his writing and if his book takes off then he could be right back there with all the attention, and he won't have room for me. And I'm already too busy, I don't have the time to give to a relationship. I don't need someone texting me every hour wanting to know when I'll be home and what's for dinner. Wanting me to pick up after them and keep their life in order.'

Olivia felt disloyal for even saying the words. Somehow she had a picture of how life might be with Tom in it, and she knew it wouldn't be the one she had just described. They both liked their space and their time alone, and when they came together it was fun and easy, as if they'd been sharing together for years rather than weeks. And then, last night. Another step and one already making her feelings for him even more complex.

'So you don't do it. You lay down the ground rules at the start and you stick to them. It doesn't sound like he'd be so bad to live with.'

'You make it sound so simple.' Could it be, really, for her and Tom? Olivia felt a flicker of hope amongst the doubt, and it wasn't easy to dismiss the sense in Gina's words. Maybe it would be foolish to assume she and Tom couldn't last beyond Christmas. Maybe she was rushing, but what if it was in the *wrong* direction? Away from him when she should be giving them a chance.

Their meals had arrived, and she and Gina thanked the waiter as he poured water and left them alone. Gina's smile was caring. 'I understand why you're worried and trying to compare your relationship with Jared against a possible one with Tom. But they aren't the same, Liv. Not the same men. Would you want to be held up against Tom's ex-wife and cast aside because of something she'd done?'

'Of course not.' Olivia knew how unfair that would be as she picked at a forkful of her food.

'I know why you're doing this, it's perfectly obvious.' Gina finished her cocktail and put the glass down, her look unflinching on Olivia. 'Because you've fallen in love with him. That's the part you're not telling me and you don't need to, I can see it.'

Olivia's mouth opened and Gina held up a hand. 'Don't bother denying it. If it was just a bit of fun, a pause as you said, then you'd be sitting here all merry and telling me what a good time you'd had together. Instead you're agonising about whether to end whatever it is you have before he does it first.'

Olivia's forehead was in her hands. 'I knew I should've let you have brunch on your own,' she said helplessly. 'You talk far too much sense for this hour of the morning.'

'Morning?' Gina smirked. 'You surely don't need me to remind you it's practically midday? It must have been quite the night. Despite the glow you look exhausted.' She paused, serious again. 'I think you should tell Tom how you feel, Liv.'

'I'm not doing that, at least not yet.' Olivia was vehement as she reached for her glass. She wasn't quite so hungry now. 'He'll probably be horrified and run a mile.'

'Like you're threatening to do, you mean? What if, and here's the thing you haven't thought of, he feels the same?' Gina's next words were kind. 'Only you and Tom can decide if you can have a life together after Christmas and you're not going to find that out by pretending it's only a pause. Have the conversation before it's too late.'

Olivia nodded doubtfully and Tom wasn't mentioned again as they caught up on their news. Once their meals were finished, Gina stood up.

'I'll be back in a minute. Let's have something sweet to finish, I totally trust you to choose me the perfect dessert if they come over whilst I'm gone.'

'Absolutely. About a billion calories at least.' Out of habit, Olivia pulled her phone from her bag; she'd barely looked at it this morning. She turned her email notifications back on and saw the number piling up without opening the app and her response was a sigh. There were a couple of text messages and she ignored those to listen to her voicemails first.

She had the dessert menu in her other hand, idly perusing it as she played the oldest voicemail first. It was from her assistant asking her to call him back and she rolled her eyes; that was the last thing she felt like doing in this moment. Her mind was full of Tom, and it was a stretch to even decide on a pudding right now. She wanted to go back to the house, to see him and find out how he was feeling too, after last night. She wanted to be with him, and the thought was a happy one which began to banish the doubts.

The second voicemail was also from her assistant and he sounded concerned, asking her to call him as soon as possible. He'd rung nearly an hour ago and Olivia was impatient as she waited for the call to connect. Gina was back and Olivia pointed to her phone with apologetic eyes. Gina nodded as she sat down. The restaurant was still packed, and Olivia had to ask her assistant to repeat himself once he'd picked up, not certain she had heard him correctly even second time around.

'What? It can't be!' Her eyes widened in horror and she was already fumbling for the iPad in her bag, almost dropping it in her haste as it clattered onto the table. 'I scheduled that myself and it's tomorrow, I'm sure. It was awfully close to Christmas but it was the only time they could give me.'

Worry was already racing through her mind, shock making her heart bump as anxiety began to prickle on palms becoming damp. She frantically brought up her calendar, staring at it in dread and knew her assistant was correct as she checked the confirmation email as well. She'd planned her last online client meeting before Christmas for this morning, not tomorrow as she'd thought, somehow assuming it wouldn't have clashed with her and Gina's brunch. In her distraction and fun with Tom for his birthday, she'd clean forgotten to check.

Utterly mortified, Olivia apologised as her assistant explained that he'd managed to reach Julian and her business partner had taken the meeting with a demanding and important new client instead. Her assistant had covered her back by saying that she had been unavoidably detained, and she knew Julian would be wondering exactly what was responsible for this most uncharacteristic mistake.

She apologised again, thanking her assistant gratefully for dealing with the situation and trying to look after her in the process. She was already typing an email to Julian to thank him too, suggesting that they speak later so she could explain her oversight. Gina was waiting patiently and had ordered dessert for both of them.

'I'm so sorry, Gina' Olivia muttered, trying to compose herself as she put the iPad away, her eyes still flicking over her phone in case there were other horrors waiting. She just didn't do this. She didn't ever let the balls drop, she made certain to keep everything in the air, it was how she got by and stayed in control. 'What a rotten brunch this is turning out to be for you.'

'Not really. I've had worse meals out, you know that, what with four boys to bring up. At least we got to see each other and catch up.'

'I promise I'll make it up to you.' Olivia smiled weakly, her heart still finding its way back to normal. 'A spa weekend on me at the very least.'

'You don't need to do that – we've always been there for each other and that won't change, however many brunches you mess up.' Gina reached across the table to squeeze Olivia's hand. 'You made a mistake and missed a meeting. Don't beat yourself up, the sky didn't fall in because you had something else on your mind.'

Gina's voice dropped sympathetically. 'And Liv, however much you love your work and I know you're damn good at it, do you ever think about what all those extra hours cost you? What you might be missing? I understand it makes you feel safe and secure, and that falling in love is so unpredictable, especially when you weren't expecting it. But you can still be the best in the business and have someone wonderful in your life if they come along. It's allowed. You've guarded your heart for a long time now, and just maybe it's time to let someone else have a go.'

Chapter Twenty

Olivia saw the lights on in the annexe when she returned to the house and guessed Tom must be in the shop. Her dad was coming home tomorrow, and she had preparations to do in readiness for his arrival, and then there was book six for the Twitter hashtag to decide upon and tweet. Neither she nor Tom knew how much longer they would be here but it was certain that this would be the last Christmas spent with her dad in this house. The thought was a melancholy one that pressed in on her even more than it had a month ago.

She pushed thoughts of all that aside as she sat at the kitchen table with her laptop. Julian had already replied to her email and she ran her eyes over her other correspondence before calling him. She wanted to go to Tom, to seek him out, and ignored the desire as she settled into work instead, trying to compensate for her mistake.

She was still at the kitchen table when Tom came in, the door shutting noisily behind him. She'd meant to do some cleaning but had decided she needed to be up to speed with work instead. She didn't want any other nasty surprises. Olivia felt his presence like a touch on her skin the second he spoke, unable to forget a moment of last night with him and how they had spent it.

'I didn't see you there, Liv. If I didn't know better I'd think you were trying to scare me off again.'

No, that's me, she wanted to say. Scared of how I feel and what I'm going to do about it. Trying to picture my life with someone as amazing as you in it. How I'd be if you left. He came up behind her and she sensed him hesitate and then his arms went around her shoulders, the chair an awkward barrier between them. Tom leaned around to place a kiss on her cheek.

'It's been a long afternoon without you. I thought you might pop in but obviously you've been busy. The shop was busy too, the word on Twitter has got around and I did quite a few selfies. As my publicist I hope you're happy, I even mentioned my book once or twice.'

'That's nice.' The knowledge that he had been recognised again didn't please her in the way it had before, as she thought of his public life, their separate realities drawing him away from her. 'I decided to stay in the house, I had some unavoidable work to do. And I really should be sorting out my dad's room for him.'

Olivia heard her coolness and wished she hadn't spoken in quite the way she had. Those things were not Tom's responsibility, and she was already doing it – pushing him away and using her fear of being left like before. Maybe it would make the situation easier for both of them, measuring him against her marriage. She ignored the small voice that told her Gina was right and this wasn't fair.

'I would've helped if I'd known.' His arms left her, and he stepped back.

There was worry in his tone and she regretted her words even more, still unable to stop herself from putting more distance between them. 'You can't, it's work. Sorry Tom, could you give me some time?'

'Of course.' He moved away, flicked the light on, making her blink. 'You haven't forgotten about book six, have you? I had a sneaky peek at Twitter and people are wondering. And I've got my choice ready for you.'

'You could just tweet it then.' She pushed her glasses into her hair to run a tired hand over her face. 'I can give you the password.'

'I think it's better coming from you, in your voice. You've written all the others so beautifully.' Tom was at the fridge. 'Glass of water? Wine? I'll make you something.'

'No thanks, I had a coffee earlier.'

He closed the fridge door and crossed the room to turn on the tap. 'Liv, what's up? If I had to make an educated guess, then I'd say it has to do with last night and how you're feeling now about what we did.' He paused. 'Where it leaves us.'

She ignored him for a second, her heart beginning to thud. She was trying to focus on a property she needed to view and it was hopeless, she couldn't think about work with Tom here now and the trace of hurt she'd already recognised in his voice.

'Liv? It won't go away, we have to talk.' Tom put the glass down to pull out a chair opposite her. 'And I don't like how this feels, now.' He went to reach for her hand and she drew it away. 'Okay. I think I'm beginning to see.'

'Can you give me a few minutes to send this email?'

'Of course.'

He sat in silence and she was feeling crowded, the sense of him being in her space, not allowing her the freedom to work in peace. Six minutes later Olivia put the phone down and turned it over, took her glasses off.

'Tom, I, last night, it was…'

His eyes were narrowed on hers, the blue seeming sharpened by surprise. 'Wonderful? Significant? Or a mistake?'

'Possibly all three.'

'Right. Good you've cleared that up for me. If I were answering that question then I would have left out your third point.'

'I don't think we should do it again. I was thinking you were probably feeling the same.' There it was. The opportunity for him to take, to say it was fun, finished. He could walk away and Olivia would make herself get over it, she'd done that before.

'What if I don't feel the same? And are you going to share a reason for this decision with me?'

'Because neither of us live here, not really. This isn't our real life. I have to go back to Manchester and you're probably going to be in London.' She wanted to touch him, to reach out and hold his hand and try to make him understand, hating the hurt she already saw outlined on his face.

'Tom, I believe your book could be a big success and you might decide to act again. And that would be wonderful, and I don't want to be someone holding you back. And I won't be the one left behind again, keeping everything together.'

'Holding me back?' His laugh was harsh. 'I think you mean it the other way around. That I'd be the one holding you back. I've got nothing I can bring to this, to us, except a future I want to work for. Why do I get the feeling that matters to you?'

Olivia couldn't find the words to tell Tom that it didn't matter. That she didn't need anything from him, didn't need him to have a house or even a job. He was all she wanted. Maybe if he did think that was her reason then this would be easier. She didn't share that after these weeks together and then last night she felt as though he'd brought her back to life, one which she didn't yet know quite how to live.

She looked down, turned her phone over and back again. Felt herself drawn to the notifications she saw there, the safety in her work and the demands it made that didn't need her to feel anything more than professionalism. 'You know how important my career is to me and I missed something crucial today.' She couldn't meet his gaze now. 'I took my eye off the ball and messed up because I was distracted.'

'What did you miss?'

'A meeting with a new client, one my business partner has wanted for ages. He had to step in and I've never let him down before.' Olivia hesitated. 'I need to see a property for them and I'm going to do it tomorrow.'

'But you're meant to be on holiday, and we've got this party to plan.'

'I know. But I have to go.'

'Do you really?' There was a suggestion of bitterness in Tom's voice. 'The day before Christmas Eve? This client, whoever they are, can't possibly wait a few days?' She didn't reply and he exhaled slowly. 'I see. You want to go, to be there for them. Not us. Or your dad.' Tom didn't attempt to disguise the cynicism now. 'So was last night all just part of my present? Some gift, Olivia. You're quite the party planner.'

'Of course it wasn't part of the plan!' She stood up, her chair scraping across the cold floor in her haste. 'I wanted to do something nice for your birthday and things progressed. What happened between us was a possibility, we both know it's always been there.' She hesitated. 'Maybe it was just unfinished business, something to get out of the way before we move on.'

'Unfinished business?' Tom drew out the words incredulously. He jumped up so quickly that his chair fell backwards, and he didn't attempt to right it. 'Ticked me off your list, have you? Told your friends already? Tom Bellingham, failed actor, writer. Failed man. Was it all part of your publicity plan, to make people feel sorry for me?'

'What? No, of course I—'

'After these weeks here and how we are together, the way you took care of me that night. The way we laugh. I thought we were a team, planning this party. And maybe so much more.' His eyes were glistening now and she knew she'd wounded him, that somehow her attempt at reason had failed them both. 'Now I find out that I was only unfinished business for you. Was it even me you saw, Olivia, or just that guy off the TV? A character?' Tom's voice dropped and she was devastated at what she'd done. 'And fool that I am, I seem to have fallen in love with you.'

Olivia's phone was in her hand and it hit the floor with a sharp clatter. She wanted to confess, to tell him it was how she felt too but she was afraid of saying it out loud to someone she had known for so little time. It couldn't possibly be real, couldn't last or amount to anything more than a holiday fling. Or could it? She was struggling to make sense of their situation, her mind racing as fast as her heart was pounding.

'I know it's madness, the last thing I expected. But here I am.' The short laugh which followed from Tom was ironic. 'Don't worry, I'll learn to live with it. I daresay this little chat we're having might go some way to changing how I feel.'

He stormed across the room, his hand on the door. 'I wasn't planning on going back to London.' The desolation in his words rattled through her, making her want to cry at his admission. 'I was going to tell you tonight that I've accepted the job of programme director with the retreat. A new beginning, a chance to start over, or so I thought. But there's obviously no reason why you would be interested in that.

'I've been without a proper home for most of my life, Liv. And being here with you has felt more like home than any I've known since I was a kid. I love how we are together, and I thought maybe we had a chance. Could find a way. But I can't blame you for not wanting to take a chance on someone who's a failure, it doesn't fit your life.'

The words fell like hammer blows on her already fractured heart and Olivia gasped at the pain radiating from her chest – pain she'd also caused this wonderful, sensitive man.

'Tom, please, let me…'

'No need, I think you've been quite clear. When you said that it's okay to fail, to get stuff wrong as long as you try again, you meant everyone but you, didn't you? You made a mistake today and you're blaming us, me, for letting it happen. You don't do failure because it happened to you before and that's why you won't give us a chance. You won't let yourself stand still long enough to try. It seems I can't make you fight for something you don't want either.' Tom's reply was crushing, weighted with regret. '*The Polar Express*, by the way. For book six.' He was still staring at her. 'For fools like me who were starting to believe.'

Chapter Twenty-One

For our sixth #BradshawsBooksAtChristmas
Tom has chosen #ThePolarExpress. For all
those who believe, and those yet to discover
the miracle of a silver reindeer bell, the magic
of a Christmas journey. Join us to share your
memories and make new ones.

It was by far the worst evening they'd spent in the house.
After last night, the fun, the flirting, the ending, Olivia
couldn't believe she'd brought them to this atmosphere of
tension and torture. She still hadn't found the right words,
the ones to tell Tom how she felt about him and how
afraid those feelings made her. She'd lost someone she'd
loved before, had been the one at home picking up the
pieces, and she desperately didn't want to do that again.

But she'd also been unfair to Tom and knew that she'd
hurt him, something that made her whole body ache.
She'd tweeted the book and followers were engaging with
the choice of *The Polar Express* and wanting to know what
they were planning for Christmas Eve. Olivia had already
tweeted earlier in the week to say that they were planning to finish that night with one final book. Speculation
about it was growing, as was the realisation that it was
Tom Bellingham, former actor and writer, who was the
mystery man in the shop.

After a separate, restless evening she was up early and going over the list for the supermarket. There was quite a bit of shopping to do for the party and Mrs Timms had been overjoyed when Olivia had popped into the cafe yesterday to ask her to bake for Hugh's homecoming and goodbye to the shop.

The word around the village was out and Olivia was aware that people would want to take the opportunity to see her dad and wish him well before the house was sold. Fifty still seemed like a sensible number to cater for and that took planning. She wished she hadn't offered to drive over to Lancashire to view the property this afternoon. She knew she'd rather be here, with Tom, but she'd promised and after yesterday's fiasco she couldn't back out.

Already the house seemed layered in melancholy, a gloom seeping through the rooms where before there had been happiness. Thoughts of her own company, the luxurious if empty apartment, and Ellie heading for Australia in the summer, filled Olivia's mind and Christmas was something she now wanted to be over and gone. Breakfast done, she was ready to go and at the front door when Tom came down the stairs. Her gaze flew guiltily to his, searching for any sign of the love he'd confessed, and found none.

'Morning.' He reached for a coat, pulled a hat out of the pocket. 'I'll be in the shop this afternoon and then I'll start on the food we talked about. Those two recipes of your dad's.'

'I'm just about to go shopping, I'll be back as soon as I can.'

'I'm coming with you. It's a lot of stuff to fetch and I didn't intend to leave you to do it alone.' Tom wasn't looking at her as he pulled the hat on. 'You're not planning to cancel the party then?'

It had crossed her mind. 'I can't, too many people have been invited and Mrs Timms is on the case.' That didn't make him smile in the way it usually would. 'And Dad's looking forward to it. It's not necessary for you to come with me this morning. I can manage.'

'Yeah, well, you don't have to. Why do you find it so hard to accept help and insist on doing everything on your own terms?'

There wasn't an answer she could give him to that, at least not in this moment. When they arrived in town, they'd barely exchanged another word and collected separate trolleys to gather all they needed. The supermarket was crazy busy, and Olivia just wanted it to be over.

Tom pulled his hat down, drew the scarf higher and she knew he didn't want to be recognised. Half of the fun of the party they were holding for her dad had gone now. There was no joy to be found in silently loading her car, stuffing bags of food and drink into every corner of the vehicle. It was no better when they reached Thorndale and emptied the car of the same things. There was time for coffee before the shop was due to open and she had to leave to see the house. She made a drink for Tom and left it on the table.

There were just two afternoons left in there now and Twitter was busier than ever. Olivia replied to notifications, helping to increase interest in the final book. She also noticed a steady stream of people making their way through the garden to the shop, including a few she recognised from the village.

She messaged her dad to remind him that she would collect him tomorrow before lunch to bring him home and received a cheery reply. He was planning to go back to the flat on Boxing Day in time for a lunch with other residents and Olivia felt now as though Christmas was going to be excruciating. She'd have to pretend to her clever dad that all was fine and hide the uncertainty and the fear she was concealing about how she felt about Tom. What she'd done to him, to them.

Gina was checking in with her daily and Olivia called her from the car to say that she was okay, trying to find a way forward. Ellie and Logan were updating the family chat group with fabulous Caribbean photos and Olivia was thrilled they were having such a wonderful time. It wasn't very many days since they'd been here, but that feeling of being happy with Tom then, of possibility and enjoying his company, had deserted her now and it was her own fault.

She was relieved to have an excuse to avoid the bookshop, not wanting to be part of whatever was going on in there. She wouldn't be able to do that tomorrow and would have to find a way to get through that final opening. She wasn't her usual wholly professional self when she viewed the property and checked in with Julian and the new client to inform them.

The house wasn't right, and she was about to suggest that she continue searching over the holidays when she changed her mind, remembering Gina's words about what it cost her to always put work first. She reminded Julian that she was on annual leave, and he offered to take over before his usual New Year holiday. She thanked him, feeling a mixture of relief that the client was no longer hers to deal with, and strange that she had passed the search to someone else.

Tom was busy in the kitchen when she returned, the shop already closed. She helped him clear up after he'd prepared the recipes, a coldness to their silence that hadn't been present between them before. She told him how much her dad would appreciate the festive twist Tom had applied to the dodgy sausage rolls, adding sage and onion, and the famous prawn and lentil dish he hadn't been able to resist, and he thanked her politely.

She had come to know the man – not the actor – so well, and every time she thought of him, she thought of a different decision for herself, one which allowed them a future together. But then memories of the look in his eyes and the hurt that she had brought about followed straight after and she didn't know if she could ask him again. He had given her a chance and she had ruined it; he surely would not give her a second one.

–

Happy Christmas Eve! Thank you for taking Bradshaw's Books into your hearts again. We have one final #BradshawsBooksAt-Christmas to see us out. Join us live at 5 p.m. – all will be revealed by Hugh Bradshaw, without whom we wouldn't be here.

And isn't that the truth, Olivia thought sadly as she pressed the blue button. If her dad hadn't invited Tom to stay, hadn't provided him with a home when he'd needed one. If her dad hadn't insisted that the house, and he, needed her attention and that he wanted her here whilst Tom was too. Had her dad done all of it on purpose? Had he wanted her to make space in her life for something more than her clients, her career? Had he known how she and Tom would feel about one another? How they would laugh, fight, tease, share and finally love one another?

There was so much to do today, and she felt the hectic distraction of it replaced by a new sadness. Sadness for her and Tom, as well as for the very last time that Bradshaw's Books would be open. She'd become used to seeing villagers and visitors popping in and out of the annexe, and she knew some of them would miss it once it was gone for good. She wondered how many people who'd heard about the shop on Twitter had been attracted by Tom: his presence, his celebrity amongst them.

'Morning.' Tom appeared as she was still staring at her phone and Olivia looked up. Saw the hint of sorrow before he blinked it away. 'So I suppose we've got a lot to do today.'

He was slicing bread to make toast and he added another piece for her. She appreciated how he still did that, included her in what he was doing for himself. It was another small detail of his character and one she'd liked from the beginning.

'What time are you collecting your dad?'

'About twelve, so we can be back in time for the shop at one.' She thanked Tom when he slid the toast across to her. 'He wants to be here for the whole afternoon in the shop.'

'Right.' Tom was standing at the sink to eat, his back to her. 'I'll rearrange things in there a bit if you don't mind? There's barely enough room to swing a cat, never mind extra customers.'

'I like how you refer to them as customers whereas I still think of them as visitors. And of course I don't mind,

274

you know you're free to sort the shop as you wish.' Olivia paused. 'Have you thought about what you'll do with it, the collection, once the house is sold?'

'Why? Are you worried you're missing out?' Tom sighed, and she heard the splash as the plate was dropped in the sink. 'Sorry, Olivia, that wasn't fair. I'll keep some and sell the rest. It's the most obvious thing to do and I haven't got the space to store everything.'

No more Liv. 'Tom, I'm so pleased about your job. The opportunity, here.' She brought her own plate across, wanted to stand beside him and be near him.

'Thanks.' He glanced at her. 'They've offered me the first six months as a residency, to see how it goes and give me time to find somewhere permanent.'

'That's wonderful.' She couldn't help touching his arm, saw his eyes fall to watch. 'So you'll actually be staying on in the house, then?'

'Yes. It won't be the same here without you.' His smile was bleak, brief. 'Less of a home.'

'Tom, I...'

'Right.' He was brisk. 'I'd better get started. See you later.'

'I'll help. There's not much I can do with the food until later and it's too early to go and get Dad.'

It was well over an hour later before they were done and Olivia was happy that the shop looked as welcoming and festive as possible. She and Tom had cleared some of the stock out of the way and brought in a standard lamp which should throw enough light over her dad to enable him to read.

Afterwards when she drove into town, the roads were busy with people setting off for the holidays. Her dad was ready when she knocked on the door of his flat, a small bag sitting in the hall. Back at the house, Tom was hovering in the library and her dad was so pleased to see him that she almost cried.

She watched as the two men hugged, immediately falling into chat about books and the shop. There was an exuberance, an energy her dad was giving off, and she was satisfied they'd made the right decision on hosting the goodbye party, even if things between her and Tom were now at an end.

After a quick lunch which Tom made, they settled Hugh in the shop beside the fire, glasses and a book at hand, a blanket over his lap to keep him comfortable. He was so happy to be back, even in such a small way, at the heart of the bookselling trade he adored.

Olivia hung around the shop most of the afternoon, greeting people, replying to Twitter notifications and tweeting again, reminding followers that Hugh was planning to speak live at five p.m. There was a steady stream of visitors, most of whom bought books and were in no hurry to leave. Despite the sales she was certain that they had barely dented the overall level of stock still left and that Tom had a big job on his hands to prepare it for sale.

Her dad was in his element, and she wondered again how he was settling into his flat and if he truly was happy there without the bustle of people around him. Many of the customers knew who Tom was now, and he seemed happy to pose for a few selfies and even sign a couple of autographs as he chatted about being here on retreat to write his new book, ignoring Olivia wherever possible.

Lots of villagers popped in too, and so she opened the house early, poured drinks and pointed them to the food which was rapidly disappearing. Mrs Timms had outdone herself on the baking and was holding court in the dining room, dispensing mince pies and slicing the huge Christmas cake she had produced. Sam and Charlie Stewart arrived with Esther and made themselves useful topping up drinks and clearing plates. Gina had a houseful for the holidays and had already sent her apologies.

It was a window into the days when Hugh had welcomed guests for the literary festival and she couldn't dismiss the contentment in knowing that the house would still be a home to more writers in the future, with Tom at the helm. It was also a swift reminder that her own connection to Thorndale was diminishing just as Tom's was increasing. With her dad in town and her apartment in Manchester, she would have little reason to visit other than to keep in touch with Annie and Jon.

The party was only really supposed to start at five thirty and last for a couple of hours but as five p.m. approached and Twitter notifications kept arriving, speculating on their final choice of book, Olivia was busy greeting visitors with Tom and replying to tweets.

Twitter seemed to have taken on a life of its own and Tom's stay in Thorndale was definitely public now as people speculated online about his next book and remembered that most famous of roles he'd played so beautifully. Some of the comments about his performance were decidedly cheeky and she knew they would have laughed about them together had things between them not changed so drastically.

She and Tom emptied the shop of people, persuading everyone to head up to the house instead. Olivia wanted the shop quiet for her dad so he could speak live on Twitter and introduce the final book. She was finding it hard to meet Tom's eyes as they tried to avoid each other in the confined space and she was sure her dad would have noticed their politeness and lack of ease with one another. She checked her phone yet again, the book already on Hugh's lap, almost ready to go. Tom was sitting on the armchair opposite his.

'Liv, we've had a change of plan.' Her dad cleared his throat.

What? Olivia felt her pulse spike with worry. Words like that from him always had the capacity to alarm her.

'Tom and I have spoken about this evening, and we thought it would be nice to read the book live as well as introduce it. It's out of copyright now so there's no issue. And Tom would like to be the one to read it.'

It took Olivia a moment to process her dad's decision. 'You can't be serious?' Her gaze flew to Tom, to her dad and back to Tom again. 'You don't want to do that, surely, Tom? It would bring even more attention and I'm sure you must have had enough already.'

'Actually Olivia, I do want to read it.' Tom gave her a smile and she saw the way her dad was looking at him, speculative and assessing. 'If you agree?'

'Of course, the hashtag was all your idea anyway. But why, what do you hope to achieve?'

'There's just something I want to say, that's all.'

'Come on, Liv, it's almost time.' Her dad was getting impatient and she knew they couldn't be late, not with the expectation growing. She opened Twitter, prepared to go live. She checked and saw that both men looked relaxed and comfortable. Right. So it was just her hand that was shaking then as she tried to hold the phone still, nerves tumbling in her stomach. She pressed the button and gave her dad a nod, capturing the two men in her screen.

'Welcome to Bradshaw's Books at Christmas.' Hugh was smiling, clear and confident as ever. 'Thank you for joining us for some fun over the last few days. I'm sorry to say that this really is the end of my shop after all these years but those books that are left are going to someone who will know which ones to keep by his side.

'I want to thank two people whom I love dearly for all they've done in looking after the shop and letting me go out with a bang, as it were. They are my daughter Olivia, the brightest and best of women, and Tom Bellingham, who is not only a brilliant actor and a better writer but someone I'm proud to call my friend.'

Hugh reached out to grasp Tom's hand for a quick squeeze before letting go again. Olivia was struggling to keep her phone still and she blinked furiously at the sudden rush of emotion on her dad's face.

'So tonight it seems only right that Tom should be the one to read our final choice to you. As it's Christmas Eve, that choice can only be *The Night Before Christmas*. Tom?'

Olivia felt the nerves in her stomach launch into real fear as the two men shared a grin and Tom opened the book Hugh passed across, and she tried to gulp back the worry. She prayed nothing would go wrong and Tom wouldn't regret this most public of readings, even if he did have the lines in front of him.

'Hey everyone. I've not performed in public for a while and I had no plans to ever do it again.' Tom also seemed perfectly comfortable and relaxed, and Olivia huffed out a breath, wondering if she was the only one here suffering from fright.

'But someone I love has reminded me that it's okay to fail and get stuff wrong, so I hope you'll forgive me if I get my words mixed up.' Tom smiled and she knew it was for her. He sounded wonderful and she heard the growing confidence he was already portraying. Her heart was pounding and she knew it was too late: she was lost in love for him and she would have to find a way to let go of what was holding her back to be with him, if he would still have her.

'I've been reminded that it's not our failures or our mistakes that have to define us but how we respond and whether we let them prevent us from trying again. So this is me, trying again, feeling a bit like that kid who didn't know who he was, how he'd ever succeed until somebody believed in him and told him he was worth a shot. To give it a go.

'Something else I've been enjoying this Christmas is new old traditions, and maybe reading Christmas books together is something we can all keep on doing. The books we chose for the hashtag are all close to our hearts and have reminded me that our lives are made up of many experiences, ones that help shape who we are and help us not to repeat past mistakes but learn from them. That love is at the heart of everything in our lives and we all do better when we are loved and love in return.'

Tom began to read and Olivia knew at once there was no reason to worry for him. He was perfectly confident, natural, and any suggestion that he might struggle was gone. Tears were already sliding down her face as he continued, instinctively finding the right tone for his voice, the moments to slow down, when to go just a little faster. By the time he read of Santa rising up the chimney and whistling his team of reindeers, her phone was going crazy and she ignored everything to focus on Tom wishing a Happy Christmas to all and to all a good night.

He was smiling as he closed the book gently, and his gaze met Olivia's for a long moment. She ended the broadcast and flung her phone onto the nearest table to rush over and wrap her arms around her dad. She held him tightly, the narrow shoulders slight beneath her arms.

'Get on with you,' he chuckled, letting her go as he got slowly to his feet. 'I think someone else needs you more than I do just now, Liv.'

Olivia turned to face Tom as her dad shuffled into the next room. Tom stood up as she found her voice, overflowing with a love for him that was impossible to hide.

'You were right and I'm sorry. I'm so frightened of failing again that I've just let myself give up trying. What if I love you too?' She whispered the words, wanting to hold him and be held. To comfort him in the way she already had these past weeks, to be supported by his strength and to have him beside her whenever they needed one another. 'I didn't want to.' She sniffed and it turned into a helpless laugh. 'You're far too famous and annoying and generous and clever and amazing, and I just do. I want to try, with you, if you'll have me? If it's not too late?'

'Oh, Liv. Never.' Suddenly their arms were around one another, holding each other as tightly as they could. 'I just want to be with you.'

'You didn't have to do that, the reading.' Olivia said, unable to hold in any more tears. She hadn't cried properly for years and couldn't seem to stop now that she'd started. 'You've well and truly blown your cover. Twitter is going mad.'

'You helped me to decide that I should try again. That what happened is part of me and I need to just accept it and move on.' Tom tipped his head back, his thumb brushing away a tear hovering. 'Have you even been reading our hashtag books? Charles Dickens and his haunted man?'

'I skipped that one. Sorry.'

'You're a terrible bookseller.'

'I know.' She reached up to touch Tom's face, feeling his mouth against her palm when he kissed it. 'Maybe you can read that to me next Christmas.'

'You're on.' He ran a finger down her cheek. 'Acting is over for me, Liv, but at least now I feel as though I've ended a performance on my own terms.' He grinned. 'Anyway all I really need to do is give my detective an even hotter love interest and ramp up the sex in my next book, and then it'll be all about that and not me. I'm thinking of making her an estate agent who is utterly immune to his charms. He doesn't have many, admittedly, but he is wickedly handsome.'

'That definitely lets you out then when the producers come to cast the part.' Olivia loved teasing Tom, the mischief she saw in his expression and how he didn't take himself too seriously. 'And I think my role as your publicist is now officially redundant with that statement.'

'Good,' he murmured, letting his arms fall away to grasp her hands. 'Because I'd much rather have you as my wife. You're far too unpredictable as a publicist.'

'Very funny. You'll be telling me I'm your fairy godmother again next. Are you going to put this in your Christmas movie?'

'What, the bit when the guy gets down on one knee and asks the girl to marry him?' Suddenly Tom was kneeling on the floor, looking up at Olivia with eyes full of love and a hint of nerves. 'I think I'd have to, wouldn't you say? Happy endings, and all that.'

'Tom, I… What are you saying? You're not serious! Are you? Really?'

'I came from nothing, Liv, and I haven't got much to offer you but me. Maybe a book that'll amount to something and a job I want to make a success of. If you'll have me on those terms then will you marry me, make that wedding night in the honeymoon suite we didn't get official?'

'What about my terms?' Her voice was faltering and Olivia had to swallow, she needed to make him understand. 'If we're going to be together then I want to share all I have with you, Tom. For us to be equal in everything.'

'Half of nothing is still nothing, Liv. You can't risk your home and your business for me. I wouldn't want you to.' Tom stood up and Olivia tugged his hand impatiently.

'You don't understand.' She could hear the tremor in her voice as she rushed on. 'If I can trust you with my heart then I trust you with everything else. My life, the home we'll make together. And besides.' Her hands went to his face, holding him gently. 'I want to be there for you, to come home to you. For you to come home to me. I already know you love me, and I love you. Can we do this?'

Tom's eyes were blazing on hers, the fire crackling behind them. 'I think we can.' He leaned forward to murmur into her ear. 'You do throw the most amazing birthday parties.'

'Can we put that in the movie?'

'Nope. That was our evening, I'll have to think of something else.'

'You're really going to write it?'

'I think maybe I really am. It sounds like a lot of fun and as you said before, we've done most of the research. But you still haven't given me an answer.'

'To what?'

'Liv!'

'The proposal? Was that what it was?' She drank in the expression of exasperation and love as Tom stared at her. 'What would happen in your movie?'

'They would declare undying love to one another and she'd say yes without torturing him.'

'Right. Yes. Just a bit of torture, I don't want to be a predictable wife again, I'd much rather be an unpredictable one. Yes, again, just to be clear. But there's no rush, right? We should maybe try dating first, even if we are sort of engaged and already living together.' Olivia was still laughing as Tom pulled her back into his arms and she had to mutter her next words into his chest. 'Do I get to choose what you wear when we do eventually get married? Can it be...'

'Olivia Bradshaw, if you say breeches then I'll...'

She silenced him with a kiss she planted on his mouth, murmuring innocently against his lips parted in a smile. 'I wasn't going to say breeches. I was going to say maybe a white shirt. What's wrong with that?'

'Right.' Tom seemed relieved. 'Good. A white shirt sounds fine.'

'Unbuttoned, of course, we definitely should have a nod to Harrington. I'm thinking white sand, turquoise seas, sunset, barefoot.'

'Sounds perfect. Your dad's always told me that he wants to see more of the Yorkshire coast. Haven't you, Hugh?'

Olivia heard her dad clear his throat as he returned from the other room with a book, swallowing down the emotion he didn't often display. 'Don't be ridiculous, Tom, I said nothing of the sort. It was the Amalfi coast, if you remember. I have an author friend who's based there.'

Hugh was beside them and he held out a hand to shake Tom's firmly. 'Congratulations. I do love it when a plan comes together.'

'Dad! You're worse than Ellie. What plan?'

'Never you mind. Just get on with living it.'

Chapter Twenty-Two

Olivia felt bleary-eyed but still elated when she walked downstairs on Christmas morning. Twitter had gone wild since Tom had read the book and she was replying to notifications in all her free moments, which were in short supply. The party last night had been a huge success and Mrs Timms had been a star, dashing home for extra mince pies from the freezer, which made Olivia laugh whenever she caught Tom's eye. They had yet to make their own mince pies and she was looking forward to the opportunity.

As it was so late when they'd managed to wave off the last of their guests, Hugh had suggested they all go to the eleven p.m. church service. Candlelit, it was as beautiful as before and Olivia left her phone at home and strolled through the cold, frosty night with her dad on one side and Tom on the other. She had been sorry to miss Annie and Jon at the service but being just home with a tiny new baby took priority over everything else.

After the service Olivia had made sure her dad was settled in his room, watching him whizz up to the first floor on his stairlift from the landing. When she'd come back down again Tom had opened champagne and was waiting for her. They'd sat up to finish the final two staves of *A Christmas Carol*, taking turns and reading one each. Christmas Day was already a couple of hours old when they'd finally crept up to bed in Tom's room, the turkey roasting gently in the oven to maintain the Bradshaw tradition of cooking it overnight, the table laid for breakfast.

This morning Tom had suggested that Olivia take her time and join him downstairs when she was ready. She had her phone in her hand and was messaging Ellie. It was too early for the Zoom that was scheduled for after lunch when Ellie and Logan's morning had got underway. Tom was at the range when Olivia walked into the kitchen and she went over to slide her arms around him, sniffing appreciatively at the smell of turkey almost ready.

'Merry Christmas.' She glanced at the pan he was gently shaking. 'Pancakes?'

He let go of the pan to cup her face and kiss her. 'Yes. I remembered you said you used to like coming downstairs for pancakes on Christmas morning. Merry Christmas, I love you.' He let go with a grin, reaching for the pan just as the contents began to catch. 'I think it's fair to say that this Christmas is turning out not at all like the one either of us expected.'

'Agreed. And I love you too. Even more than I did yesterday, if that's possible, now I know you can make pancakes. No, don't say it, I know there must be an end to your talents somewhere.'

'Yes, but it'll be ages before we get that far.' Tom flipped the pan with an expert hand. Olivia could watch him cooking all day: his quiet confidence in bringing a meal together for the three of them, taking care of her just as much as she loved taking care of him. 'This is ready, is your dad on his way?'

'No, he's in the bathroom.'

'Then it's yours.' Tom slid the pancake onto a plate and Olivia settled at the table. 'Buck's fizz?'

'Perfect.' She stood up again. 'We're a team, remember? I'll get it.' She shook her head in wonderment as she crossed to the fridge, and he laughed. 'Look at how well you've already trained me.'

It wasn't long until he joined her and they clinked glasses. 'What do you think Ellie will say, about us?' He sounded worried and Olivia wanted to reassure him.

'She did tell me to go for it, that nice people like you don't come around that often, especially as I'm crap in the kitchen, according to her.'

'You're not really, not totally. You don't think she'll think it's too soon?'

'Doubt it, she was at pains to point out how incredibly old we are when she was here.' Olivia saw the relief and then amusement in Tom's face. 'How do you think you'll like having a firecracker for a stepdaughter?'

'A stepdaughter?' His voice caught for a second. She left her place and Tom pushed back his chair so she could sit on his lap, and their arms went around one another. 'That sounds wonderful. I hope she will think so too.'

'Oh, she will, and she'll let you know if you're getting it wrong.'

'I'm just so looking forward to being part of your family.'

'You already are.' Olivia touched his face with a hand. 'And you might want to include a stepson-in-law in there too. I don't think Logan's going anywhere in a hurry, although I hope they don't rush into anything.'

'Like us, you mean?'

'Tom, we haven't talked about practicalities.' Her voice was suddenly small. 'What we're going to do, where we'll live.'

'You could live here, with me,' he said. 'I've got six months, but I don't plan to stay on in the house forever. Once I'm working then we could search for somewhere to share together. Apparently you're pretty good at that.' Tom was laughing as she raised her eyebrows. 'Unless you want to be in your apartment?'

'I absolutely don't. Manchester is a great place to live but it's never really felt like home, not like Thorndale. Living here with you sounds amazing until we find something else. I can work from here and travel when I need to.' She was quieter still. 'Tell me you didn't take the job because of me?'

'Not entirely. I want to have a go at the role and I think I can make a success of it. There's the possibility of acting workshops too and you've always been right, Liv, about my profile. It will help if I use it in the right way and it was one of the reasons the board wanted me.' Tom was stroking her hair in a way Olivia found entirely too distracting and it was harder to think about work in this moment.

'My dad will be over the moon that you've accepted. Congratulations, I'm so pleased for you. I think you'll be wonderful and they're so lucky to have you. You'll bring such a lot to the job.'

'Yeah, like writers and more readers, hopefully. If I can encourage people, help them write, then that would be amazing. Teach maybe, too.'

'I think you'll be perfect at that. And you have your book to look forward to. You'll need to make time to write another.' She tipped her head, lips hovering over his mouth. 'I think the turkey might be ready.'

'Oh?' Tom's hand was in Olivia's hair, drawing her closer. 'It can wait.'

'I'm not sure it can.' Her lips were against his mouth now and she kissed the corner, felt his other hand tightening on her back. 'We might burn it. And it's Christmas Day, we won't get another.' She kissed him again and freed herself as he pulled a face, reluctant to let her go. 'I'm telling you, it's done. Someone needs to keep this meal on track.'

Olivia crossed the room, carefully lifting the turkey from the oven and leaving it to rest on the top of the range. 'Perfect. Just in time, good thing I didn't let you keep on distracting me.'

'When are we Zooming Ellie and Logan?'

'After lunch, about three, before they get stuck into their meal. They were planning to go swimming first thing.'

'Then when we've spoken with them and shared our news, I'll give you your present.'

'You've got me a present?' Olivia had finished checking the turkey and she whirled around to face Tom. 'But what if I haven't got you one?'

'That doesn't matter. I wanted to give you a gift, I'm not bothered about me.'

'But I am. Luckily I did get you one too, because I like giving gifts as much as I do receiving them.' She started to laugh. 'I think I've just worked out what yours is going to be.'

'Have you been rummaging underneath the tree?'

'Don't need to.' Olivia was still merry. 'It's obvious, isn't it? It's a DVD of your series with all the extras and behind-the-scenes stuff. Because I haven't seen it yet.'

'Busted.' Tom was grinning as she continued.

'That's something to look forward to, spending Boxing Day with Harrington and watching women swooning.'

'I can do better than a DVD.' Tom left the table to walk towards her and Olivia swallowed down her giggle at the look in his eyes.

'Oh?'

He caught her, swinging her around as she half-heartedly tried to make him set her down again. 'You're going to be spending the day with the real thing. Breeches, shirt, boots, whatever you want. On or off.'

'Seriously? You've actually got them here?' Olivia was gasping with laughter now, her feet almost back on the ground, and she was still smiling as she kissed him. 'I don't want any of that. Just you. Only you.'

–

The lunch that Olivia and Tom produced together was a triumph. She'd insisted on doing the roast potatoes and he'd made the gravy, and her dad had pronounced it perfect. The little shop at the end of the garden was in darkness and she began to realise she didn't mind so much now. She'd realised how tiring yesterday had been for her dad and he had accepted the changes in his life, had begun to embrace them with the new friends he was making on his rambles around town. Living here with Tom, at least for now, meant that they would be able to see her dad more often.

Over Christmas pudding Olivia stunned the pair of them when she announced that she'd taken the rest of the week off too and had put an out of office on her email. Family time, even with Ellie and Logan far away, plus this burgeoning relationship with Tom, was all too new and precious to let her clients call her away. Work could wait for the New Year and then she would be able to help Tom sort through the books and they could clear the house together, readying it for the handover to the arts consortium.

She tried and failed not to cry when they Zoomed Ellie and Logan and saw them sitting outside in the sunshine on the beach in Tobago, looking healthy, relaxed and fit. They were having a wonderful time and two of Ellie's stepbrothers were visiting too so she was enjoying getting to know her younger siblings better. She was thrilled about Olivia and Tom's news, even if she did give them a sideways look when they said they were planning to marry at some point but there was no immediate rush. Hugh was with them and it was over an hour before they said goodbye.

Her dad was still tired from last night's activities, and he wandered off to his library for a snooze, book in hand. Olivia covered him with a blanket and returned to the sitting room to see that Tom had topped up their champagne flutes with the last of the bottle they had opened over lunch. He set the glasses down on the coffee table.

'Would you like your present?'

'Yes please. I can't wait any longer to give you yours.'

Tom reached for a package under the tree and handed it to her. 'Merry Christmas.' He followed it up with a kiss, his hand gentle on her neck, both of them sitting on the floor. 'I hope you like it.'

'I will because you gave it to me. Thank you.' The present was beautifully wrapped and Olivia took her time, pulling off the bow, snapping the ribbon and finally tearing the paper. Inside was a beautiful cashmere scarf in navy, heather and burgundy.

'You need a proper scarf of your own, you can't keep borrowing that old thing of your dad's any more.'

'I love it. Thank you.' Olivia lifted it to wind it around her neck, halting as an envelope fluttered onto her lap. 'What's this?'

'Open it.'

She did, tearing the envelope and lifting out a gift voucher, one she soon realised was homemade and tears followed as she read the words Tom had written. 'Paris? For our first proper date?'

'Absolutely. I'm not risking that Operating Theatre museum and the stinking cheese again. There is one catch, as you'll see. It's only a voucher, a promise to take you when I can – I don't really know when that will be, but we're going. Hopefully when the book is an instant bestseller.'

'That's the most perfect present I've ever had.' She reached up to kiss him again. 'Thank you. After Twitter and your reading last night, I don't think there are any doubts about the success of your book. I still haven't replied to everything, and people are desperate to know more about what you're doing.' Olivia pulled back, still wearing her scarf as she reached under the tree. 'Now it's your turn.'

Sudden nerves were fluttering in her stomach as he unwrapped the paper slowly, his gaze going from hers to the gift. He opened a narrow box to reveal a beautiful silver and navy ballpoint pen.

'For all those books you're going to be signing. It's engraved.'

Tom turned the pen over to read the inscription. '"Believe"? Oh, Liv.' He edged towards her until she was in his arms. 'That's just wonderful, thank you. I love it. I appreciate your confidence in me.'

'You're not the only one who loves *The Polar Express*.' Olivia was sniffing, and she pointed at the wrapping paper he had discarded. 'That's not quite everything, you might want to check in there. It seems we were on similar lines with vouchers.'

He did, pulling out an envelope, watching her as he opened it. Tom's eyes fell to take in the voucher she had made him.

'A domain name? Liv, that's so thoughtful and generous.'

'You like it?' Suddenly she was worried that perhaps she had gone too far. 'I should explain that I haven't actually bought it, I didn't think that would be fair. I checked and the name is available, so if you want it then it's my gift to you. I quite understand if you'd rather not.'

'"Tom Bellingham Author dot com". I love how that sounds.' He kissed her, holding her close. 'And you're right, I am going to need a website.'

'I'm so pleased.' She was hugging him fiercely, trying to imprint her faith and her love onto him. 'It's not like your bio pic has to be one of you in breeches, is it? Although…'

Olivia didn't get any further. She squealed as Tom pulled her down on top of him and forgot all about Harrington. Her heart and her hands were full of Tom Bellingham and she knew he was more than enough.

Acknowledgements

This book was inspired by a house I found, a window to the right of the front door giving a view of an old leather chair and a library. Along came Hugh and the life he was living, and Olivia and Tom soon joined him. Creating their back stories was a lot of fun, especially Tom's, and I'm still wondering about Harrington's story and who might have written him. Or even who might still...

To Susan Yearwood, Emily Bedford and all at Canelo, including the fabulous cover designers, and Katrina Power, thank you. I was delighted to be able to complete the Thorndale series at Christmas and I very much appreciate the opportunities that working with a brilliant team brings.

I'm very grateful to book bloggers and readers, and all they do to share the books they review; I'm so pleased that readers are discovering and enjoying the Thorndale series. Thank you to the RNA, its members and volunteers for the support and encouragement we share in this most wonderful of genres. Friendship with other authors is a pleasure and I'm looking forward to meeting in person again when we can.

The similarities between my dad and Hugh are very few but they do share a love of cooking and we never say no when my dad rings to suggest a roast dinner. Thank you, Dad, for all the meals, memories and early morning Christmas Day phone calls to talk turkey.

I had a fairly small window to write Olivia and Tom's story and it wouldn't have happened without the unstinting support I have from my husband Stewart. Thank you, once again, for all you do and delivering delicious lunches to my desk so I could keep on working. And for the memories we've made together, all we share and the very best Christmas cake.

Christmas is a very special time in our house, and we've created our own traditions down the years, some from our childhood and some of our own. The search for the perfect tree to decorate whilst we watch an old movie, reading *The Night Before Christmas* every Christmas Eve and the mince pies I never liked until I tried my mother-in-law's. All play a part in how we celebrate, from being in the choir and huddling around the tree outside to sing carols again in the dark, to the brass band strolling through the village pausing to play and the dash home from church on Christmas Day to cook the lunch. Each of these and more have their place in our traditions, and I hope we've passed some on to the next generation.

Olivia and Tom's Cocktail Recipes

Olivia and Tom have fun sharing cocktails over a couple of evenings; here are two of their recipes, including Tom's favourite.

Olivia's Espresso Old Fashioned for Tom

- Double shot (6oml) espresso

- 5oml bourbon (Elijah Craig Small Batch – Olivia's gift and one of Tom's favourites)

- 1oml brown sugar syrup

- 2 dashes Angostura bitters

- Ice

- Orange zest, to garnish

Mix the espresso with the bourbon, sugar syrup and bitters in a shaker with lots of ice. Shake and strain into a short glass and garnish with a twist of orange zest.

- 50ml vodka

- 25ml coffee liqueur (like Kahlua or Tia Maria)

- 1tsp Cointreau

- 2 dashes Angostura Bitters

- Ice

Spoon the ice into a short glass and add all the ingredients; stir gently before serving.

Tom is planning to make a Christmas cake next year and Olivia has promised to take mince pie baking seriously. Mrs Timms is trying to persuade Tom to direct and star in a revival of the Thorndale pantomime and Olivia has polished his boots, just in case. She's also ordered a wand.